DATE DUE   JUN 0 5

AUG 11 '05			
2·2-0b			
APR 07 '06			
2 25/10			
GAYLORD			PRINTED IN U.S.A.

HEDWIG
AND
BERTI

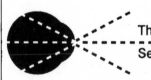

This Large Print Book carries the
Seal of Approval of N.A.V.H.

HEDWIG
AND
BERTI

FRIEDA ARKIN

WHEELER
PUBLISHING

Published in 2005 by arrangement with
St. Martin's Press, LLC.

Wheeler Large Print Hardcover.

The text of this Large Print edition is unabridged.
Other aspects of the book may vary from the original edition.

Set in 16 pt. Plantin.

Printed in the United States on permanent paper.

Library of Congress Cataloging-in-Publication Data

Arkin, Frieda.
    Hedwig and Berti / by Frieda Arkin.
        p. cm.
        ISBN 1-58724-956-1 (lg. print : hc : alk. paper)
        1. Refugees, Jewish — Fiction.   2. London (England) —
Fiction.   3. Child musicians — Fiction.   4. Jewish
families — Fiction.   5. Gifted persons — Fiction.
6. Immigrants — Fiction.   7. Pianists — Fiction.   8. Large
type books.   I. Title.
PS3551.R44H43 2005b
    813'.54—dc22   2004030854

To the merry memory of
Anne Ratner

As the Founder/CEO of NAVH, the only national health agency solely devoted to those who, although not totally blind, have an eye disease which could lead to serious visual impairment, I am pleased to recognize Thorndike Press* as one of the leading publishers in the large print field.

Founded in 1954 in San Francisco to prepare large print textbooks for partially seeing children, NAVH became the pioneer and standard setting agency in the preparation of large type.

Today, those publishers who meet our standards carry the prestigious "Seal of Approval" indicating high quality large print. We are delighted that Thorndike Press is one of the publishers whose titles meet these standards. We are also pleased to recognize the significant contribution Thorndike Press is making in this important and growing field.

Lorraine H. Marchi, L.H.D.
Founder/CEO
NAVH

* Thorndike Press encompasses the following imprints: Thorndike, Wheeler, Walker and Large Print Press.

My thanks and gratitude to
William B. Goodman and Katie Boyle

This is how Harry gets into it.

He's alone in the flat now. A year ago, in the spring of 1938, Edwina asked if he'd agree to a divorce, and of course he did. She was apologetic, she knew it was a bad time for Jews, the things one heard going on over there, if one could credit the stories. She hated to add to his discomfort. She's not Jewish, of course, not religious in any sense, but she felt bad — really bad — and if he wished, she'd stay with him at least until all the nastiness was past. Ought she? Though actually there was no point in it, was there?

Of course no point, Harry agreed. Why she brought up religion, he had no idea. Both of them know he's no more religious than she. Nor does divorce itself bother him. They've no children and there's little family on either side to be considered. He's got none to speak of, having while still in infancy lost his mother, who went to sleep in a dentist's chair and woke up in heaven. And when he was twelve his father, on a long-anticipated holiday in Rome, walking close to a wall of the Colosseum was terminally coshed by a sizable falling chunk of antique stone. There are no brothers, no aunts, no cousins, only his father's brother, Uncle Jack, who from then on reared him awkwardly and, as soon as decently possible, shed him.

(Yet Harry, fleetingly, had had an aunt once. Not so many years back, Uncle Jack married a widow under the impression she'd inherited a packet from a dead husband. She'd had somewhat similar illusions about Jack, so for a time there *was* an Aunt Julia until the mutual folly was amicably put to right, an honest mistake.)

So there went Edwina and, though he'd always been a man used to living narrowly, Harry's since gone a bit to pot. Still in the pawnshop, of course, in the job he'd once taken to keep himself in paints and brushes. Now, he depends upon it utterly.

But with Edwina gone and his painting done with, there's little to do with his evenings and he's at a loose end more often than not. He's generally back at the flat at around five and from force of habit has a look in the kitchen, though he's come to view eating with pure indifference and can put it off until his stomach growls like an irritable dog. Then he downs something or other, walks into the sitting room and throws himself at full length on the sofa.

Napping, unlike food, is important. Until lately, he'd found this early-evening bit of shut-eye purifying, it cleansed him of the day in a way he imagined a miner must feel, bathing after eight hours in the pits.

But today, still early in the evening, Harry wakes like a shot from another of his dreams of Nazi storm troopers, dreams he's been having too many of lately. He suspects this comes of his refusal to believe the constant talk at the shop, about the most bizarre atrocities they say are happening. Can they possibly be true? Yet why would anyone invent such stories? At the same time, believing them surely puts a terrible burden on one's shoulders, of a sort Harry can't quite name. Perhaps this is why he'd rather not credit them? That is to say, if one doesn't believe them, they're not on one's conscience. But why ever should they be on his conscience? Why should he credit these accounts any more than others he's heard from customers in the past? For he's often been struck at the oddity of people who walk into pawnshops and pour out their life stories while parting with the pitiful tangible bits of their histories.

His boss, Mr. Preger, now emerges several times a day from the back room of the shop following hoarsely whispered conversations with men and women whose very manner of opening the front door proclaims they've not come on regular business. And daily Mr. Preger's face, with the constantly unquiet eyes, is becoming grayer and more haunted-looking.

Actually Harry must suppose the stories are true. Every one of the people entering with that special tread of theirs is hustled quickly into the back room, from which Mr. Preger later emerges more heavily weighted, as the customers are heavily weighted, as Harry's dreams have become heavily weighted.

He's not had a dreamless sleep in months . . .

It's more than the dream that's wakened him. They're actually at the door!

Harry knows how dreams go beyond waking logic, containing utter impossibles. The moment his eyes are closed in sleep, his dreams leap upon him and seize on reality, as though it were a flat sheet of paper which his dreams bunch up and crumple, so that surfaces normally separated by time and space become suddenly and impossibly contiguous, even superimposed on one another. A thing the waking mind cannot contain.

The brute knocking comes again: bahrah-ram! bah-rah-ram!! Chillingly German. Still riding his nightmare, Harry rolls himself from the sofa, and with knees that refuse to straighten, hobbles toward the door like an old man. The rapping comes once more before he reaches it. Exactly as before.

He wants to shout "This is England! This is London!" as he throws open the door.

No Nazi thugs. Instead facing him is a woman easily six feet tall. And in spite of the wan light in the hall — his dream must be coloring his vision — she's got Germany written all over her. She's immense in a fur coat and hat that now put him in mind of a Russian Cossack. But no, actually what he's beholding might have just stepped out of one of those Wagner operas he so detests. *Lohengrin?* No, the noisy one with the bloody flying witches in helmets. Valkyries.

Harry and the Valkyrie consider each other in silence.

She's much too tall. Yes, easily six foot. Harry himself is barely five-five. One of her hands is thrust into a fur muff and all three — coat, hat and muff — are of a dark brown substance that looks to be expensive. Her coat is open down the front and shows a dark dress beneath it, and a bosom so monumental that Harry nearly cringes.

The woman at first appears amused at what she sees and then her look becomes suddenly — what? Condemnatory. She continues to regard him, her arms folded, and examines him from his face to his feet. Has he done some awful thing? What right has any human being to look on another in this way?

The dream still in his throat, Harry can't bring out a word. Now she's staring beyond him, into the room. The expression on her face remains the same. A large face, pinkly German. Northern German. Scandinavian, he'd say. Her eyes — large, pale blue — seem to be taking the measure of his flat. And then, like some perishing building inspector, she looks the doorjamb up and down and turns her majestic head slowly to survey the passages on both sides.

He knows perfectly well it's a nasty little flat, it was all he and Edwina could afford when they married, and now if anything he's worse off still. Well, what does the woman expect? This is Hackney, not Mayfair.

Might someone please tell him who in the hell this female is?

She speaks. "You are Harry Eisenstein." Her voice, advancing from the gloom, is formidable, it goes perfectly with the Valkyrie tits: heavy, Teutonic, straight from his dream. She leans toward him and Harry can almost feel her eyes sweep his face, like a violent caress. Never mind the frightful light, she seems to have found what she's looking for, now she stands erect.

"Absolutely you are Cousin Harry. I would know anywhere those ears." She gives a deep — indeed, a melodious — laugh, and Harry is aware of a heavy elegance in her thickly accented voice. Rather like her body.

"Absolutely it is the Kessler ears." Now there's a tenderness in her smile. "Do you know, you are the exact picture, the *exact,* of Cousin Manfred? From Hildesheim. Only, Manfred has so little brains. You, Harry, do not seem so. Do you say few? Few brains?"

Suddenly she clasps her hands, bringing them to her chin, at the same time raising her eyes upward, so that Harry's positive she's about to break into one of those monumental soprano solos filled with rocks and lightning bolts. No. She's brought her look back to him once more, again scanning his face.

He's never had an experience to prepare him for this. Some idiot lecturer he'd heard once at the Academy — Sir Charles Humbert, was it? — speaking of the world and the painter's eye, had kept going on about "creative confrontation." Here's the woman who knows exactly what he meant.

"No," Harry hears her say, "you do not look so, I am glad to see."

He's lost the thread and regards her blankly, whereupon she laughs like a fruity flute. "You are wanting to know who I am. I am your cousin Hedwig. Hedwig Kessler." Meaningfully. "And now you will ask us to come in?"

That magnificence of body deserves the royal plural. He steps back, and now sees two immense leather suitcases standing behind her, which she lifts as though they weigh feathers and brings in with her over Harry's threshold.

It's only then, in the uncertain light, that

18

he sees a little man standing there. Like the luggage, he has been absorbed by the gloom. A frightfully small chap, shorter than Harry himself. He holds his hat low in front of him as though shielding his genitals, smiling up at Harry with mild brown eyes, like a bashful child or a gentle dog.

For a long moment Harry waits. Some bond is immediately established. The shy smile still on his face, the little man turns to retrieve a valise, and then two umbrellas tied together that are leaning against the wall, and follows the giantess meekly into Harry's flat.

"And this," Hedwig Kessler says when Harry's closed the door, "is Dagobert. He is happening to be my husband." She turns majestically, and putting a hand behind the little man's shoulder, presses him firmly forward. "All call him Berti."

Berti's head does not quite reach her shoulder. At once Harry accepts the fantastic union, it's entirely in line with this unbelievable encounter. He extends a hand to Berti, who reaches out but barely touches it. Possibly they don't shake hands in Germany? Do they kiss on both cheeks? That's French. Rub noses? No, Eskimo. "Berti has no English yet," Hedwig says, and turns to regard the room. The presence, the spaciousness of this Brunhilde in his sitting room has shrunk everything surrounding her to doll size.

She begins to remove her wrappings. Like the rest of her, her clothes are impressive. She carefully lifts the immense brown velvet hat from her head, revealing an astonishing mountain of white hair done up high, in braids that surround her head like a battlement. She's not old. Possibly an albino? That dead-white hair. Also, albinos have pink skins and so has she, though hers looks to be rather the bloom of health. But of course not. Her eyes are an incredible blue.

Next, off comes the coat, an expensive fur of some kind. Harry doesn't know furs, though they get them occasionally at the shop, or fur-collared jackets, but it's Mr. Preger who examines them and writes the names on the tags.

With the coat off, she still looks muffled, her large body swathed in a long brown dress with brown lace at the throat. She turns to find somewhere to deposit the coat, then drapes it over an arm of the sofa. That done, she looks at Berti, purses her lips, and makes a sharp gesture toward him like a silent snap of the fingers. Instantly the little husband unbuttons and removes his own coat and stands, holding it.

Though she's called herself his cousin, Harry won't for a minute believe a woman like this one can in any way be related to him. She'd fit more likely into what he remembers of Edwina's family, actually, Harry thinks, and for a minute he tries to pin her there. They're a tall lot, though on the reedy side. In fact Edwina, slim as a weasel, has no figure at all. He throws another awed look at that thunderous bosom. But what nonsense he's thinking. Edwina certainly has no German relatives. This woman said her name is Kessler. His mother's maiden name.

Only, wait — it's the *husband's* name that's Kessler! Now Harry feels as though he's been let for the moment to touch royalty, only to have it swept loftily away. Berti stands, staring at him somberly.

They are all standing. Belatedly, Harry says, "Won't you please sit down," and wonders uneasily whether he ought not go to the kitchen and cook some tea.

She seems an extraordinarily dense woman — not in the sense of stupid, of course, but that she seems most firmly and healthily packed. With heavy grace she deposits her body at one end of the sofa, near her folded coat. At the same instant the husband seats himself in the chair opposite.

"So then." Brightly, smoothing the brown skirt over her thighs, "I am Hedwig. This is Berti." And as though she's been reading Harry's mind: "Besides that Berti is your cousin because he is married to me, he is also your cousin himself. What I mean, I have married my . . ." She hesitates, leans toward Harry: "You understand maybe a little German?"

"Hardly any, I'm afraid," says Harry. He is still standing. Since the only other refuge is the heavy armchair beside the door next to the kitchen, he seats himself at the other end of the sofa.

"How do you say in English . . . wait! I think I am remembering!" Again that operatic look aloft. "You say first cousin, is that so? Yes. Berti and I are first cousins. I was Hedwig Kessler before I married, and now I am *still* Hedwig Kessler!" She sits back in amused triumph.

That makes her his again. But Harry will still not believe it. She leans forward once more and says tensely, her eyes the deepest cerulean blue, "You do not know your relatives in Germany?"

"I'm afraid not."

"You do not even know" — her strong voice trembles — "that Hyman Kessler was your Grossvater?"

"My Grossvater." Harry says the word carefully.

"It means grandfather." She enunciates the three syllables as though speaking to a child, or perhaps that other cousin she has mentioned, the hen-brained Manfred.

"You see" — Harry is apologetic — "I was very young when my mum died."

"Yes, that I have already known. I will tell you, then." And readjusting her handsome bulk, she pushes herself against the back cushion and clasps her hands composedly in her lap. Berti likewise resettles himself — he's too short, rump-to-knee, to sit properly in an adult's chair — then looks down on his shoe tops with absorption. She asks him something sharply in German and he shakes his head quickly. Does he want the loo? Probably.

"Your Grossvater" — she turns to Harry — "Hyman Kessler was the brother also of *my* Grossvater, Bertholdt Kessler, who is also Berti's Grossvater." She folds her arms and smiles pinkly, full-face, at Harry. "You are, then, *you* — Harry Eisenstein, our cousin. Cousin Harry." This she says meditatively, as though tasting the words.

"I see," says Harry.

"And we have only now come from Berlin."

"*Today,* you mean?"

"Today. Of course today."

He will set aside the Grossvater issue to examine later, though the name Hyman Kessler doesn't sound even a distant bell.

"Now?" Harry says. The storm troopers clank forward in heavy rhythm. "The two of you actually . . . I mean to say; from what we've been hearing . . ."

She speaks smoothly, pleasantly. "First we went to Hoek, and then we have come to Dover," ticking the names off on her strong white fingers as though she and this man with her have just returned from holiday. "And then we have taken the boat train to here, to London. We have come to where you live, you see how I have your address." She pulls her fur coat toward her and extracts a folded white paper from the fur muff that dangles like a leashed animal from one sleeve.

"Here. On this paper. Your name and where you live."

"What I don't understand," Harry says, "is how you come to know of me."

She will gladly tell him how she comes to know of him. She comes to know of Harry because that is the kind of family the Kesslers are.

They have never misplaced a relative. Even the impoverished Harry Eisenstein — insignificant, a nothing, actually (her manner implies), living in a seedy bedsitter in what is probably the meanest corner of London (her manner implies),

25

even Harry is in the family books. Because Rosa Brauer, née Kessler, had a friend who had known Harry's dead mother. And information about him was sent to Rosa, and through Rosa — as Kesslers have always done — to the family record-keeper. This was Grossvater Bertholdt, the last to inherit the books. "Grandfather, that means," she tells Harry again.

She looks stiffly down and appears to be tracing the figures in Harry's dirty blue carpet. Something stirs the little husband — Berti pushes his body forward in the chair that could easily hold two of him, and cupping his hands over the ends of the chair arms, says, "Tot," barely audibly.

Harry knows that word. "Tot," in fact, has always sounded the dread and finality of death so much more than the English word.

Bluntly, Hedwig continues with her story. Grossvater was plucked from the Street two weeks ago by a band of brownshirts . . . Harry has heard of the brownshirts? . . . while he and Grossmama — oh, yes, Grossmama also, fragile, tottering Grossmama, without even her medicines — while taking their evening walk in Charlottenburg. That is where they lived, all of them, she and Berti too.

When she has finished she turns toward Harry, the movement bringing her strong face out of the shadow. It has lost most of its pink and looks almost carved. A cold face, Harry decides, who's been trying with no success to get a handle on her temperament. Her pallor suggests that near-translucence certain stone has — alabaster, perhaps. No, it's a kind of ivory he's thinking of: a skin quality he'd never quite succeeded in getting from his brush. He shakes his head to rid it of the thought. He's still trying to wean himself from the compulsion to contemplate the world as though it were a spread of canvas. He accepts the fact that he'll likely spend the rest of his life in this exorcism. Hedwig's broad face looms at him like a pale moon against the obscurity of his walls, and he notes raptly, as though they're illuminated from within, fine deep-pink capillaries at the tops of her cheeks: at the sides of her nostrils, too, there is the same delicate spiderwork. Is it possible this new cousin of his is a boozer?

Hedwig, leaning forward, seems about to
pull her body from the sofa, and Harry realizes it's high time he showed the two of them
the small bedroom at the kitchen end of the
flat. But his cousin hesitates and then sits
back. "It will be all right if I tell the men to
deliver the boxes here?"

"Boxes?" Harry asks.

"It will not be for long." She speaks
hastily. "Berti and I will look soon for somewhere to live. Here is too much crowded for
so many, such a small place . . ."

"Boxes?" says Harry again.

"They are at Victoria Station."

"Actually, you were able to bring boxes
with you?"

"Two only," says Hedwig. She transfers
her gaze immediately to the far wall, as she
had before when he'd shown surprise at
their managing to leave Germany. And
now with boxes? Recalling the stories at
the shop. Horrible. Horrible beyond de-
scription. She continues, still addressing
the wall. "They have told me when first we

28

came there, as soon as I will give them a place where to bring them, they will come with them."

"Of course!" Harry says. "Certainly have them brought."

"And then!" She turns to him, and suddenly there's a world of joy in her face. "You will see about the family you have come from. The books are all there, in one box. Eight books!"

"Ah."

"Then you will see how we go back more than four hundred years." She's raised her white-braided head which now trembles faintly, again staring off into a corner of the sitting room. The light in her face is positively fierce.

"How many families do you know who can say such a thing?"

They're to take the little bedroom, Harry insists, leading his magnificent cousin, trailed by the little husband, to the far narrow end of the kitchen. "Not much of a room, I'm afraid," as he pushes open the door. This is the room Edwina had moved into — leaving him the larger sitting room sofa they'd been using — when she announced for divorce. He's barely stepped into it since.

Hedwig comes to stand beside him and look in. Through the murk she can see a longish, narrow room, small and dark. It smells of mice. A divan-bed stands snug up against one wall, a low chest of drawers beside it. There's hardly space for anything else. A bit back here, perhaps, behind the door? She moves a little forward to peer in, but only slightly, as though more might indicate endorsement of a room like this. Some grainy light enters through a window which hasn't been cleaned in years, giving, very probably, onto an inner court, though there's light enough for her to see that behind the door there's the space she needs.

She wouldn't give a room like this to a *Putzfrau,* a scullery maid.

The room's only lamp had departed with Edwina. He can still call up her sharp figure, the lamp clasped close against her, on her last departure from the flat. Still, Harry can see well enough that a woman of such large dimensions as this one, even alone, can scarcely make do in a room this size. Quite drenched with shame, he says: "I haven't been in here in months. I'd quite forgotten how small the bed is. I think the two of you ought to take the sofa, it opens out quite wide, you know. Actually, the bed here will do fine for me." It's quite impossible the two of them can sleep in it.

"No. I will not allow that you put yourself out. You must live as you lived before we came. And please to know we do not mean to stay long. But so long as we stay, here we will sleep. And here, behind the door is room for the boxes when they will come. They will fit, one on the top of the other."

"Oh, no need for that, you know. We've a box room in the basement."

She looks at him with scornful eyes. "In the basement! You think we would put — but I forget. Of course you do not know what is in them."

31

The old Grossvater, probably. "But it's quite safe down there," Harry insists. Hedwig gives him a look and turns away with a disgusted flip of the hand — the identical look Edwina had flashed at him when he'd said nothing to her wish to remove herself to this little back room. Sometimes it occurs to Harry to wonder how he must look to women. It's always the same, always the same: each time he's tried, he is found wanting. No matter.

"The boxes will go behind the door." Hedwig, firmly. And the matter is settled.

She will trust the English government because she has no choice. She will trust the railway men with the boxes, again because she has no choice. But as for these boxes, to imagine that this donkey-headed cousin of hers even thinks she will put her trust in anyone living in this shabby set of flats in this *dreckige* neighborhood!

She and Berti carry their things into the room.

Objections? He's got no objections at all to his house-guests, probably because he never really settled down to the enjoyment of living alone. Not that he's missed Edwina, exactly. He can't complain of the abandonment of love. But certainly her going has removed a small something from his life, as though he'd mislaid a jacket he'd become accustomed to, or a piece of furniture that fit perfectly into a particular space in the room. Being a man of painful honesty, he's tried to face this truth, as he has a few others lately; Edwina's going hasn't really touched his interior.

Harry suspects he has no interior.

One doesn't turn away relatives who've managed to flee barbarians. One rejoices they've managed to escape, one is grateful to be able to do a little something in a world which, Harry now suspects, may be speeding to a splash.

He asks her how it is that her English is so good, for she's told him she's never before been out of Germany.

Hedwig is standing in the cramped

kitchen where she's just finished making noodles. The surface of the table, her large pink hands and her arms halfway to the elbows are floury. Even so, she still maintains the opulent air of a queen in exile. Harry, standing in the doorway, watches her slice what looks to be a folded sheet of pale yellow rubber into ribbons, a scene this kitchen has certainly never beheld before.

Hedwig laughs. "You think my English is good? I am glad to hear so. I will tell that to the Fraulein that Grossvater got for us, if I meet with her again."

The "us" includes her brother Bruno, who she says was sent to America when he was eight years old, though she's never said why. And the Fraulein was no Fraulein, but a young Englishwoman who'd lived with them for several years in the house in Charlottenburg. Until the day she left, the two children were made to speak in three languages. "Miss Love." Hedwig gives a bark of a laugh. "Isn't that a name!"

Her tone darkens. Harry gathers that the English governess was sent packing in a cloud, a sexual cloud, something in his cousin's pink face — suddenly a mask — suggests this. It may have to do with the old Grossvater, possibly, or the butler — from her descriptions, it sounds like a house that would have the German equivalent of a butler. Or even diddling around with the little boy; governesses do those things.

"Always we spoke English in the mornings." Lovingly, she brushes the flour down from her confident arms onto the table. She has set the noodles to dry on a piece of linen draped over the cooker-top.

"We spoke only English from *Frühstück* to *Mittagessen*. You know what means that?" — flashing him one of her blue looks he's got rather used to by now, half-amused, half mildly derisive. "Of course, no. From breakfast, it means, to luncheon."

His education is filled with holes and Harry knows it, but that's because he'd never really applied himself to anything in life but his painting. Not even Edwina, he sees now.

He often wishes he could like his cousin more. And then, ever scrupulous, has to remind himself that what looks to be a heavy comfortable arrogance is probably, beneath it all, defensive. She's come through a bad time — the two of them have — and what she has left behind her won't bear looking at. Stories in the shop that have been trickling out of Switzerland are goose-pimpling. Yet, but for the one time she'd spoken of her grandparents' being hauled off by those Nazi apes, she never speaks of the Germany of the present, never.

"German we were let to speak during the afternoon," Hedwig continues. "But later, after that, French. From *le dîner jusqu'à l'heure du dodo.*" Her French words as heavily accented as her English, there comes again the juicy self-pleasure of her laugh. "That means from dinner to bedtime. Even to fall asleep, do you know, I must count sheep in French!"

He compliments her on her English.

"Oh I have read many books!" And she begins to enumerate authors, her shrewd eyes amusedly on this English cousin of hers who, she correctly assumes, has never read any of them. John Galsworthy. Arnold Bennett. Virginia Woolf. (But how could he have read them? When he hadn't been painting, the only things he'd read were what critics and painters wrote about painting.)

But one she had not read — her nostrils dilate distastefully — will never read, is that *schmutzige* Irishman and his Mr. Bloom. She'd found the book in a drawer in the Englishwoman's room after she'd left, and, following one look at it, threw it

36

out. Never mind the dirtiness; who could understand such a kind of English? Which in any event gives people the wrong idea of someone who is a Jew.

The word galvanizes Harry, it's as though he's been waiting for her to mention Jews; he's frightfully keen on hearing her speak out about . . .

"Also he has spelled the name wrong."

Once Harry Eisenstein hadn't the slightest doubt but that one day he'd be recognized as a fairly competent painter. Perhaps a bit more than that, actually, though he supposed his chances of becoming an immoderate success might be on the slim side. No matter. What did matter was that with a brush in his hand he'd felt he could reconstruct the world. Possibly all painters felt that way? But he'd been at the Slade and had had great encouragement from McCulloch, for one. And Hammels, certainly. And others. Not all, but most. But above all, how else to interpret those fifteen years of the most absolute and profound excitement — frightening, sometimes: that mad itch to paint, paint, paint, continually! The feeling, each time he picked up a brush: positively erotic; a started canvas — after his later marriage — more inflaming than Edwina ever was. No fault of Edwina's, of course.

He'd shared a studio with that Czech chap, Jan Pachta, who had the place days; Harry, evenings. Each black night, passing the rows of black houses in the black streets on his way home to the flat, it was natural that he found the streets lifeless, the houses silent and remote. Dead. Even that his footsteps made no sound. True life was back in the studio. He lived only for the evenings. And when he reached the flat he'd oftener than not find Edwina asleep, or pretending to be. From her point of view, Harry acknowledges, he mustn't have been much to wait up for.

All gone now.

He's never discovered what triggered his
universe to turn itself upside down, but he
knows it's irreversible and now he gives it
little thought. The world of painting he'd
known, the pell-mell drive to put life on almost any receptive surface — have totally
evaporated. Shriveled away.

This is how it happened, and he remembers the evening well. His current model, a
girl who clerked in the next-door shop, had
been unable to appear that night, but he
was so close to the finish that he knew he
could manage the last touches without her.
The portrait had been giving him an enormous and sensuous pleasure for weeks. It
showed a quick-smiling girl with flowing,
luxuriant hair the color of an Irish setter's.
He'd worked a dozen colors into that hair,
every one of them necessary, each ab-
sorbing the other, and the whole thing had
been . . . well, he'd known what they meant
when people talked about crowning glory.
Her pale skin had the kind of incandes-
cence so common with that sort of red-

head. He'd first seen her on a bus, and when she alighted at his stop he'd followed her smart, quick steps to a shop nearby his own. She hadn't at all minded his request, and in his studio, after an initial hesitation, unfastened all that eloquent hair.

This night he'd just put on a touch, the merest point, of vermilion . . . there . . . and was applying over it a brush only ticked to chrome yellow when he realized quite calmly, his arm still raised, that he'd done the same thing before: the exact motion, the exact color on the same spot on the same painting of an amiable, rather vacant-looking young woman with red-setter hair who wasn't even, he'd already discovered, a natural redhead. A poster girl, actually. And at that time, too, hadn't he perceived that he'd done the same thing before? With a hammering in his chest, Harry stepped backward to look at the canvas. He leaned and turned it on its side and looked at it again. A nail drove into his heart.

Coming forward, he turned the thing upside down, scrutinizing it long and anxiously.

Yet again, over on its other side.

Truth seen from any direction is truth. Not that it came blazing at him with a soul-searing refulgence. Quietly, unmistakably, he saw that what he owned at best was a shabby talent. He had just finished a rather pretty picture. Yes, poster art. And not the very best poster art, at that. A bit clumsy here . . . here, too. He'd tried to put grape-bloom on her skin, but the colors were raw. Moreover, he'd done it before and it hadn't been frightfully good then either.

The prolonged déjà-vu experience left him slowly, trailing away like the drawing-off of the tassels of a shawl. And whatever it was, it took with it everything that had once sparked him. The exalted discoveries about painting which he'd once believed inspired and original were, Harry saw, the discoveries every student painter comes upon. Oh, but more: it was now magnificently clear to him that everyone lived his life over and over. The same life. Over and over. He'd already lived, painting frenziedly, foolishly, emptily, lived and died times without number. Two thousand times, perhaps? And was destined to trace again and again that copper arabesque of hair over the right ear — what had once seemed to him an audacious little ear, fragile and flowerlike, but now with a newly educated layman's eye, he saw cruelly as merely pink, and rather commonly shaped, at that — as he'd already done two thousand times before?

Quietly he put away his things and let himself out of the studio and walked toward home. The streets were packed with fog as dense and nearly substantial as the feet he walked on, which were rather numb and touched the ground like sponges.

He woke next morning cleansed and calm. The pawnshop job he'd once taken on lightly to pay for canvases and stretchers and tubes — for it had always been Edwina, a secretary at the BBC, who'd carried them along — he has now settled into permanently. And more and more rarely now thinks painterly thoughts.

To Harry, his cousin Berti's journey through life looks like a constant push through water. Even the way he breathes suggests effort. The few words of English he knows he speaks haltingly, but he seems incapable of learning to read the language: every word appears to remain stuck outside his eyes and refuses to enter his brain. Largely by gestures, he manages a few shy exchanges with Harry. Yet it's clear that the little fellow is more than passably intelligent. Why, Harry wonders, that air of low-keyed, doomed desperation?

He does, however, have one source of gratification: sneezing.

Berti has sneezing fits that are deep, melodious and orgasmic. They generally come upon him shortly after midday. Hedwig — and Harry, when he's present — recognizes the first premonitory tickle almost at the instant Berti does. Immediately a handkerchief is plucked from a side pocket and Berti holds it, waiting, with an almost cheerful expectancy.

This is the time of the day when Hedwig is usually in the sitting room sewing, or with a book on her lap. Like her grandfather, she reads Goethe or Schiller or Stefan George for an hour each day. Occasionally she'll direct something to Berti, in English. ("I say to him he will learn English only when he *hears* it always," she's explained to Harry. "So I ask when you speak with him you will use only English, please." "I have to," Harry says, "I only know one or two German words. I can say 'wunderbar.' And 'Gesundheit.' " And he smiles at her, hoping perhaps for a congratulatory smile, but she's looked away. He's pronounced the words execrably.)

"What a monster you sound!" she shouts at Berti one Sunday afternoon. They are all three in the sitting room. Beautiful smells come from the kitchen, where Hedwig is cooking something she calls *Hühnerbrust,* and the aroma embraces everything — even the furniture — lovingly. She closes her book with a sharp snap.

"To sneeze in such a way is common! Very common! Hold tight the nose! The nostrils together!" She demonstrates vigorously.

Obediently, Berti presses the sides of his nose together, then, after a spasmodic inhalation, sneezes deeply. *"Bitte verzeih' mir,"* he says, wiping his eyes.

This appears to be one of the days when anything Berti does can fill her with fury, and on these occasions Harry would like to club her. The poor little bastard, he thinks, born to be hounded and hectored to the end of his days.

These sneezes, now — Harry rather thinks he's got a handle on them. Somewhere inside Berti Kessler there is a robust and a mighty clamor for life. His sneezes bring release to his soul.

While she waits for the boxes in the days that follow, Hedwig Kessler reminds herself often that she and Berti are beggars. She pushes every late memory of the villa from her mind. The two of them are beggars. Exactly that. Beggars.

Of course this is only temporary. Her inner eye roams continually among the contents of the boxes, sorting out every object, wrapped, shrouded and bedded against the shocks of transportation, folded in down comforters, rolled in linen towels and hand-embroidered tablecloths. She has already accepted that she will have to sell some of the rare things she has brought with her, but like the flashing visions of Charlottenburg which, do what she will, still pierce her daily, she forces the agonizing thought from her. How can she allow a single one of them to become the property of a stranger? It is like cutting with a knife an opening into a blessed dominion, it is like laying bare the sleeping souls of the family.

Her voice severe, she says to Harry one day, "You should know something of the history of your family."

"Yes, I suppose I ought," says Harry, who has a tendency to agree with any speaker, it's how one learns others' viewpoints, is it not? For it's true — as Edwina once told him angrily — he knows nothing outside of painting. If that.

"About your mother. I suppose you do not know even how you came to be born in England."

"No. Rather, yes! My father's family's English, you know."

"Of course I know." Hedwig waves this away. "Here is what happened." And she gives him the story of his mother. Lena Kessler, daughter of Hedwig's grandfather's brother. Lena had come to England with her sister Leopoldine and their brother Friedrich to visit the Crystal Palace. The whole story is there, in one of the eight volumes that "Bookbinder" Albrecht Kessler rebound in goatskin morocco in

48

1928. The volumes are in one of the trunks.

Harry can thank his existence to something that happened in the Crystal Palace. And exactly what happens in the Crystal Palace? Hedwig sets her hands to her hips and looks firmly into Harry's eyes. Clearly, it's through the eyes that the thrust of her story will reach him. *This* is what brings Harry into existence: Lena must fall down a staircase, to be picked up by a stranger, with a broken leg. A man named Daniel Eisenstein. She is taken off to hospital, where every day he comes to visit her. Brings flowers, brings chocolates, brings English novels. It ends that he asks her to marry him and she says yes.

Terrible quarreling follows between Lena and the sister and brother, who then sensibly return to Germany. Next come exchanges of letters. A young man has been waiting at home, from a fine family in Wiesbaden, whom the aunts and uncles think highly of, but no. The quarrel eventually extends to the rest of the family, and the breach was never healed.

Harry feels a profound twinge. His mother had really done this, made her escape? He has few memories of her, none that recall even what she looked like.

Never mind all this; Lena is still in the book. Naturally. As is Harry. It's as she said, no Kessler ever vanishes. Not even Philip Levi, son of one of the aunts who'd married late to almost a stranger, in Leer, in Ostfriesland. Philip Levi, not knowing the sea was to be his last bed, had gone all by himself for a sail in a small boat and was never seen again. A piece of wood from the boat was later washed up on the shore. Not even Fanny Kessler, child of an uncle in Lübeck, who defected to Lutheranism. She is still in the book.

"When the boxes will come I will show you that you are there," Hedwig tells Harry. "Now Lena is dead, peace be with her; there is the end of another piece of our line."

"Not quite the end — there's still me." Harry grins at her. He mayn't measure up to Kessler standards, but here he is, isn't he? And hasn't he heard (though he's a terrible Jew and admits it) that somewhere in the Talmud it says it's the mother who affirms the child's line? Or has he got that mixed up with something else?

Oh, she doesn't mean to say that Harry isn't a Kessler! Yet suppose — only just suppose that it had been the brother Friedrich who had caught, falling down the stairs, a nice English — if it must be English — Jewish girl of good family, and *they* had had Harry. Harry Kessler. How right the name sounds somehow, doesn't he think so?

"No," says Harry.

Well, that is because . . . the name . . . Harry. It has more of an English sound.

"Heinrich!" Hedwig cries triumphantly. "Heinrich Kessler!"

"At your service." Laughing, Harry gives her a bow. But this is no joking matter. She knows there would be much more Kessler in Harry Eisenstein if he'd been a product of Friedrich instead of the sister Lena.

"I cannot believe that your mother never told you . . . well, but of course you were very young. But your father. She would have spoken of her family to him. He never said to you one word?"

"Not one word," says Harry, warming to the slender memories of his parents, to whom he's given little thought in years.

"That I cannot understand." She sighs heavily and shakes her head. In a way, Harry's enraptured with this cousin of his, a woman who has somehow managed to embalm her memories, which remain fresh as life. Magnificent in the half-light, Hedwig raises her hands and begins pulling silver pins from her heavy white hair. The sleeves fall back from her arms, revealing the flesh and musculature and firm roundness of a Rubens. Harry can note this calmly, with no slightest leap in the chest as he would have felt once.

Harry's met up with plenty of odd sorts —
many of them the characters who trot daily
into the shop. Like Mr. Morissey, an elderly
gentleman who comes in from loneliness
now and again to pawn a bit of men's jewelry. Nothing of much value, it's clearly for
the visit. He likes talking to Mr. Preger. Very
interested in coincidences, Mr. Morissey is.
He keeps a notebook filled with them, im-
pressively long. The latest has to do with his
greengrocer, whom he'd been surprised to
meet on a train just pulling out of Liverpool.
Mr. Morissey himself had managed to catch
it by a hair; if he'd missed, he'd never have
known the man was on the train. Or just
suppose he'd jumped into a different car?
Then, not a week later, he and the greengrocer had met again on the upper deck of a
tram near Kensington Gate. Once on, suppose the other fellow hadn't climbed the
stairs and seated himself across the aisle
from Mr. Morissey? And both of them carrying the same newspaper. Coincidences
mean something, there's no doubt about it.

Mr. Morissey has hundreds in his collection.

Another strange one is the middle-aged woman who'd come into the shop less than a week ago with a strand of yellowed cultured pearls, again not of much value — she'd been clearly disappointed at what Mr. Preger offered her, but she took it and stayed, chatting. They'd just moved house, she said, they lived in the neighborhood now and she could use a bit to see her through the end of the week. The pearls had been a wedding gift from her mother-in-law, and she'd somehow thought they were more valuable. The talk had got onto the subject of marriage. Lately, she said, she'd given much thought to what she'd do if her husband died. Even now, after thirty years, they loved each other deeply. If he should die, how she would nurture his grave! She would visit it weekly and freshen its flowers and weed its grasses; she would sit and talk to him, and gain thereby peace of soul. They would both be the better for it. The husband had not died yet.

So Harry, recognizing the lean and the fat of the flesh of the soul, can accept Hedwig's passionate hobbyhorse of family pride and history. He relishes, rather, that look her eyes take on whenever she speaks of the Kesslers, as though she's viewing faraway mountaintops.

And he has to admit to being impressed by the antiquity of his own underpinnings. It seems that Kesslers were settled in Pomerania and Brandenburg by the sixteenth century, possibly earlier, and now of course are scattered throughout Germany and Austria and God knows what is happening to them. Probably just a few tatters of family left. And then, there's that one who's got to America, Hedwig's brother Bruno. All, all, she's told Harry, every one of them in the books she's got in the trunks.

How do they survive in that wretched room. Harry wonders. The bed must be a horrible, an impossible squeeze for two people. Possibly Berti sleeps on top of her, like a flea on an elephant? Harry imagines the poor wretch amorously, laboriously, perhaps dutifully mounting his splendid wife. Needs pikestaff and pitons, probably. What wouldn't he give to watch the acrobatics, just the once.

Berti. Each day is exactly like the last: Harry returns from the job in the evening to find his cousin sitting in the feeble light of the sitting room, where he appears to have spent the day dreaming out the window. This window gets more daylight than any of the others. Berti never turns on the electricity in the flat, not even in the pinched bedroom where, perched on the bureau, there's now a quite handsome lamp Harry's brought home from the shop.

Hedwig has decided that Berti is to learn English. "He must find a job sometime soon," she says, "so of course he must learn to speak."

"What sort of job, do you think?" Harry can't imagine any work the little man is capable of doing. What would have become of him in Germany, if none of this Nazi thing had come about? Possibly there was a family business he'd been bred to, perhaps the sausage factory Hedwig's grandfather had owned. Harry can't ask about this because Hedwig still refuses to talk of the present.

"I don't know. Something. It doesn't matter. Whatever it is, he will have to speak English to someone." And heavy with her own knowledge, she sets herself to teach her husband English.

Late at night, as Harry closes the kitchen door ready to throw himself on the sofa bed, he can see the two of them in the raw glare of the kitchen light, a pile of books on the table between them, where Hedwig sits with folded arms opposite her husband.

On the Sunday last he'd heard them through the closed door — Hedwig's voice sounding almost masculine, belting out the German words for Berti to fit the English incongruities to. When she's teaching Berti, Hedwig handles the words like rocks.

"*Tisch!*" she shouted from the kitchen. "*Tisch!*" And then came the sound of the table being thumped. There followed an interval. "Table!" Hedwig boomed. More thumping. "Speak it! Tay-bull!"

It's not exactly a subject Harry's well up on, but he can think of better ways to teach English to someone like his timid cousin. In the general way of living is how he'd handle it, as when he says "Good morning" to Berti each day receiving from him an entirely recognizable repetition of

58

the words, accompanied by a briefly brilliant, friendly, but melancholy smile. More's not required, of course, Harry not being his English teacher.

He's getting rather fond of the poor wretch. It's not pity — more like admiration, actually. Imagine sharing a — There was the sound of the scraping of a chair and then a tapping on glass. "Win-dow!" The poverty of her nature had never been so clear to Harry as in what he now detected in the timbre of the voice that came through the kitchen door. A pause then the usual strangled sounds not unlike a parrot beginning an utterance, or the hesitant gurgle Harry recalls coming from the speaking tube in his father's old barn of a house at Harston. This was followed by Hedwig, screaming in German. How could a language so fashioned of bricks and boulders, Harry remembers thinking, be spoken so fast! Then, distinctly, there came a sound. A slap? Then silence.

Berti is to be enrolled in a Beginners' English Class for Foreigners, two streets away.

The boxes have actually come; two men stand at the door waiting to see what's wanted done with them. Swiftly Hedwig walks forward — today she looks particularly majestic, with that Scandinavian hard beauty that comes to her sometimes. Her hands are clasped and there's a great heaving of her rich bosom as she leans to examine the trunks — battered and scratched though they are, the locks appear intact.

Where would she like them put, missus?

"In the room at the back. Come! I will show you." The men lean down and each hoists a box on his back and, bowed low, they stagger through the flat into the kitchen, where she waves them toward the tiny bedroom. "Behind the door, over there, behind!"

They scrape into the room singly and Hedwig gasps with a hand to her chest as the second box is heaved heavily up onto the first.

She had labeled ridiculous Harry's offer to have them stacked against the side wall of the sitting room. His only concern had been to save his cousins the abominable crowding in there. But she seems to need to sleep on them, perhaps against thieves coming in the night to pinch some of the family bones. So the things are put where she wants them and now one can't take a full breath in that room where she and Berti sleep.

Harry knows what is in the boxes. Those perishing volumes of family history, as well as every treasure from the house in Charlottenburg that could be packed in (she has described the villa's rooms twenty times over, that backdrop to the immaculate memories of her childhood): paintings, rugs, tapestries, many prized family documents, Meissen, linens, even embroideries brought back from some great-great-great-aunt's honeymoon in Venice, a woman already five generations in her grave. Harry's read somewhere of a family of Sephardic Jews who two hundred years ago had fled to Germany from a city in Spain, taking the doorknobs of their houses with them. He guesses that his cousin's trunks probably also contain doorknobs.

(All the same, how has she managed to get them here?)

Berti's come in, the lonely little man has

61

risen from his chair beside the window and padded in silently, and now the three of them stand viewing the two trunks of thick, ocher-colored leather, clearly built for turbulent round-the-world travel.

"D'you want me to open them for you? I'll fetch some tools."

Awakened from her daydreams, she gives Harry a spacious look and shakes her head. "No." She seems to want only to stand and look at them.

She's told him they contain all that's left of the family. It must be true — there can't be much hope for the Kesslers who've remained, or anything they've owned, either. The stories are daily becoming more ghastly, even on the wireless one hears about Jews disappearing — and now he believes them totally — like the grandparents, from the streets. Or pulled screaming from their homes, or forced to their knees outdoors and made to clean gutters and latrines. Stories you'd expect would at least play the deuce with Hedwig's peace of mind, though she shows nothing. Usually, when Harry turns on the set, she leaves the room to busy herself in the kitchen. And on the few occasions when she does remain, she sits — dispassionate, stolid — her eyes on her sewing or knitting or the book on her lap, not a flicker on her face. Not even her lips tighten. It's possible she knows how to turn off her ears.

He hears worse at the shop. Things not even the newspapers print.

Days later Harry, happening past the doorway when Hedwig has got the top box open and some of its contents spilled out on the bed, has a lightning glimpse of a splendid jumble. Her treasures: tobies and pitchers, he recognizes, and lying on its side rather close to the edge, an engraved tankard — heavy, ancient-looking and certainly silver, for it's nearly black with tarnish. The top is domed, much like one he's seen at the shop which Preger shows to a privileged few but has always refused to sell. If this one is as old as it looks it must be worth the earth.

Hedwig, who has been standing viewing the contents of the bed with absorbed tenderness, sees him, gives a start, then flings a wide Spanish scarf into the air, and both of them watch with appreciative pleasure as the red-black-and-gold billows sink and cover the lot on the bed. Not a word is said, and Harry leaves the kitchen guiltily.

What bothers her? Is she trying to hide her wealth from him? Ought he reassure her that, though his mother was a Kessler, he has no claim nor designs on the family heirlooms?

She says very little for the rest of that evening, but on her way to bed stops beside the chair where Harry is reading. "I have picked some pieces from one of the boxes. I will want to sell a few of them," she tells him stiffly. "Berti and I will share expenses with you so long as we stay here."

Harry sets his newspaper aside. "There's really no need of that."

"Even so." She clasps her hands tightly and raises her chin. "We wish to contribute to the house. If you will please to take some small pieces to your shop and show to your employer."

Harry will have nothing to do with parting Hedwig from even one of the family treasures. "You *do* contribute, you know! You shop, you cook, you tend house."

"Still."

They regard each other for a long moment. "Well, you won't want my sort of shop; pawnshops won't give you anything near their proper worth." He hesitates, then, as she stands immovable beside the chair, he rises, takes paper and pen and writes down for her the names of some reputable dealers in antiques and old silver.

It may appear to Harry that Berti spends the day in the sitting room's only upholstered chair looking disconsolately out the window, but this is not the case. When breakfast is over and Harry's left for work, Hedwig goes into the tiny bedroom. There, no matter what the weather, she flings up the meager court window, which will remain open for half the day, pillows and bedclothes piled on the sill. Then she fastens her hat firmly over her plaited hair, wraps herself against the whipping autumn winds and, with her purse and string bag, departs for the day's food shopping, accompanied by her husband.

There's very little conversation. Bearing his best interests in mind, Hedwig will speak to him only in English, therefore Berti rarely talks. He's beginning to comprehend the language, thanks to the beginners' course, though still almost every English word comes uneasily to his mouth. He values the class mainly for his fellow students, all German-speaking and, like him, fugitives from a native land turned nightmare. He's made one or two good friends, and they speak only German to one another outside the classroom.

He takes a fragile pleasure in these walks with Hedwig, who sets the pace, which is a speedy one, so that Berti almost trots beside her. She can't wait to leave these shoddy surroundings, every street is an affront to her. Never once has she walked into a single shop in the immediate neighborhood of Harry's flat.

Berti sees as well as she how sad and dirty the streets are. But where they fill her with distaste, he discovers a certain excitement: everything is very raw, very human. This fried-fish shop, for instance. These are honest, living streets, and Harry's building, as shabby as any of them, is an honest building. Also, he has a presentiment that it's in some such place as this one that he and Hedwig may well have to live permanently. They are unlikely ever to return to Germany, though this is apparently something Hedwig will not believe. She is wrong. Things are bad at home now? As bad as they can be, one thinks? They are getting worse.

"Here we cross," Hedwig says abruptly, making a turn to the left, though on other days they have always proceeded straight on for some distance, to the better section. Her sudden swing interrupts Berti's body and his sorrowful train of thought. *"'S tut mir leid,"* he apologizes hastily, and she looks at him with rage.

What's been occupying Berti's thoughts is something Marcus Koppelmann told him yesterday — Marcus, who is also in the English class. All over Germany they are continuing the breaking of windows of Jewish shopkeepers, and houses, and synagogues, and burning their houses, and forcing the fleeing people back inside them. Berti sends a sidewise look up at his wife, plowing grimly on beside him. The news, Marcus told him, has been on the wireless and in the newspapers for several days. Hedwig must know of it, but she has said nothing to either him or Harry. Not until now has Berti — living in the midst of a language he knows little of — felt how like it is to being deaf and blind. He will work harder in his class. He will ask Marcus and the others if maybe they shouldn't try to speak in English when they are in the *Kaffeehaus* near the school. A little.

He and Hedwig have come to a new section now, one strange to them both. It has the same air of general decay as Harry's area, and in the sharp autumn air the people he sees put him in mind of worn rugs walking, which he knows is a foolish thought. Yet as he scans their faces they do not appear to him more unhappy than the better-dressed ones in the shopping district Hedwig prefers. "Walk faster," says Hedwig.

At first Hedwig thinks it's perhaps because of too much *Schnaps*. She likes a drop in the afternoons, just as Grosspapa had, and also a drop at bedtime. Perhaps another, now and again. She has even brought with her, and carries in her purse, Grosspapa's little green *Schnapsglas*. But two weeks later there is still pain and nausea, and she limits herself to the small glassful at night, to help with the sleeping. Now even that she has to stop. Another two weeks, and still it is no good. If anything, the pains in the belly are increasing. It must be cancer.

Keeping the fearful symptoms to herself, she goes to consult a doctor in Eaton Square recommended by a woman shopkeeper she trusts.

When the doctor finishes his examination he asks her some questions, then looks at Hedwig thoughtfully, but says nothing until she is seated across the desk from him in his consulting room. He is wearing what seems to her to be sporting clothes. His bronzed, seasoned bald head and face suggest frequent riding on horses or playing the game where a small white ball is whipped across close-cropped green fields. Not, to her way of thinking, what sight of a doctor should bring to someone's mind.

"My dear young woman," she hears him saying, "you are, I should say, approximately three months pregnant." There is a touch of asperity in the way he looks at her. "Surely this doesn't come as a total surprise to you?"

She receives his words impassively, letting her eyes rest on his walnut-colored brow, which reflects the green-shaded light from the desk lamp. "Yes," she says. "A total surprise."

Throwing her a skeptical glance, he opens a drawer, takes out a prescription pad and plucks a pen from the jug on his desk. "You surely must have . . . I mean to say, you've missed three periods, you know. It's not a thing one wouldn't notice."

She watches the pen fly swiftly across the paper. "I thought it must have been . . . I have been now under great . . . great . . ." Hopelessly, she seeks the English word.

"Strain?" he supplies, scribbling, and she gives a short, vigorous nod. "Strain. Great strain. I — my husband and I — have recently come here . . ."

"Yes. Well . . . that does happen. You've just come away from Germany, have you?"

"Three months."

"I see." He throws her a quick glance, then resumes his writing.

"And then . . . the pain, I have thought . . ."

"Nothing of importance that I can see now." He tears off the sheet and pushes it across the desk to her. "This will very likely take care of the pain. Also the nausea. One tablet three times a day. With meals. I'd like you to do away with all salt, if possible. And I want to see you in a month. Sooner, if the pain persists. Shall we say two weeks?"

So. A child.

Hedwig is a strong woman, as witness the means of departure from . . . as always, immediately down comes the curtain.

So, Hedwig thinks. A child.

She gives the matter much thought.

A baby, as a baby, has as yet little meaning for her. With the passing days what goes on in her head rarely relates to what may be transpiring below her rib cage. She pictures no tiny developing homunculus, feels as yet no maternal pulse of warmth.

A child means the priceless treasures need not, after all, turn green or fall to brittle crumbs in musty cases in dark museums G—d alone knows where. Now she can do more than take over from Grosspapa the role of guardian of the books. She can hand them on.

There are other things to consider.

To start at the beginning, she has no intention that she and Berti will stay on in this *unreinliche* flat with their cousin Harry.

She won't say she cares greatly for this cousin of theirs, never mind the ears: a man of few interests who reads no books, listens to no music, knows nothing of art and appears content to live each day as he has lived the day before. It is the English father in him. The instant he'd opened his door to her knocking she had recognized something of the sort in her first glimpse of that London face of his, the color of brass. Clearly, this is not a healthy man and she is not surprised. See what he has been eating, buying his food at cooked-meat shops, *schreckliche* pies of kidney, and soups from tins and a thing that here they call liver sausage that would have made Grosspapa vomit — yes, vomit! — only to look at it. And there is also the air, another thing she caught instantly at first step out from the train. This city is very bad for breathing. She remembers what Grosspapa has told her about oxygen and carbon monoxide and how lungs should always be — shiny-red and slippery.

And that manner Harry has, as though he stands off one hundred meters and looks at you through a *Teleskop*. Always, always examining and saying nothing. Measuring, always measuring, that one. Is he wishing to read her soul? She has done her best — she and Berti are both of course grateful to him — and she has tried to open herself out and take him in, but something in him does not let her. Harry is of the family and at the same time he is not of the family. The mean little job he has — even in a neighborhood where workingmen come out from their houses at dawn carrying their lunches, Harry does not stand out, though he leaves two hours later. His work she does not approve of. His employer may be Jewish and even has a German name, but she looks coldly on pawnbrokers, into whose illiberal hands forever vanish the cherished possessions of generations. She knows this not because of what Harry has told her but because, without consulting him first, it was to a pawnbroker that she made a visit, carrying two silver spice boxes, the day after opening the first trunk.

And this building. From every open passage comes the smell of phenol, like from a public lavatory. And the flat itself. From every window comes in nothing but gloom.

She's given some thought lately to her brother Bruno and to America, where he was sent at the age of eight, to be raised by their mother's people. Mistily, Hedwig can recall great discord between Bruno and

Grosspapa, seeming somehow having to do with Bruno's head of brilliant red curls.

Yet America will be even more foreign in its ways than England, and even farther off. She knows from the way both Harry and Berti look when she sometimes speaks of Charlottenburg in her natural conversations how they perhaps think she still lives in the ashes of the past, but it is not so. Who can cut, like with a scissors, such an important tie? In any case, she knows they will in a few years return to Germany, when the madness will be over.

From America, her brother Bruno writes rarely, usually in answer to a letter from her, and not always then, and when he does, he writes only in English.

"Can't you see the signs? Are you blind?" he shouted at her in Charlottenburg three years ago. "Listen to me and get yourself out of there while the getting is good!"

She'd read the letter with shock and incomprehension. Leave Germany? Leave Charlottenburg because of some monster stories people are telling? Grossvater to leave his wurst works? Who could know then, Hedwig has a hundred times asked herself since, about the gorillas — that is what Bruno called them, gorillas in black boots. (Yet how can it be that the Americans knew?)

"What the hell are you waiting for?" Bruno shouted again, later, from across the ocean. "Nonsense," said Grosspapa when, again troubled, she spoke to him. Nothing is intended for them, not to their kind of people. To agitators, loiterers, traitors, Communists, maybe yes. And others who would debauch the Fatherland. A new Germany is being built, a thing that some find hard to realize. Some are saying bad things about Jews? These are the kind of excesses one finds in any new movement. He even made jokes about the Nazis. She will see, things will arrange themselves in time, and Hedwig agreed. The dinner-table arguments with relatives and friends. Some were Zionists. To be a Zionist in Germany is to be a lunatic, said Grosspapa. It is to hack at the very ground beneath one's feet. The stories? Over-blown. Their good friend Oberst von Heisermann — the von Heisermanns and the Kesslers have been close since Grosspapa's own grandfather's day — even Oberst Otto von Heisermann, who is a *grosses Tier* in the National Socialist Party, says the same. The stories are extravagance spread by the enemies of the new Germany. Grosspapa sent the new party 25,000 Reichsmarks.

They could not believe it when the racial laws were proclaimed. Hedwig refused to credit them, she had continued to patronize the *Feinkostläden,* the luxury food shop on the Kurfürstendamm, where since girlhood she had accompanied her grandmother on food-shopping trips. The thick cables of her beautiful hair wound round her head, she continued to walk imperturbably into the shops that refused to serve dogs and Jews, and where her queenly presence was acknowledged. She continued to give her orders crisply, sending clerks scaling the walls like lizards. No ordinary Jewish woman would have dared it — but, for that matter, how many women look like Rhine maidens?

"Still sitting on your keisters? Begging for it?!!" Bruno raged in a still-later letter which Hedwig never received.

Only when Grosspapa and Grossmama were swept away like a couple of dried leaves in a high wind did Hedwig realize that the ailing old man had no more judgment than a baby. And after a night spent in an inconsolable passion of sorrow and fear, she went to call unannounced at the villa of Otto von Heisermann.

This time, Otto made many things clear.

Now they are here, in London, and it is plain that except for what lies lovingly in the boxes, there will be nothing left, historically, of the Kessler dynasty. Physically, she and Berti may be the only survivors. Oh, and Harry, of course. Perhaps Bruno, too, who will not even say the word Germany. He has long ago been adopted by their mother's family in America, who live in some place with a French name. Saint Louis. And has changed his own name to that of their mother. What he calls himself now — Bruno Brodsky — can only make a person laugh. But the *Grosseltern* did not laugh. They never spoke of him, never, not even on the days when his rare letters to her arrived.

Bruno was eight years old in early 1914, when the elder Kesslers booted him out of Germany. He hadn't the remotest idea of why he was being shipped off. His and Hedwig's mother's family, already established in America, received him with open arms, and the matter of the Kessler rejection was never brought up. Could it be, Bruno asked himself, because his mother came of Russian people? From living in the Kessler household he knew with what scorn German Jews looked upon Russian Jews. But why was this? Because Russian people didn't read Stefan George? Or didn't eat *Apfelbettelmann?*

Yet the old folks kept his sister. Because, Bruno decided at the time, Hedwig had blue eyes like their father, and also his pale, pale hair.

Now he knows. Hedwig, three years younger than he, didn't remember — as he did — how their parents died. An auto accident, a terrible auto accident, they told the children, and then couldn't get rid of Bruno fast enough.

He can still recall the grandfather very well. Straight and glossy-whiskered, a man who rose at six every morning to do his calisthenics, followed by a bathe. Then down the back stairs to the kitchen where, a half hour before he took breakfast, he spooned psyllium seed into a cup of boiling water and drank it down.

A heavily family-conscious man. A pious Jew with German roots. A pious German with Jewish roots. In his sixties when Bruno was a boy, Bruno remembers him as an old man upright and steely, who somehow managed to pour blackness into every room he entered. That was at home. At the wurst works, where he'd taken the boy a few times, Bruno had once seen him smile, and glimpsed the man his employees saw — a stiff, courteous, elderly gentleman.

They never saw the man he became once the library door was closed.

The library was a sunless room which, but for three narrow ceiling windows, was separated from the world. Though Bruno visited it daily, all he can recall of it now is its total atmosphere of leather — a heavy, near-suffocating smell: massive leather chairs and a long couch, all with the black, malevolent shine of the licorice dice one of the visiting uncles used to bring from Vienna. Instead of walls, shelves of dark-bound leather-swelling books climbed to the ceiling. Bruno cannot recall a single title.

Here, into this room, every evening shortly before dinner the boy was pushed, then grasped — usually by the collar — and thrust onto the leather couch whose chill immediately began to eat into his bare legs.

Then the old man began to talk, pacing the room jerkily, one arm behind his back, crooked at the elbow; the other flailing, cutting the air to ribbons as he spoke. At intervals as he passed through the slanted late-afternoon light pouring from the high narrow windows, each momentarily engulfed him in a shaft of golden book-dust — the fierce finger of God stabbing home the grandfather's every word.

The lecture always began softly, the grandfather taking purest pleasure in his finely
modulated German: the voice of the dinner
table, the voice of the parlor, the voice of the
wurst factory. Circling the room as he
talked, walking in and through the golden
slanting pillars of light, shortly the tone
began to roughen, and here came the moment
when the boy sitting stiff-legged on the
couch saw the shelves of black books begin
to tip slowly and perilously toward him from
the top, like the inner walls of a pyramid.

And then suddenly the grandfather's
voice was hoarse and, his arms unglued, he
began punctuating the air, shouting at the
grandson. If the day's behavior had not
been rich enough in infractions — a rare
thing — old ones were hauled from the
past. Now the voice became exalted in its
brutality, unrecognizable, and his hatred of
the child shone in the room like a radiance.

At the end of these evening sessions the
grandfather strode to the heavily studded
library doors and flung them open and

stood with blazing eyes as the boy crept in silent misery out to the hallway.

Did any of this carry beyond the walls? Furtively, Bruno tried to glimpse, on the faces of the others in the house, some acknowledgment of the sounds from the leather room. But the two women servants continued impassively about their duties. Hedwig was always upstairs with the nurse, having her bath. With regard to the grandmother, Bruno could never make up his mind. To this day she remains a sepia-colored figure in his mind: thinner and straighter than her husband, always dressed in shades of brown with an ecru-colored something at the throat and a row of tiny buttons down the middle of her chest to the waist. Though he can't recall her features, her face is astonishingly white in his memory, due — he used to think — to her powdering her face with flour. And though she must surely have spoken some words to him during the first eight years of his life, he cannot, as with the book titles in the library, recall one of them.

Came the day they dressed him in his short German jacket and attached a shipping tag to his collar and, with two valises, dispatched him like a parcel to his mother's people, who many years before had left Russia to live in America. The Brodskys met his ship in New York.

"He looks like Elena," they told one another, "only see the hair!" and took him in their arms and hugged him unmercifully and carried him with them to Saint Louis. When they arrived at their house, his jacket had barely been removed before they thrust letters into his face. Could he read Russian? Here were the letters his mother had written before her death two years earlier. They translated them to him, and Bruno stashed the nightmare of their message permanently away beside his own German memories, so that even up to quite recently, though he's now a married man and Hedwig herself is married, he's been fearful of what the grandparents might do to his sister, who is, like him, half Brodsky.

The Brodskys wrote to the old man, asking the Kesslers' permission to adopt the boy legally and have his name changed to theirs, and at once Herr Kessler sent his consent in the spider legs of his elegant German calligraphy, on the stationery of the wurst works.

Practically everyone coming in now has a story
to tell. Yesterday Mr. Preger was at home with
a cold and his wife took his place in the shop.
A woman came in to ask the price of a har-
monica in the window. Though her English
wasn't frightfully good, she had an accent similar to Hedwig's. Before leaving she told them
about a little Jewish child in a village near
Frankfurt, who was ordered suddenly from
her ballet class. She had no business being
there, a new sign — in German, of course —
had been put in the window: "It is forbidden
that dogs and Jews study the dance."

Her parents were sent for. Only the
mother was at home, and she came quickly
to pick up the little girl, who was waiting
for her outside, wearing only her tutu.

"Oh she must have been cold!" cried
Mrs. Preger.

Two Nazi thugs stood beside her. "Let us
see the little girl dance," they ordered the
mother when she arrived. "Let us see if a
little Jew can dance." So the child danced.
She was a very young child, she missed a

step and stumbled, and they shot her dead. In front of her mother they shot her.

"Oh God!" Mrs. Preger exploded into tears. No. No, she wouldn't believe such a thing. Such a story is like a splinter in the heart. She wiped at her cheeks and said "Those are the sort of things people like to tell nowadays. They are too terrible to be true."

The woman paused with her hand on the latch. "They are true," she said softly.

The stories. The stories.

Even suppose, Harry thinks, only some of them are true. Or a part, only, of all of them. And now he looks guardedly at Hedwig, wishing he could like her better. It's likely that she and that mite of a husband of hers have had some experiences that are half this side of nightmare. There is still nothing to be got out of her. She remains closed off. But for the tale of the abduction of the grandparents, she has never spoken of their recent life in Germany.

Nor will she lend herself to pity.

Actually Harry gets more out of Berti, who still barely speaks English. Each time their eyes meet, Harry reads a sober message there, a message that surely accounts for the little man's bleached energies. It's really all very simple, Berti's eyes tell Harry. The world is chaos.

Harry comes from work one day to discover Berti in his usual place at the window but now there's a newspaper in his lap, and Harry shouts joyfully, "What's that you've got there, the *Times*, isn't it?" How delighted he is to have found a conversational gambit — positively the first since the cousins' arrival.

Slowly, Berti turns his sad dog's eyes on him.

"English coming along?"

Now Berti's look is almost rapt, and his lips tremble as he strives to fit English words into the puzzle of his reply as though he's picking up pieces of glass. "Nicht . . ." Berti says, and then rustles the paper disconsolately. He recovers: "Not . . . sehr . . . gut. Gooood."

"It'll come, it'll come," Harry says, "bit hard at first go off, just you give it time." And to end this infliction of pain on the two of them walks quickly on into the kitchen. In any event, he's keen to investigate a spicy odor his nose picked up the moment he came in the door. Hedwig's fixing something lovely; the old trout's a magnificent cook.

Harry has now accepted that the two of them will be with him for some time. Actually he's rather glad of the company, for he's never really come to terms with solitude, so far as life in the flat is concerned. And though he still occasionally feels a flash of something very like fear when faced with Hedwig's massive indomitableness, she's mainly on a level he can relate to. It's Berti who continues to bewilder him. A man fashioned without condiments. That air he has of transience. His manner of seeming to look at life as though the world hurts his eyes. What, Harry wonders, has so denatured him? Though every bit as much a Kessler as his wife, it's Hedwig alone who wears the breastplate and helmet. Poor chap, poor chap. A dwarf in the hall of the Mountain King.

She is seven months gone before she makes her announcement.

Harry beams. "Unbelievable!" Isn't it, though? For actually he's never been able to bring himself to really believe in any physical communion between those two. Who could imagine Berti — Berti, with the pained, secret eyes who sits folded over the *Times*, wrestling with English while mournfully relishing his daily sneezes — who could see that little chap successfully scaling his monumental wife?

Still, he must have accepted the off-chance of it, otherwise why the delicacy of his refusal to step into the kitchen, once they'd closed their door at night? Many's the time he waked into a long bout of sleeplessness, yet denied himself a cup of tea or a look into the fridge lest he overhear acrobatics, however unlikely, from the tiny room.

So it turns out after all that Dagobert Kessler knew Hedwig his wife; and she conceived; and will shortly bear a child and boast: I have gotten a man from the Lord. For, again, when Harry comes to think of it, the Lord seems infinitely more likely to have fathered a child upon Hedwig than her mouse of a husband.

Hedwig walks four kilometers a day. For the baby. On different days, selecting different directions. It's also a way of getting to know London, those parts beyond the radius of Harry's street that she already knows. Occasionally she leaves early in the morning while Harry is still at home, and he stands behind Berti at his window, and the two of them watch her strong, rapid strides which take her swiftly out of sight. He's heard that Germans are great walkers.

"Where does one find milk from goats in London?" she wants to know. "Grosspapa says only such milk has the proper minerals for bones. All the Berlin and Frankfurt aunts drink it when they are making babies. You would not believe such children they have!"

Those would be the athletic Kesslers she's speaking of. Harry's heard about all of them many times over, he can almost give faces to the familiar names. He's had to climb the family tree with her and examine every leaf and fruit on it, before clambering out on the insignificant limb where he himself hangs, thanks to a dab of family cement.

The admiration he feels for his mother's defection now verges on reverence.

On this, the sporting side of the family, were the tennis Kesslers, the swimming Kesslers, the pole-vaulting Kesslers, the discus-throwing Kesslers — two from this clan had even been in the 1924 Olympics. All very big on health. Even Hedwig's grandmother: Friday mornings, without fail, Hedwig has told Harry, a physical therapist arrived on her bicycle at eight o'clock sharp and mounted the steps of the villa, her knapsack filled with professional paraphernalia, to give Grossmutti her high colonic.

There were Kesslers of other sorts as well, of course: philosophers, poets, Talmudic scholars. Kesslers were scientists, mountain climbers, revolutionaries, mathematicians, rakehells, historians, musicians . . .

Musicians! Almost every Kessler was also a musician. When meeting for birthday celebrations or family dinners, they arrived with instruments, and immediately three, four, half a dozen were seated in the living room behind the music stands which were kept in one of the hall closets.

Harry sees them and almost can hear them, tootling or sawing away at Vivaldi and Telemann. On the brink of extermination.

Kesslers manufactured microscopes and played the cello. They published religious texts or ground optical lenses by day and practiced the violin by night. They were diamond cutters and flutists, otolaryngologists and oboists . . .

One of the Kesslers — Grossvater — played nothing. He had been an athletic Kessler, in his youth an Alpinist and a hiker, and lately the only music he liked, Hedwig told Harry with heavy merriment (the recent years and his disappearance had no place in these recollections), was the song of healthy blood coursing through healthy arteries. He found the music of a sound digestion more rollicking than Rossini. To be sure, he had been a physician once — did Harry know that? — before retiring and taking over the family's wurst factory, hence could be allowed certain vulgarities. There is a rather coarse little verse he is fond of, Hedwig says, and if Harry will give her a minute or so she will turn it into English.

She discovers she can even make the English words rhyme. It goes like this, if

Harry will only please excuse the words, and she recites in her Berlin-accented English:

When the farts are loud
and the urine is clear,
then the doctor's knock
you will never hear.

Her face red, she's laughing. It is a vulgar thing, not? but a thing Grosspapa was fond of. "Always he takes very fine care of himself, one whole hour every morning before breakfast he sits on the machine you ride like a bicycle but it stays in one place. And in the evening he walks, with Grossmutti. Always they have their . . ." Here she falters, she has reached the walk from which Grosspapa and Grossmutti did not return.

Harry no longer feels alarmed when she speaks in this manner. She may or may not have trouble with her tenses, but if she'd only let herself speak a bit about what's going on over there she might be able to remove the blockage that closes off one of her passages to reality. But she still appears numb to what's in the papers or coming over the wireless. How is it possible to live this way? Clearly, she never looks into her husband's eyes to see what Harry sees.

The birth of the little girl comes off quite suddenly, a bit a head of its proper time, but smoothly.

When the child's sex is announced to her Hedwig gazes reflectively at the ceiling and says nothing. She is lying in bed looking very tired and very pink, her mass of white hair hidden by the towel bound round her head. But she is frowning. This has to do with Berti.

He'd been deeply apprehensive during her labor, which — but for one very loud groan at the outset — turned out to be miraculously easy. Berti heard the groan, the whole thing having come on her rather suddenly while on her hands and knees scrubbing down the lino in the kitchen — the only position, she said, in which she felt comfortable during this last month, and therefore why ought she not get some work done while she was about it? It was undoubtedly surprise more than anything else that had made her cry out.

Harry was able to find a taxicab at once,

and with exaggerated care he and Berti helped her in. During the ride to hospital she sat very straight — composed, even, except for the deep rhythmic heaving of her breast. Calmly, she explained to the two men regarding her worriedly that this is how the Berlin aunts and cousins always breathe at such a time, deep down in the abdomen, it is for the easing of labor pains.

Berti sees their child before Hedwig does. He is standing worriedly in the corridor when Nurse emerges from the delivery room with a wailing white cocoon in her arms. Down the hall she sails smartly on her rubber soles, and after a moment's hesitation in the cool wind-scallops of her wake Berti follows in silence. He sees her disappear through the doors of the nursery and then throws a quick, haunted look up and down the corridor as though he has it in mind to follow her. But a moment later he is leaning against the opposite wall, his eyes fixed on the nursery doors.

The passage has the feel of a subterranean hall and the cracked corridor walls, the color of cheese, have an unpleasant resinous smell that agitates him. More than anything he's experienced since coming to London, the odors throughout this building seem to have the power to revive his past. Often ill as a child, he'd been twice removed to hospital, and now even the emanations from these green walls stir pains in his chest.

Nurse has abruptly come out again and is startled to see him. "And what might *you* be doing here? Who are you? You'll have to leave; no one's allowed in this passage, you know."

"Excuse me, I am the father."

"Oh, it's your baby, is it?" She is young and blond and homely in a comfort-giving kind of way, and she flashes Berti a searching look. "Want to see her, luv? You've got a little girl, did you know? Stand over here next the window and I'll show her to you," and she's gone through the doors again.

Now she is visible inside the broad glass window, the white bundle in her arms. Tenderly, she lifts a flap at the top, displaying a tiny, dark, round knob — wrinkled, and looking as though someone has pressed from top and bottom to push the tiny face together. Berti sees one of the rubber gnomeheads on Japanese pencils that schoolchildren buy. The baby's mouth is open — undoubtedly it is crying. It has also an unbelievable amount of coarse black hair.

Holding her, Nurse smiles out at Berti through the glass, but when she glimpses his stricken look she quickly withdraws with the child and is out the door in almost no time at all.

"You mustn't —" she begins, but Berti's anguish interrupts her. "Not our baby," he says in a low voice.

"What's that, luv?"

"Is not our baby!" he nearly shouts.

"Not your baby? Whatever are you saying? I'd like you to know I'm not even allowed to show her to you this soon, but you looked so . . . so *forlorn,* standing out here like that!" She puts her hands on her hips, studies him and shakes her head reprovingly. "That's a beastly thing to say. I just brought her in, didn't I? You saw me just bring her in. You have a dear little girl!"

Berti looks into her face for a moment, then turns and walks miserably back down the passage. She calls down after him: "Ain't none of 'em beautiful when they're first out, you know!"

Harry's come to the hospital and has a look at the baby too, and can't find a scrap of relationship to either parent. Even imagining so farfetched a thing as Berti's not being the father — an impossibility, surely an outlandish baby isn't required to make such a notion plausible — it's hard to understand how nothing of Hedwig has come through.

The baby's an oddity, practically a ball of fur, with a head of spidery black hair and a covering of down on her arms and legs that's actually comical. Harry imagines his cousin Hedwig mating with an ape, an idea that delights him, and he indulges in all possible aspects of the fantasy, brightening a day which has been otherwise quite horrible.

That morning, crossing the road opposite the shop, he'd run into his old painting colleague whom at one time he'd shared his studio with, known with affection among their friends as the crazy Czech. Jan . . . Jan . . . Harry searched for the other name. Pachta! Jan Pachta. But how changed. His face, which had used always to be crinkled with a strongly infectious silent merriment, was gnarled with the kind of suffering Harry was becoming used to seeing lately. The planes of the face he'd known were rilled into the gaunt longitudinal lines of El Greco's *Saint Louis*. He'd gone hollow and grey, and the eyes didn't bear looking at. They recognized each other at the same moment and then Pachta had stumbled and Harry had practically to catch him in his arms.

"Jan, in God's name what's happened to you? You look positively frightful. Are you ill?"

"They have killed my brother and his wife."

The two stared at each other. "My little brother," Pachta said. Tears streamed down his face.

"Who?"

"The Germans. Who else?"

"But what were they doing in Germany? I thought . . ."

"At home. It was at home. In Kladno."

"Are you sure . . . you said Germans . . ."

"Germans! Germans! Of course the Germans! No one seems to know they are already in my country and they have killed Emil and they have killed Annie." Pachta covered his face with both hands and his voice came choking, thick and wet against his palms. "And they are not even Jews . . ."

Nurse has just taken baby away after Hedwig's attempt to give her the breast. This has not gone well, but everyone knows such a thing takes time. Hedwig pushes herself up among the pillows, then announces to Berti, sitting beside her bed, that she wants to call the baby Waltraut. She is wearing one of the treasures from the trunks, a fine bed gown of raw silk, its bodice inset with handmade lace that had certainly brought blindness to some seamstress in one of those dungeon ateliers in Venice. Two fat white plaits of hair trail down the length of her rich bosom. She is pink and totally restored, childbirth a minor incident of yesterday.

"Always there has been a Waltraut in the family." As though defending the name against Berti's silence, her voice becomes sharp. "You remember Urgrossmutter Waltraut from Jena?"

Berti lifts his eyes from the scrubbed stone floor to the tent formed by the double humps of her feet under the bed-clothes. The hospital smell is especially dense here in Hedwig's room, everything gives him a pain in the chest. The green walls, the floor, the bed linens, all exude that terrible smell. He pulls a handkerchief from his pocket and holds it tightly against his nose.

"And then the niece, Grossmutti's cousin. From Minde. The one who was cut in two pieces by lightning. It is in the book. Waltraut Goldner." Slowly, contemplatively, she strokes down her braids of hair.

"And after that, Cousin Hannelore Waltraut from Hanover. Waltraut was her middle name. It is right that we name this one after Cousin Hannelore Waltraut; she even looks like her."

"No," says Berti in a tight voice.

"Yes. A little." Hedwig gives him a swift look.

Berti says, speaking through the handkerchief, "Cousin Hannelore was pale. Always. I remember. And her hair. Like yours."

Hedwig says serenely, "You have a bad memory," as she continues smoothing down the ropes of her hair.

"Is not our baby."

"What is that you say?" At once Hedwig sits up.

"Is not our baby."

The doctor who has delivered her

chooses this moment to enter the room to see how his patient is doing. He looks cheerily at the two of them and is not prepared for the moody little husband sitting beside the bed. "Everything is going well, is going well," he says, in a Germanic accent thicker than Hedwig's. "In seven days you will be going home, you are doing very well. And the baby too. All going very very well. You have any questions?"

Hedwig shakes her head. Berti stares at the floor.

"I will stop in again later today. Rest. Sleep. I have nothing else to tell you. Everything is going very very well." And the doctor leaves. Before the door has closed behind him Berti has risen from his chair and follows him out into the corridor. The two walk down the hall until they reach a nurse's desk, whereupon the doctor turns and regards Berti with surprise.

"You have a question?"

"Is not our baby."

"What's that you say?" Nurse looks up expectantly. "What do you mean, not your baby? Of course it is your baby!"

"An exchange. This one . . . a gypsy child." The doctor glares at him, but, tightly, Berti stands his ground.

Nurse breaks in. "She'll get lighter, luv.

They're often dark first off this way."

"She will not. By the ears I can tell."

The doctor, himself a refugee from Munchen, now cries out at Berti's suspicions. "Not your baby!" he almost screams. "How can you say this is a gypsy's baby? There are no gypsies in this place. Babies cannot be mixed up here! You have a baby *geistreich!* Absolutely *geistreich!* This I could tell you the moment he came out. The hair will all fall away, it happens sometimes, in a month you will not know your baby!"

Berti murmurs something.

The doctor knows positively that he received this child from between this woman's own legs.

"The moment he came out. To look at him is to know one day he will do great things!"

He has already forgotten what is between the baby's own legs. Nurse leans to whisper in his ear; flustered, waving his hands in the air, the doctor flees down the corridor.

"She'll have a thin time of it here with a name like that," Harry says.

He considers himself the baby's god-father — out of pity, one might say, considering how neither parent seems overly concerned with the tiny thing itself. It still looks like a muff. He wouldn't exactly have expected childbirth to loose a flood of maternal emotion in Hedwig; but it seems to have awakened in her little more than a need to give the family tree another shake. If he confers upon the brown little girl no other gift, Harry feels, let it be said he's spared her the agony of a name that will make people laugh.

"Mightn't it be wise to choose a name that English people have heard before?"

He keeps trying to see in this baby some mark of authorship by even one parent. Its gnomishness is perhaps faintly reminiscent of Berti. But the little thing, four days after its birth, is as dark and furry as ever.

"It will lose the hair, it will lose the hair!" the doctor has told them testily again, refusing to meet Berti's stunned eyes. "In a few weeks you will see I am right. This sort of thing happens with babies now and then, it is in fact quite common!"

Harry supposes he may be right. What does he know about newborns? All the same, he has little patience with his cousin's fanciful absurdities; the little girl had ought to be given a name that will help her dissolve in a crowd. Mildred, Millie, he thinks. Brenda, perhaps.

"Gertrud," suggests Berti one day.

"It is better a name we already have in the family," Hedwig responds. "Let me think some more." Yes yes, Harry sees, she's still climbing the tree, and still will not see the ax being taken to the limbs.

Then she says dreamily, "There is also a very old name, far back, and also in legends. Mechtildis. A beautiful name."

Harry's impulse is to grab his cousin by her beautiful hair and shake the teeth out of her for the damnable insistence she has of living at right angles to reality. The explanation must be that she hates the baby.

They finally decide to call the little girl Gerda. "I hope such a name is acceptable in England?" Hedwig says tartly.

"It's a fine name!" Harry says with enormous relief. "Quite pretty, actually. Sounds German, too, rather. I mean to say, one might know . . ." Though anyone would think by now she'd want to get properly away from everything German. Only last week the three of them had sat in the darkness, listening to the wireless. The brutes were looting Jewish shops and burning down synagogues with the people in them, to the applause of crowds.

Immediately afterward, no word was spoken. Hedwig, hands clasped over the vastness of her belly, had sat in silence, then leaned and snapped on the lamp and took up her sewing, and Harry had a quick glimpse of Berti as he resumed his seat near the window, his face, in the lamplight, a glistening sheet of wet.

Berti has got his Alien Registration Card, and is looking for work. In a day or two Hedwig will be back in the flat with the baby. Inexplicably, she appears unable to nurse it. She may have shared these several days of Berti's agitation, which might explain why her opulent bosom refuses to produce milk. Consequently the dark little mite has a bottle popped into its mouth whenever it opens it in a thin piercing cry. And it appears the doctor was right, the little thing is fast losing its furry covering and is, in fact, becoming quite presentable. Harry in particular, who visits the hospital daily, is immensely taken with it . . . her.

Hedwig, entering the flat, carrying the new baby into the sitting room, stops when she sees the pot of asphodel and the other, of cineraria, that Harry's bought to welcome them home. She regards the plants thoughtfully — and he has to admit they have an alien look in the comfortless room. Possibly this prompts her next spoken thought: "Berti and I will very soon now find a place of our own," she says, turning to Harry. Before leaving to have the baby she'd managed to wedge a tiny cot between the bed and the window of their room. Beyond this, she vowed, she would allow the baby to intrude no further into Harry's life.

"Oh, we can talk about that later, can't we?" Harry says.

"Why later? Why not today?"

"But you've only this instant got back! You've still your coat on! And now there's Gerda."

She looks down upon the infant in her arms, its blue-black eyes fastened in anxious absorption on her face. "The baby will be no trouble, I will be able to take it with me to look for a flat for us."

"Take *her* with you!" Harry cries, enormously upset that neither of these parents seems to have any regard for this new human being, whom his cousin will not even credit with a gender. Hedwig smiles at the anguish in his voice.

"Yes. I will be able to take her with me." She deposits the bundle on the divan, and as though she's just pulled an alarm pin, a thin, high wail pierces the air.

Berti has come in last, as usual. *"Hier hab'ich die Flasche."* He pulls a packet containing a filled nursing bottle from his jacket.

"So feed her." She turns her attention back to Harry. "We have intruded long enough on you."

"It's no intrusion at all, really not!"

Berti, holding the bottle uncertainly, approaches the divan, leans, and gently pushes the nipple into the baby's face.

The fact is, Harry's only this moment realized that until his cousins' coming, he'd been hungry for years. Only when Hedwig took over the kitchen had he had any notion that eating might be more than a narrow perfunctory pleasure, on much the same level as his rather tepid sexual appetite.

The fact is, Hedwig cooks like an angel. Edwina had never pretended to be even a passable cook. In fact, she could never really be said to cook. She'd come back from the shops with things like sardines and tinned meat pies and Turkish delight, and, boiling the water into insensibility, couldn't even make proper tea. She was an uneconomical shopper, besides, though of course it was her own money she spent.

He's never understood how Hedwig does so well on the little money he can give her, the marvelous things she can do with foods that are off the ration: potatoes and carrots, for instance. Meat is scarce, of course, and even bearing their three ration books, she never comes back from marketing with much of it; yet she somehow transforms what she brings home into heaping platters of food, pungent and hearty. He suspects she sells a little thing here and there from the boxes — trinkets, probably, she's not likely to release her relatives into the London air — for ready money when she wants it for some of the lovely things she makes. She is indeed a remarkable, and thoroughly German, cook. Her dishes were new to him at first, but their succulence appears to have wakened memories from somewhere deep within him, possibly from

114

the part of him that is legitimately Kessler. And those moist, rich gâteaus she makes, filled with nuts, wherever does she find the ingredients? Since her entrance into his kitchen the entire flat has a new depth, an aromatic dimension which daily gives sharp expectancy to his return journey from work. Now she's talking of leaving, and there's a dull thump in his belly at the new, purposeful firmness he detects in her voice.

"Well," Hedwig says, "we will speak more another time. Tell me something. Do you think there will be war?"

He's been smelling war for months. "Of course," he says.

From Bruno:

A fine time to have a baby. Listen, the two of you are lucky to have got this far with your skin. Only tell me what's the point of escaping from one butchering pen to stand in line for another. You think where you are now is safe? In a pig's eye. In a year England's going to look like a piece of cheese. Can't you two fools see what's in the cards?

Of course not. That bird on the family shield is an ostrich.

Anyway, congratulations on the baby. What do you mean, she looks like a kobold? Have you decided on a name? How about your m——r's name? Do you even remember our m——r's name? She was called Elena.

By the way, do you hear me telling the three of you to get out of England? You can come here and live in Drummond, this is a nice little town. Let me know and I'll start the paperwork. They've asked me to design a new auditorium building for the college.

Begin taking steps now. Before you know it the fish in the Atlantic ocean are going to start gobbling up Jews.

He knows damn well why she chooses to stay in England. It's closer to das Farterland, he can see her straining at the starting line, her head hanging over the water. Hitler will blow away in a year or so and then it's back to the castle in Charlottenburg, where Rhine maidens guard the heavy square furniture and the ankle-deep rugs. She's only waiting for the Chormans to wake up, the good, honest Chormans who'll suddenly realize what they owe to all the fine old gentlemen like Grossfarter Kessler, who killed his Russian daughter-in-law and who so enthusiastically with the rest of them poured his own gold into the new Chormany.

No matter how strenuously he tries, Bruno can't exorcize the old man. It has taken him a lifetime to learn that the dead are not dead.

The rise of the Nazis — barring some of their excesses, of course — seems like an inevitable outgrowth of everything the grandfather stood for. Grosspapa, whom he hasn't seen for twenty-five years, still lives with him daily. As though he's just stepped out of it, Bruno sees the special room up-

117

stairs filled with physical-fitness paraphernalia. There, each morning Grosspapa rides
his bicycle contraption and emerges from
the room glistening and smelling of old
man's sweat. Twenty minutes later he's in
the breakfast room, clean and rosy black
beard oiled and gleaming. There he eats his
muesli and his figs with honey, thoughtfully
and rhythmically Fletcherizing, thirty-two
chews per mouthful. And after this — a
man of regular habits, thanks to psyllium
seed — he walks in majesty the twenty-two
steps to the little room built into the polished oak under the front staircase *wo selbst
der Kaiser zu Fuss hingeht* — "where even
the Kaiser goes on foot" — for a timed
squat of fifteen minutes by the clock. On
the days when he's in a jovial mood, his
voice — deep and melodious, Bruno admits
it grudgingly — pours from the white-tiled
cloister, always in the same song:

> *Ich bin der Doktor Eisenbart*
> *Zwilli, willi, wich, bum bum.*
> *Kann machen dass die Blinden sehen,*
> *Zwilli, willi, wich, bum bum.*
> > *Lautoria, Lautoria,*
> *Zwilli, willi, wich, bum bum.*
> *Kann machen dass die Blinden sehen*
> *Zwilli, willi, wich, bum bum.*

She's actually done it. "But it's been a *pleasure* having you here!" Harry cries in disbelief when Hedwig tells him.

She'd been leaving the baby with Berti, mornings, and had gone out flat-hunting for weeks, often staying away the full day, and now, she says, she has finally found a beautiful ground-floor flat in a very proper street in a piece of London called Stepney.

"We should speak the truth, yes?" To Harry's ears, her voice vibrates with what almost seems to be relish and her face is a deeper pink, and even her white coronet of braids has new regal glints in the lamp-light. She walks to Harry and faces him firmly. "You have been very good to have us here, but we have outstayed our visit."

"But I've never felt that!" Already Harry sees them gone, the air in the flat no longer rich with Hedwig's cooking. Loneliness to come rests an icy finger on the back of his neck.

She is saying, "I even tell you that you do not altogether like me. How can a person not know how another feels? Only a fool, and I am not a fool."

What's she bloody getting on about? He's held his rather lukewarm estimate of her in check, hasn't he? Quite willing to put up with her for the sake of the meals, and for the husband's sake — he really likes the little chap now. Not that he can't understand it — he has to credit her with the perception to see that he recognizes that transparent warmheartedness of hers, that motherliness of face for what they are: nothing more than a trick of the flesh on the bone. The capaciousness of her body, which often suggests amiability, is in Hedwig an illusion. The most that can be said for her is that she is momentarily sentimental. And see how abominably she treats Berti.

"Grossmutti always says, never stop long as a guest in any house. *Any* house. Feelings begin. It cannot be helped."

So it's her own feelings she's speaking of. Harry hasn't considered that. She dislikes *him*, then? A nasty shock.

All the same, he wishes they'd stay. The three of them.

The baby. Harry doesn't quite know what to make of it. A few of his and Edwina's friends had had babies; he can recall excited invitations to examine the eruption of first teeth like little rice grains on the pink gums; he'd watched them being fed, sung to, bounced about . . . but this one, with its tiny goblin face, is out of his experience, though he's rather oddly drawn to it. It gives absolutely no trouble, it cries rarely, perhaps knowing it's unwanted, and has made its peace with this knowledge, sleeping its tiny existence away in its corner. How many times has he watched Hedwig regarding the baby dispassionately as she applied the bottle. A baby must sense the absence of some necessary something, even though it's still very young. *She's* very young, Harry reminds himself sternly.

Hedwig hasn't finished with her everlasting Grossmutti, ". . . guests destroy the routine of your house. Always under the feet." She gives a harsh laugh. "And then when finally they go, Grossmutti says, you are left with nothing but debts and dirty linens."

Now that, of course, is absolute rubbish. Her thrift and her cooking have more than repaid the minor expenses Harry's been put to but he daren't say so, she'll know it's his stomach talking.

How will the two of them manage? Berti

has his Alien Registration Card but will never manage to find a job. What on earth can he do? How will they survive?

The boxes. Of course, the boxes. Again, he suspects she's already parted with some of the things in them, and now she'll sell even more of the ancestral bones.

"When we have settled ourselves in you will come many times and have a good dinner with us." The unpiercable knowing creature smiles at him broadly.

Boxes, baggage and baby, they move to the new flat which, Hedwig discovers now, seems not to be on such a charming street after all. They are on the ground floor of a smallish, sooty-brick house, and there is definitely a smell of cockroaches, though she has yet to see one — but at least it will get them away from that one with his pale face like unbaked dough, always looking at her with his camera eyes.

Sometimes Hedwig has the feeling that the earth has pulled away from her feet and she is suspended in air. She has at present put Germany behind her and now there is no home anywhere for her. She doesn't like England, she doesn't really like the English people — it is surprising how much they are like Miss Love.

Yet daily she considers the possibility of an eventual return to Germany. This terrible war that is happening, surely it will burn itself out in a year or two, maybe less. Yes, very likely, Germany will one day soon be cleaned of Hitler. Hitler is not Germany, he is scum, a maniac, he will die soon. In the meantime letters keep coming from Bruno shouting to them to come live with him. She reads them and tears them up with grim satisfaction, knowing she will never go. She and her brother can never — as Harry would say — hit it off. She has known this since she was seven years old.

Harry accepts immediately Hedwig's first formal dinner invitation, and takes a rather sour pleasure in noting that the flat she's found is on a rather rubbishy block, rising slightly in the middle and weighted at either end by a pub. Judging by the tatty shops and the peeling stucco fronts of the houses, he doubts the street can even be said to have seen better days. On the way he passes in front of When All's Said and Done, which one would expect to be blazing with life and juice, but today is strangely quiet. He listens a little, then proceeds up the hill to the house.

Emanations from her kitchen greet him the moment he steps into the entrance hall. Sauerbraten. Anticipatory juices nearly dribble down his chin. Hedwig opens the door immediately to his knock, perhaps she's seen his approach from the window. She leans to receive his kiss and he detects a faint odor of gin. The whites of her rich blue eyes are slightly pink. Hastily, he asks after the baby.

"She is awake, come in, you will see her."

A pale grey perambulator stands beside the door. The rooms are quite bare still, though she's bought some chairs and a table. It's not much better than his own small airless flat, Harry thinks — a bit lighter, perhaps. But then, they do have the extra room for the nursery.

She's off to fetch the baby, and Berti appears. No longer the colourless little husband — he looks quite jaunty, actually, with rather a spring to his step. He smells of iodoform.

"How are things going?" Harry asks.

"I am very well." Berti's answer is prompt and proud. English is accruing to him, finally. Wonderful.

And here's Hedwig, the baby in her arms. Gerda fixes an intent gaze on Harry, a thing she's always done with him. Still ugly, but more recognizably human. Rather charming, in fact, and her eyes have lost the pale blue vagueness of early infancy, suggesting now a brown or possibly hazel future. Hedwig appears lightly affectionate and quite comfortable with her — she has not only the body for maternity, but now quite possibly the soul.

The baby, continuing to stare fearlessly at

Harry, is carried off uncomplainingly to the nursery. When Hedwig returns, they toast the new house with *Schnaps*. "It should be sherry, no?" Hedwig says. "But I do not like the taste. You English" — she laughs — "always drinking port or sherry." She looks about her with a stolid complacency. "So what do you think of my Englishman's castle?"

Everything looks very well scrubbed. They toast the house again while dinner waits. The meat must settle. Its fragrance makes Harry weak with longing, for at home he's gone back to tins of baked beans, kippers and biscuits. He sits, cupping the glass between his palms and studying the curved perfection of the windows in the amber whisky. They are silent. Yesterday the Germans sank the *Athenia*, and it seems to him ridiculous, the way they are sitting here. "Well," Harry says, "so we're in it."

Berti lifts his hands, then drops them in his lap. "We will eat now," says Hedwig in the same instant, and stands up.

At dinner she leans to Harry earnestly. "This war. I do not think it will last long, do you? The English have wonderful ships. Of course we also —" She lifts her water glass and takes a sip from it. "But the whole world knows of the British navy."

"I rather think it's not so much a matter of the navy, you know." He doesn't care to say what it's a matter of, this time round. The buildings they've been sandbagging, the gas masks they're issuing, including the ones for children, even babies, zip-ups with Mickey Mouse faces and floppy ears, show pretty clearly that war has changed. The picture as he sees it is quite sort of scaring, but there's no point in discussing it at Hedwig's dinner table.

Hedwig turns to Berti and says brusquely, "Tell him."

Berti smiles his gentle smile and tells him. "I have found a place."

Harry feels exactly as he felt when informed that Berti was to become a father. "Oh, I say — wonderful! Wonderful! What sort of a place?"

Berti looks to his wife.

"He is working for a . . . how do you say a man who cares . . . like a doctor . . . for animals?"

"A vet? You're working for a veterinarian?"

"Ah, that is it. Veterinarian." Hedwig says the word slowly and nods, storing it away in her English arsenal. "He has a practice on the Brompton Road. When he is examining them, Berti holds them, and when he gives them . . . you know, with needles?"

"Marvelous!" Harry nearly shouts. "I can't tell you how delighted I am. D'you like the work?"

Berti turns his brown eyes, rapturous, on Harry. "I like it," he says shyly. "I like it very much."

"He is very good with animals," Hedwig says. "Dogs like him. Cats also."

Harry has joined up. Leaving on the next day but one, he comes over to say good-bye. He has a strong desire to hold the baby, of whom he's grown quite fond. That way she has of looking at him. And that amusingly imperious gesture she has, a way of turning her head that is like a microscopic glimpse of Hedwig herself, but gone in an instant like a whiff of scent from a passing woman. In this tiny dark creature he finds it immensely funny.

He discovers she's been brought back to sleep in Hedwig and Berti's own room, and that the nursery has been let off to a pair of young men, factory workers.

Earlier, Harry had suggested evacuation to the country, but Hedwig refused absolutely. "We stay here. Who can say where is more safe? There are bombs out there too, waiting in the fields, I have heard about them." She holds her head high and speaks with dignity, nostrils dilated, her face faintly scornful. "You take a chance wherever you are. Besides that, Berti has his work —

they have been sending dogs in, did you know? For special training."

In spite of being hard at it to keep the flat clean, caring for the baby, shopping, cooking for her boarders, she continues to look magnificent and indomitable.

"Actually, it's Baby I'm thinking of," Harry says, smiling at Gerda, touching her on the cheek. She's been brought out in her nightie to say good-bye. She has become, at eight months, a cranky, untoward child, at war with all the world. Because she's never actively scowled at him, he is her slave. From time to time he brings her little things from the pawnshop, and tonight fetches out from behind his back another such, a small mechanical bunny that looks made of pink marshmallow, and twitches its nose.

"It is bedtime, we will put it here until tomorrow," Hedwig says, setting the thing on the sideboard beside the Mickey Mouse gas mask.

The child wants it now, however, reaches for it and starts to cry. "Tomorrow you will have it," Hedwig promises. Gerda cries more loudly and kicks mightily, propelling herself into a rage so vast and suffusive that her thighs become a mottled red. She is carried screaming off to bed. In the kitchen, Berti is sneezing.

"I know some people in Suffolk have got a small cottage to let," Harry says when Hedwig returns. He can't stand the sound of the child's shrieks, which even from this distance are ear-splitting — the new flat has the acoustics of a concert hall. He raises his voice. "I'm sure you could have it. You and Baby might go while Berti stays on here."

For Berti has also become an air-raid warden. He has a tin hat and when the siren wails, is off with the speed of a dog after a rabbit.

"And who can afford a cottage in the country!" She looks at him with infinite scorn, as though he's suggested a Riviera outing or an African safari. Immediately Harry has a vision of the trunks, so filled with antique tobies and Dresden figures that their lids will scarcely close. She's got, besides . . . well, who knows what else is in there — jewelry, most certainly, she's told him so. And things from off the villa walls — hasn't she mentioned a small Renoir? Yes. And war or no war, there's always a market hungry for such things. But no, everything she's got in those trunks is padded, thickly cobwebbed, still surrounded by the shades of the family — a family that clings to every thing she possesses.

Watching him, Hedwig reads his every thought. He believes, does he, that the contents of her boxes will allow her to live on an estate with gardeners too old and worn out to fight a war — and a Miss Love, too, if she wills it, to care for the child? Let him think what he wishes. And it's not entirely true that she has great wealth, though there are a few things — yes, a few; if museums suspected what the boxes contained they would come on their knees to her. Old menorahs (two of them) . . . spice boxes . . . alms boxes . . . He may think she can sell what she has, but she will not. It's that pawnbroker's head of his that makes him see the world this way, it is the Englishman in him, here is where the father's side of the family comes out. She looks at him sternly, arms folded, and all this is in her eye.

"Where we are, here, is fine for us. We have found this flat and here we stay. I am not afraid of bombs. Besides, I do not believe this war will last long. You will see."

What Harry sees is that this is more of her daftness. Perhaps she imagines they'll declare a truce next week? They're bombing every night nearby — how can she not be afraid? He'll be lucky if he gets home tonight. On the way here he'd had to detour round some roped-off rubble which only yesterday had been a row of good houses. The end one alone remained standing, its facade sliced cleanly off and every room on prim display: chairs, tallboys, wardrobes, dining tables, sideboards, all in place. Look at me, the house proclaimed, this is how an interior is meant to look — this room, and this room, and this.

He thinks of bombs and the baby. Hedwig, more immovable than houses, arms still crossed, is regarding him with a fixed, tolerant smile. He'd like to break her bloody neck. What he'd ought to ask her is, has she thought of what a bomb might do to those boxes of hers.

The ugly elf of a child spends half her day now beside the magic box. She knows how, by turning the knob, she can usually make music come pouring into the room. Hedwig herself has never before had any notion there was such an amount of it in the air, ready at the movement of a finger to come crashing through the netting-covered window. That's because she has never cared for the wireless, and does even less so now. She feels better if she doesn't hear the news.

"It cannot be good for her to sit glued by the ear always to that box," she complains to Berti, "her hearing will grow sidewise." Frowning, she looks through the doorway to where Gerda sits enthralled, listening to a toy orchestra and a tin piano — the wire-less set's a cheap one — play a Mozart concerto. Hedwig allows the silver fork she's been cleaning to fall — it makes a light chime — onto the heap of others already done, and Gerda looks her way ardently. Overnight, she has discovered pitch in everything: a chair scraping across the lino, a spoon scratching the side of a mixing bowl. Overnight the world has become a paradise, an Elysium, filled with the immoderate wonder of sound.

Why is it that suddenly Hedwig begins to see people she's known, relatives and friends from Berlin — and even from as far away as Kiel — on the streets of London? Always she hurries quickly to see, peer into a face that has just passed, or examine for a second time a man or woman whose reflection in a shop window belongs certainly to someone she knows from home.

Never once has it turned out to be the one she thinks it is, and the sudden onset of these hallucinations makes her wonder whether she has a new disease, something in the head this time. Or maybe these are *Gespenster,* visitations? That one who came to give Grossmutti her high colonics, Frau Golze, seen buying gloves at Harrods and wearing a grey coat and a lobster-scarlet scarf, only of course it isn't Frau Golze . . . perhaps Frau Golze has just died? And the same for Onkel Karl, whose face she saw for an instant peering moodily down at her from a passing bus, but this one was Onkel Karl as he had looked ten years ago . . .

perhaps really this means Onkel Karl is dead? The wireless last night told how Americans have dropped bombs on Kiel, where he lives.

She will allow herself to go no further in opening the door of her mind to death at home. Not one of the letters she had written to her cousins and aunts and others, before the war happened . . . not one has been answered. Of course she knows the stories since . . . Immediately the shutter closes.

It's because the woman standing in the queue in the confectionery looks so very like Cousin Lena from Offenbach that Hedwig responds to her smile. This one's teeth are grey and spotted — why do the English have such very bad teeth? Her name is Mrs. Markey and hasn't she seen Hedwig in dozens of lines? On the strength of the otherwise uncanny resemblance to Cousin Lena, whose teeth are beautiful and very white, Hedwig accepts an invitation to tea on the Sunday, and may bring Gerda and Berti with her.

"You're lucky to have your husband with you, mine's God knows where, they've sent him off to the north is all I know. Won't it be good to hand a man a dish of tea again!"

On their arrival, Hedwig — as though proffering pearls — holds out a paper bag of fudge, which is in high demand and short supply. But first Mrs. Markey stoops to welcome the little girl. Now four, Gerda is an undersized imp entirely without delicacy. Her eyes are an odd color, too — deep green, or are they brown, or are they hazel? — and she stiffens her body distrustfully when Mrs. Markey attempts, from very pity, to put her arms around her. For there's certainly nothing attractive about the child. She's really rather dark, isn't she? . . . and the woman throws a swift look from Hedwig to Berti. Hedwig is used to this. "Your own, is she?" she can read in every eye.

Gerda tears herself from the embrace and sprints across the room to where she spied an old square piano in the corner.

She seems to know the keys are meant for striking, and hits at them. The instrument, long overdead, makes the room reverberate with the tinny sounds from its jangled, rusted strings. Gerda is utterly enchanted — this clangor is her own creation. The world changes for her unspeakably.

"Enough!" commands Hedwig, her hands over her ears. The room positively shakes in an ecstasy of dissonance. Dust puffs leak from every seam of the old wooden box.

The child persists. Reaching the keys with difficulty, she stands on her toes and strikes where she can, throwing looks of frenzied joy behind her. She can move the earth.

"I have said to you to stop!" Hedwig's rare voice, the one deep as a man's.

"Sha, sha," Berti says through the bedlam, affected by he knows not what in the look of his daughter, and he makes waving, soothing motions in the air toward his wife. Gerda has now moved down toward the bass, her skinny arms hitting wildly, looking at her parents in exaltation. The room booms. What is she playing? She's playing hit my mother on the nose till the blood comes, break the dishes on the floor, no, on my mother's friend's head, she's playing things one cannot even think of in the mind, but on the keys it's another thing. Mrs. Markey can see now that the little girl's eyes are the color of deviltry. She motions for Hedwig and Berti to seat themselves as she pushes her own ample beam into a Victorian horsehair rocker. She nods knowingly. "Needs to have her bottom smacked," she says loudly, her words drowned in the thunder.

Again it happens, this time in the Portobello Road. Hedwig imagines she sees Lajos Rado coming out of a public house and turning toward her. Of course it can't be possible. She hasn't seen Lajos in nearly ten years. Grosspapa never liked him, not because he is Hungarian, but because he came to Berlin from that village whose name no one can pronounce, to study musical composition with Kurt Weill, whose music Grosspapa says is brutal and dirty. But somehow the Fürstenwalde Kesslers — the music Kesslers — adopted him, and each time they came to Charlottenburg brought him, along with their violoncellos, their fiddles and their oboes. She has an instantaneous vision of the lot of them seated after dinner in the *Wohnzimmer,* their bellies filled with *Rinderbrust,* piping and sawing away in a long-gone world of mauves and beiges, cellos and oboes.

But can this phantom be Rado? It seems to be . . . yet this Lajos Rado is perhaps, too, much older — a small man like Berti, walking toward her, looking neither to the right nor to the left but straight down with his shortsighted eyes that she remembers, and his face corrugated like a country road. And also the knees of his trousers baggy. Always the trousers baggy at the knees. "Lajos?" she says tentatively, as they are about to pass.

He stops in shock.

"It's . . . Hedwig? . . . My God, Hedwig!" He is trying to swallow her with his half-blind eyes, then he darts to her and grasps both her hands. He would kiss her if he were taller and if she didn't hold herself slightly back from him. He smells strongly of lager. It is Lajos, but a stranger.

"So you are here!"

"Yes. Berti too. Berti and I."

"And Herr Kessler?" Looking straight up into her eyes. "And Frau Kessler, they are with you?"

Instead of answering, she looks down the road to where a bus is approaching gingerly. Lajos follows her eyes and they watch it edge round a bomb crater at the far side of the road. It is the very bus that would carry her back to the flat and Hedwig wishes intensely that she were on it. But she turns back to Lajos, who is observing her curiously. She says quickly, "Do you know, maybe, where are Onkel

Dietrich and Tante Anna?" These are his friends, the music Kesslers.

He gives the faintest of shrugs.

"And the little girl? Sigmunda?"

Staring at her in that odd way, Rado says slowly, "About Sigmunda I can tell you. You remember her."

"Certainly I remember her, Anna's daughter."

"Such a tiny little girl." A wind has come up, ruffling his sparse black hair, making it wild, and as though soothing it, he passes a hand over it.

"Yes. She plays the violin," Hedwig says. "I remember that violin, such a small one I never knew they made."

"She was a little demon on the violin, you are right, it was even smaller than half-size, yet on it she played Tartini. She would grow up to a bigger one. Only . . . she will not."

Hedwig stands very still.

"They took her, with the other Jewish children on the *Strasse*. It must be now three years."

Hedwig doesn't want to hear more. Of all the people from home that she might have met on a street in London, why must it be that Rado is the one? The unspeakable is grinding inside her again. No, she wants to hear no more. As though in answer, a lorry comes rumbling by and Hedwig stands, eyes closed, allowing the noise to wash round her. It passes, and Rado, who appears to have waited patiently, says, "You know, she wouldn't leave without it, the violin. They laughed and let her take it. So she carried it, with the bow, under her arm, no time even to put it in the little case."

"How do you know this?"

"From Max Ruland. The tobacconist. I came by a week after, looking for Dietrich and Anna. They were gone. Max Ruland knew nothing about them, but he says he saw Sigmunda come out of the school with the children, the brownshirts were lining them up. You will play in the orchestra, they told her. Laughing."

"What does that mean, she will play in the orchestra? What orchestra?"

"The orchestra? All Jews. And it is true, Max Ruland says, she was seen playing at the railroad station, where the trains bring in more people. At Ravensbrück."

"I have not heard of that place."

Rado looks at her closely. "It is in Mecklenburg. You have never heard of it?"

"No, of course I have never heard of it. How should I?"

"How should you not, Hedwig?" He seems to have grown taller and thrusts his face close to hers, she will swear it is on a level with her own. "There is talk of it on the wireless. And in the newspapers they print it. How can you not?"

That way his eyes are. The strangeness in his voice. That tone, that look. They are back at the table in the *Speisezimmer* in Charlottenburg . . . She remembers now, Rado was the one who argued with Grosspapa, though he came as a guest and was not in the family. "Not everything has to be so terrible as people say," Hedwig says. "How do we know . . ." She hears Grosspapa's words coming from her own mouth.

As though she has not spoken, Rado says, his voice very quiet, "Ravensbrück. It is a place where they take women. Jewish women. And girls. Jewish girls."

She will not look at him.

"It is a killing camp."

"No," she whispers. Abruptly she flings out her hands and her purse swings wildly on its strap on her arm. "This is not . . . it does no good! Can't you see it does no good! If good could come of it, to talk, but it does no good!" And she's running toward the place where the bus will come, not caring if people stare. Before she reaches the corner she has to stop, lean against a lamppost and vomit.

The child's at the wireless again, fiddling with the buttons. The air booms and shakes, and then abruptly there is silence, followed by a thin tinkling sound — is it a piano? And as though this is what she's been searching for, Gerda, pleased, subsides on the floor below the set.

It hits Hedwig like a thunderclap. The Fürstenwalde Kesslers! And for some minutes she stands in the kitchen doorway looking at her daughter. There are things in the blood that will come out, who knows where? A memory brushes her quickly: the tiny virtuoso, Sigmunda Kessler. Gas ovens. Like a cockroach scooting into darkness, the memory disappears. She stands, regarding Gerda broodingly.

Who gives a child of four, nearing five, piano lessons? It seems to Hedwig that the music Kesslers were handed their cornets and flutes while still in the cradle. Now she goes to the trunk, lifts the lid of one, removes some things, puts some back. Considers. Then takes up two small Dresden figures, which she wraps carefully and next day carries to a certain dealer in antiques with whom she's already had some traffic.

How does one go about buying a piano? she asks her friend Mrs. Markey. Not a new one, of course, but a good one?

The matter is discussed during the next several afternoons. The two women have, in fact, been meeting almost daily for some time. They've discovered a mutual interest in gin. Since Hedwig will never put foot inside When All's Said and Done, the two of them have adjusted themselves comfortably to the round table in Mrs. Markey's kitchen, where they talk and drink neat gin. A door separates them and the short corridor to the living room, so that Gerda, hitting endlessly and passionately at Mrs. Markey's old piano, is not in the least (Mrs. Markey's words) a torment to them.

Hedwig's pink face is slightly pinker, her cheeks lustrous, her rich voice a trifle richer. "My Grossvater always says a little *Schnaps* is the best medicine in the world."

"It's jolly good stuff, he's quite right," Mrs. Markey agrees. She wonders if Hedwig's grossfotter knows what war conditions are doing to the price of the shnops they are drinking. To say nothing of its being in short supply.

"In moderation. Always in moderation," says Hedwig, pouring another small glassful.

"And quite right he is!" Mrs. Markey has fallen readily into Hedwig's manner of speaking of her German people, of her past as the present. By now she knows many of them by name, for the same ones figure prominently in Hedwig's stories. Like Hedwig's face and voice, her early life in Germany glows. And to Mrs. Markey the long excursive tales of Charlottenburg are like tales out of a book, a queer, delightful, foreign book.

The gardens, Hedwig tells her. The gardens! Mrs. Markey will never believe the roses and the lilacs.

"Oh, I do know about that sort of thing. They call it florryculture; my Henry did a bit of that for some people in Surrey before he went into the machine shop, before we were married." She can listen to Hedwig's tales of Charlottenburg for entire afternoons, and often does.

Eventually an old rosewood spinet is found, bought, and delivered. Furthermore, Mrs. Markey knows a lady who lives in the neighborhood, a Mrs. Sponce, who calls herself a keyboard artist and is willing to come to the home.

It's true, what Hedwig said. Animals are fond of Berti. He approaches them trustfully. Dr. Quillinan, with a laugh, has remarked to his wife that every beast in the place responds to Berti as though he were a particularly timid member of their own species. He arouses neither hostility nor fear, not in the sickest of them. They accept him placidly, with trust and tolerance.

As for Berti himself, if he's thankful for any single thing, it's that English dogs speak the same language as German dogs. They skulk or wag their tails without grammar. And unlike what he finds among his fellow humans, their emotions and behaviors are clear and undiluted. He loves them.

He also loves Mrs. Quillinan. Watching them together after Pansy Quillinan has come to the back seeking her husband, Berti knows surely that these two possess the very kind of marriage that the English say is made in heaven, a sentence he remembers from his adult English class. He can see this from Dr. Quillinan's way of going to her and touching her on the arm the moment she comes up to him. When she arrives on some late afternoons, she enters every room seeking him — the anteroom, the surgery, her husband's tiny office and, if she's had no success, the sunless back room, finally, with its lively smells, where Berti usually stays, tending cages and feeding the animals, except when he's gently holding them down on the operating table.

She comes in from riding — the Quillinans own horses — her face still wind-whipped and rosy. "Now where's that man of mine?" she'll ask Berti if she sees him first, her voice husky, delicately hoarse from smoking too many cigarettes. Dr. Quillinan has told Berti that quite likely his wife has little corns growing on her vocal cords. On the second and third fingers of her right hand there are deep yellow nicotine stains. For some reason, to Berti's mind, they lend a kind of elegance to her otherwise rather boyish and pudgy hand.

Tenderly, he tells Pansy where he thinks Dr. Quillinan may be found and she thanks him with her long slow smile as she leaves the room. Sometimes Berti follows behind in order to watch that way her husband has of touching her, lightly, on the upper inside of her arm. At that particular moment Berti becomes Dr. Quillinan, in quiet ecstasy at the feel of that firm round plumpness, just above the inside crook of Pansy Quillinan's elbow.

"D'you like horses?" Pansy Quillinan asks Berti. She's sitting on an upended empty cage and lights a cigarette in that charming way she has, and for a moment the smoke she slowly exhales encloses her in pale blue gauze. The room smells heavily of animals. In his surgery down the corridor, Dr. Quillinan is busy injecting a litter of Dobermans someone has brought in and Pansy sits waiting for him in the back room, watching Berti treat a sick monkey. She herself is not really one for animals, not indiscriminately, but she no end enjoys watching Berti's way with them. As for Berti, though he appears to be totally occupied with the little beast, he fears that possibly his adoration of her fans out detectably from his body like heat from a fever.

The monkey is here because of upper-body injuries, and Berti has worked down to its little black paw — its hand, rather, Pansy supposes. He touches it lightly with Mercurochrome. What bright, intelligent eyes the little beast has. Apprehensive, she can see, though it sits quite still. How wonderful, to be so graced by the trust of animals! Pansy shivers. Such a gentle man.

"I can't see, really, anyone's keeping a monkey." She crosses her legs and waves smoke from her face. "Nasty things. Peeing down at one from the chandeliers."

"I think in cages they keep them," Berti says. Working, he is filled with a happy peace. How he loves these ways Dr. and Mrs. Quillinan have — so easy, never worried, never afraid in all directions, as he is. He wishes he could be their way, but wishes it without envy. It cannot be possible to him. It is a matter of how you were bent as a sapling.

He's finished applying the medicine and he and the monkey regard each other tranquilly. Slowly it withdraws its hand from Berti's and examines its injured fingers.

"Isn't it like a child, though!" Pansy exclaims. "I don't know monkeys. I would never have dreamed . . ."

"It has fingerprints at the end of the tail," Berti tells her tenderly. She is wearing a dress the color of geraniums, and her presence is like a light in the room. She looks at him — he sees that her eyes are lavender — oh, how aptly she is named!

With both hands, he lifts the furry black body, sets it in its cage and closes the door. It knows it has been injured, it lets itself be handled, like a baby.

"D'you like horses?" Pansy asks him again.

He has never experienced a horse. "I like them very much," he says shyly because he wants to please her. He has never so much as touched a horse. "You have them? I mean to ask, you own horses? You keep them on your land?" He knows the Quillinans have horses, as he knows they have a house somewhere in a place called Surrey. He cannot imagine anyone working in London and owning horses.

"We've three of them, actually. Oh well, one's a pony, belongs to our girl Fabia."

Three horses! Berti marvels. But this is of course a special household, a veterinarian's household.

"Perhaps you'll come down sometime."

She can't think why she's said this. But the poor old thing. Not really old, of course, possibly forty. It's that sort of timidity of his, a vulnerability which she supposes has a tendency to age one. Already his hair is rather retreating up his forehead. At the same time there's something touching about him — yet, Pansy feels, he is probably quite deep. She feels motherish. No, not motherish; what *would* one call it?

"It's not too much of a place. I doubt you get out of the city often, though, do you?" She uncrosses, then recrosses her very good legs and slowly swings the upper one back and forth. One hand rests on her knee and Berti stands hypnotized, his eyes on those graceful fingers bronzed by nicotine. This has nothing to do with sex, Pansy feels. What comes into her head, oddly, is that this is like the humility of someone contemplating a perfect rose.

Something about the color of Berti's skin puts her in mind of a doll Fabia used to have, a foolish crackly thing the child had loved, made of grey-white celluloid. "Of course, there *are* people who don't care for sun."

His eyes on her beautiful legs, Berti thinks he would love the sun. As with horses, it's a thing he's had very little to do with.

She's done it out of boredom. It's that extraordinarily touching adoration in his eyes. She has a glimpse that it's the very quality of living that is, to him, something to marvel at. Regarding Berti, Pansy has an instant comprehension that some people live their lives almost entirely in their heads.

But only see how the animals here love him. She can imagine how he must be with horses. She tells her husband she's asked Berti down for the weekend. Already she can see herself leading the way to the paddock, sensing Berti following, his muzzle close to her shoulder.

Berti finds he cannot bring himself to tell Hedwig that his employers have invited him to spend a weekend in Surrey. Everything concerning his life in the surgery — each creature meeting him with its terrified beseeching eyes, every trembling furry body given into his hands, its warmth flowing into his palms to meet a mutual understanding — all, all of this belongs to a world that is his and that at all costs must remain his alone.

Strangely enough, it hasn't occurred to either of the Quillinans that he might have a life of his own, or a family. All he's told them about himself is that he lives in Leacock Road. Actually, he looks to have been fashioned for bachelorhood. What woman would want to claim him?

Pansy finds him quaint. And from the halting, thoughtful way he speaks she thinks yes, indeed, he may actually be quite deep. She's amused and rather touched to see that he adores her.

Berti tells Hedwig that he must stay at his job for three days and nights. There's been bomb damage to the back of the building (which is true, though only a window's been broken), and someone must stay the weekend until repairs are made. So he departs on the Friday morning with a small carrying case that holds his pajamas, a couple of changes of underwear, a toothbrush, a razor, and two substantial sandwiches.

They drive down at the end of the Friday workday. His first motorcar ride since coming to England. Out of the city, he gazes cheerfully through the layered haze of Pansy's cigarette smoke at the greenness of the fields. So *green* everything is. He is not used to looking at the outdoors, and this beauty of pine woods and oak trees and small lakes and dandelion-stippled meadows is a fairyland that the Quillinans have presented to him on a platter. They pass a wall of stones, and at once something very profound, very German, stirs in him. Exactly such a wall he has seen before, long ago somewhere, possibly when he was a boy vacationing in the Harz Mountains. And the sun! It strikes glitters from a stream they are passing, which hit his eyes with delicate pain. He has never been so happy. Pansy half-turns and leans her cheek against the back of her seat and smiles at him. She has the eyes of a lovely cat.

"There!" in her sweetly husky cigarette voice. "Now the sun's come out, what d'you think of it?" As though she and her husband have indeed made this land and dredged him up from underground to admire it.

Berti pulls his look from the rolling meadows — there is such a light all about! And such a green color — can there be such a color as this English green? He looks at her eloquently. He should say something, but the lively beauty of her smile, so close to him, sends every English word out of his head. The intensity of his rapture and the contemplation of two immense beautiful days ahead of him make his nostrils dilate, to Pansy they look pinkly translucent, sensitive as a rabbit's. To show how deeply he treasures this gift of the English outdoors, he fumbles with the handle on the door, unwinds the glass and loyally sticks his head into the wind, inhaling deeply. Pansy, terrified, almost ducks to the floor before realizing that the wind will of course blow toward the back. She imagines Berti is being carsick.

Not too much of a place, Pansy had said, so Berti's in no way prepared for a house of the size and magnificence of this one. They're walking him up the long path, a tree avenue — he doesn't know one tree from another — so that he may enjoy the approach. What he vaguely sees at the far end is a palace, and in the middle distance such a garden as he cannot believe. They come abreast of it and everything in it appears to be roses. Nothing but roses, acres of roses, and all with little tags hanging from them. And rising from them such an aroma as though they are walking under a thick fragrant blanket.

"We've the best show of roses in Surrey, I believe," Pansy says in her offhand way, and Berti, overwhelmed by the utter strangeness of English ways, supposes there must be a separate garden for each different kind of flower.

He must first be introduced to two rare chestnut trees, and then the three of them cross the circular carriageway and climb the steps to a lacquered wooden door high enough for giants to step through. "It's only two hundred years old," Pansy explains. "And simply a mess when we bought it."

Inside, Berti reminds himself that veterinarians, like *echte* doctors, enjoy high incomes, something he's already suspected from the number of cats and dogs and birds carried by liveried people into the surgery.

"I expect you'll be wanting to see the horses," Pansy says. "Though perhaps you'd like tea first?"

"Tea first, tea first," says Dr. Quillinan. He is a large man with hair like an Airedale's, very rugged and very kind, with little to say when he's not handling the animals.

Berti, hungry, swallows an enormous number of small sandwiches — ham and chutney, butter and watercress, butter and cucumber, he's told when he first regards them in silence. He chews them thoughtfully, it's his first encounter with such fillings. They are very good. And he drinks his tea with milk in it because that is what he sees them do. From the carrying bag in the hall the robust sandwiches Hedwig has packed, filled with wursts and cheese, signal to him in deep, muffled voices. Later he will tear the crude things into pieces and flush them down the lavatory.

"I'll show you the stables, if you like," says the Quillinans' daughter Fabia matter-of-factly. She appears to be their only child, whose age Berti has been trying to gauge since her appearance with the tea-things. She is perhaps three years older than Gerda, yet might possibly be a year younger than that — he can never be sure about these silver-haired English children, this one with her pointed little face, so fair-haired, so fragile-looking. After tea she puts her hand — it has the feel of cool soapstone — into his, and he lets himself be led out to see the horses. Especially, she wants him to see hers.

Here is the stableyard, and here is her pony Cordelia, a small light horse with shaggy legs, whose size puts Berti's fears to rest. The whole way to the stables he has been anxious, knowing that horses are generally large. They are fearsome strangers in his world of domestic animals.

"You have a very pretty little white horse," he tells her approvingly.

"She's a grey," Fabia corrects him. "I groom her myself. I expect you'll want to see Mum's and Dad's, won't you? Dad's is a gelding." She lets her light eyes rest on him. "You know what that is, don't you?"

161

"No," Berti says truthfully, smiling.

"Oh." She catches her lower lip under her upper teeth and looks at him appraisingly. "I've always wondered, does it hurt?"

"No, I am sure not," says Berti, still smiling. Does she mean riding? No, she cannot mean riding.

"I'm to be allowed to ride him next year, on my birthday. His name is Beanie. But I do love Cordelia." As they walk off she looks back with fondness toward the pony.

"Of course you do," Berti agrees. He himself has warm feelings toward this child — he can love anyone who loves an animal, even a horse, provided it is small. He carries the image of her pony with him as he follows the child, the way it had gazed at him with treacle eyes fringed with black lashes. So human. She appeared to have taken him in and comprehended Berti in his entirety, a thing he can take comfort in from such a small horse.

Fabia now conducts him to two monsters.

Each horse, he sees, has its own chamber. They are side by side and he steps cautiously back from the wooden half-doors, which appear to be far too low.

What he would like to do is go quickly back to the house. But this child is with him.

"Would you like to go for a bit of a ride?" she asks politely. "You could have Dad's — this one, Beanie. He's really rather sweet. He's a gelding, you know. Geldings are very dependable." She appears to have taken Berti's number. "But not Mummy's, I'm afraid. He's a stallion. She says she wouldn't trust Volcano with a stranger. You never know when he's going to erupt."

Berti believes it. This one, the one called Volcano, is stupendous: brown, shining, with a long malefic tube of a face. It appears to snarl at him with its eyes and he imagines he sees fire in its nostrils. "He's finicky, too. Won't drink except out of the white bucket. I expect you've brought riding things?"

"I don't know to ride a horse," Berti tells her shyly.

"Really?" Her eyes widen. "But how can you not? I mean to say, you never ride to hounds?"

Berti blinks. "Please?"

"You don't have a horse."

"No. Never have I had a horse." Never in his life has he stood this close to a horse.

"But what did you do when you were a little boy? Didn't you ride? Or was there a war then?"

"A war, when I was a little boy?" Berti regards the walls of Volcano's stall, and considers. "No. But in those times I was just being a student, I think."

"Oh." Pause. "Did you know that a rocket fell last week in Merton? Only a mile from here. Well. Pity you don't ride, though. It's awfully much fun."

He doubts it. He's busy rearranging his thoughts, removing Fabia's mother from the dainty palfrey on which he'd seated her, in a daisied field, to this baneful nightmare of a creature, standing half a thin door away from them, a mountain of brown cords and muscle, an animal that erupts.

And here comes Pansy. With worshipful eyes, he watches how lightly she steps toward them. She is wearing something pretty, a scarf and jacket whose colors seem to belong to the country. She sends her daughter off somewhere, greets Berti with her large smile and opens the door of Volcano's stall. How fearlessly she goes in! The smell of horse becomes suddenly very strong. Berti cannot believe what he sees hanging under the creature — can even so large an animal have parts so huge? — and is violently embarrassed to be standing here with his employer's wife, that in his presence she should be subjected to such a sight.

Pansy takes the animal's head between her hands and blows gently up into its nostrils. Then she strokes it on the neck, and makes crooning sounds like the wind in leaves. But her eyes are on Berti, she smiles and her lips remain slightly parted. He can feel the blood in his body pulled down toward his feet. This woman, transformed into a witch, is doing something terrible to his thoughts. To the horse's, too, for it becomes restive and abruptly moves its long legs, making a clattering noise, terrible.

"Steady on, steady on," Pansy murmurs to it, and taking something from her jacket pocket, presses it to its mouth. It makes a blowing sound and rears its head, and once more she pats the long dark face, then comes out to Berti and closes the door behind her. Putting her hand on Berti's arm, she gives him a hard squeeze, then bobs her head toward the inner gloom of the stable. "Upstairs," Pansy whispers.

Her throat, where her apricot-colored scarf is parted, is dark and vibrating, and the smell of cigarette that always surrounds her like a pungent envelope mingles with the smell of horse in Berti's nostrils. Some third thing, too, a troubling aroma that rises from the frightening pits of her body, like musk. Quickly, she walks toward the dark interior of the stables.

His arm tingles from the peremptory pinch. He catches a glimpse of skirt and foot and then the skirt flashes around some corner. He hears her shoes strike the raw wooden stairs, the back of which he can just manage to make out, ahead, in the darkness. There's hay or straw all about here, and his feet slip a little as he walks toward the narrow interior.

That stallion — he cannot get it from his thoughts. Such monstrous . . . Somewhere up these stairs, she is waiting for him in the dark and dust. He is filled with fright. She will want him to do . . . what? To remove his trousers? Yet that cannot be. Yet he does not know. It is in him to say that what he really would prefer at this moment is more of those little sandwiches with cucumber in them. He knows he cannot say this because it is not exactly what he does want. What is most terrible is that he no longer knows her. He turns and runs from the twilight of the stables to the house.

Next day he trudges glumly among the roses, which, though they fill the air with honey smells, give him no pleasure. They stand in waves of color, each melting into another, clearly as they were meant to do (how do they know, when they pat the seeds into the ground, that they will all come out the necessary color?). Pansy walks beside him, telling him their names, and more than once he finds her looking at him with mischief in her eyes. Several times, too, smiling, she takes a long suck at her cigarette and blows blue-grey clouds in his face.

In the splendored sunshine he realizes

that in fact he misses the smells and murky light of London and the sounds of his daughter's piano playing. He greatly surprises Dr. and Mrs. Quillinan by turning out to be an unamiable guest, a heavy guest to carry through a weekend. Pansy will think twice before obeying such an impulse again.

Later, upstairs, Berti stands at the open window of his room, which looks out on a pretty view. The room is thick with scents from the garden. So strong, they give him a headache. Looking down on a sundial in the center of an oval rockery that's all blues and violets, he sees nothing, aware only of a heavy consciousness of loss. Loss of delight in Pansy.

"D'you like horses?" Horses. There is nothing good to be said of them, even the smallest of them. All they do is stand there and stink.

Something Hedwig hadn't counted on: her daughter's incessant practicing. She has all she can do, sometimes, not to dash the child from the squeaking piano stool and fling her out the door to give the air a rest. Allow her own ears to return to equilibrium. Not that she doesn't take occasional pleasure in Mrs. Sponce's ecstasies over Gerda's progress — though Hedwig suspects part of this is said with a thought to her fee. One day Hedwig has all she can do not to empty a pot of the *Gulasch mit Spätzle* she's been cooking over that head of dark stringy hair: for at least one solid hour Gerda has persisted in playing over and over and over again a particularly nasty-sounding succession of notes that Hedwig is certain she'd mastered after ten minutes.

Can such a thing be natural in a child of almost five? Hedwig has changed her mind about her daughter's musical endowment. Not that she doubts it, exactly . . . yet is this the sort of thing the music Kesslers have always had to live with?

Unfortunately, Hedwig herself is impermeable to music. In fact, she and Berti both have the misfortune to own what is known as cloth ears. One evening the three of them return from a piano recital at the National Gallery which has sent Gerda into raptures. Not so her mother: How people will like to sit for two hours while up in the front, on the platform, sits a man at a long black piano that looks like a box you bury people in, and the hair falling over his face and it goes up and down, up and down like a cockatoo the whole time he is playing! She laughs deeply and derisively, as with a grand gesture she unfastens and removes her large velvet hat.

She has decided that piano concerts amuse her as much as they bore her. And on that face up there, Hedwig continues, such a look you see when they are playing you think they're sitting with the feet in a kettle of boiling water!

She's noticed such a look frequently on Gerda's pinched little face.

But it falls to Berti, largely, to accompany Gerda to recitals, those that have continued through the bombings. Since the day her teacher suggested someone take the little girl to hear Myra Hess, the child has become insatiable. Berti, who has trouble in telling Mozart from Stravinsky, has developed a deep, stubborn love for this trollish child of theirs. And patience . . . he has the patience to sit through the hours of piano playing because of the pleasure he sees it gives her.

Often, he's reflected on how different it would be if only Harry were around, who'd have taken the child anywhere, anytime. But the quintessence of indulgent uncles is gone. So is Harry's old flat — both taken, in a flash of French vermilion, by a bomb in '42 while he was home on a three-day leave.

So once and even sometimes twice in one week, the skinny little girl scuttles along on bone-thin legs beside her father, to the bus or to the tube station. Berti still walks slowly and with unsure steps, like a man who feels he occupies too much space in the world. And Gerda runs along beside him, her small muscular hand clutched firmly around his index finger.

The war's well over. Exactly as Hedwig knew it would be, they're sweeping the Nazi shards into the dustbins. Berti returns from work one evening to find two suitcases open on the bed. Bureau drawers are pulled out and Hedwig's arms are filled with clothing.

"You and Gerda must get on without me for a time."

He sits down between the suitcases. There's no need for him to say a thing, he sees the picture at once.

"Mrs. Markey will come in the afternoons and stay through dinner. You have only to get Gerda up and take her to school in the mornings."

"So you are going back." His common habit when he sits is to fold his hands together, hold them on his lap and look down on them. This he does now.

"I am going back. But I will return soon." With not the slightest interruption in the smooth swing of her activity, she deposits an armful of clothes into one of the bags.

"To go back again."

She pulls herself erect, her face flushed. "We will all go back. But first there are the arrangements to be made. Certain things belong to us. It says in the newspapers, all from whom things were taken will get them back. The new government promises it. We will get back the villa. And Grosspapa's wurst factory."

"You are going to make wursts?"

That way he sits with his hands, and his pale brown expression, looking at her like an unbright child. That imbecile patience of his. She feels an intense need to smack him.

"How would I come to make wursts? Do I know how to make wursts? Do *you* know how to make wursts?"

He smiles. "No, I like better the dogs alive."

Years back it was said that Grosspapa, swimming in Lake Leman, started to shout and sink because of a sudden violent cramp, and was tugged safely back to shore by a young stranger swimming near him. Grosspapa tried hard to reward him but the young man refused to accept anything. "Then I will make you a present of some important advice," Grosspapa was said to have said. "Never mind who I am, I know

173

what I am talking about. Never eat a wurst. Never. You understand?"

Hedwig stares at her husband for a long moment, then in disgust pulls down the top of a suitcase. "A story. You know that is only a joke. Grosspapa never said things like that. And besides, he made only *kosher* wursts." And when Berti laughs she snaps the lock noisily, irritated. Is he maybe trying to make her think he has suddenly become a man of humor?

"What I will do is, I will lease it out, the factory. Maybe sell it. It will give us something to live on."

With staccato angry movements, she finishes packing the second bag and shuts it. "I will be back Tuesday week," she informs him, and the next day leaves for Home.

Mrs. Sponce can't say she's greatly taken with the undersized, dark, tormented-looking child she's teaching. To tell the truth, from the very first day she never has done. For one thing, she's positive the girl can claim no biological kinship with the white-blond German giantess who calls herself her mother (and who clearly and not infrequently has had a drop). None of this is the child's fault, of course. But obviously there's plenty more here than meets the eye and she's dying to know the full story.

"She's come on a lot," Mrs. Sponce has told Hedwig, and this is the truth. Another truth is she's very slightly afraid of this little girl who, now eight, is in Mrs. Sponce's eyes an uncomfortably phenomenal little pianist who attacks the instrument like a demon. The piano is her enemy. So, it appears, is Mrs. Sponce herself, whose fondness for Carl Czerny and Ethelbert Nevin sends the tiny child into a rage transcending anything Mrs. Sponce has ever met up with. Nobody plays such pieces on the wireless or at the National Gallery or the Albert Hall, and in fact they sound frightful! She wants to learn this, she wants to learn that — Myra Hess played it only the last week.

Because of her size and small hands, the child has invented her own methods of getting about the keyboard, sometimes involving such lightning leaps and shifts that she cannot be said ever to sit at the piano. She plays Chopin's Revolutionary Étude on one buttock.

And not only does the girl have a questionable disposition and a nasty temper . . . young though she is, she's far from easy on the eye. Sometimes, looking at her, Mrs. Sponce, through her dismay, feels something very akin to pity. Never in her life, her teacher suspects, has Gerda been the sort of child anyone has ever swooped upon, picked up, and kissed.

There's always the possibility that her behavior and appearance may improve. And if they don't . . . well, Beethoven was all his life choleric. And Liszt had warts all over his face.

In murderous silence, Hedwig returns from Germany. She's stayed longer than she intended to. She unpacks her suitcases, sets her clothes back in the drawers, then goes to the kitchen and removes all the dishes from the cupboards. She scrubs the shelves, washes up the dishes and restores them to the shelves again.

Is this to be taken as an indication they're not to leave London? Berti waits, but receives no information. For the remainder of the day Hedwig keeps to herself.

She opens her mouth, but not until that evening. Berti has taken out his pajamas and placed them on the bed when she appears in the doorway.

"We do not get back the wurst factory," she says heavily, as though bedtime is the proper time for the announcement. "They have papers showing that Grosspapa already sold it."

He looks at her blankly. What can he say about the loss of the wurst works? He has never had so much as a thought about the wurst works. "And the villa?" he asks her. He was never once in his life comfortable in the big dark family house.

Hedwig's answer is to turn and leave the room.

Well. So they may remain on in London after all. Berti closes his eyes and smiles and thinks affectionately of the animals.

She has become, inside, a different person. Like a room, Hedwig tells herself, with a new coating of wallpaper. Entirely different, once the officials in Berlin had brought out the records and shown her the papers. Yes, there was Grosspapa's name, she knows his signature. And she saw to whom Grosspapa, without a word to anyone, had transferred the factory all the way back in 1937. Transferred the ownership to his old friend Otto von Heisermann.

On her first day in Berlin she'd walked in the Tiergarten to regard, frozen-faced, the bomb damage. And then later the streets she'd known so well, so well: now streams of gutted houses and ruins exactly like those she can see any day here in London.

After that she'd traveled to München, to Freiburg, to Nugsburg, to Mannheim. Looking, looking for Kesslers.

Not one has survived. Is there any longer reason for returning to a Germany where the air is full of holes?

The ultimate blow she can bring herself to tell no one, the most indigestible of all: the villa in Charlottenburg is gone, the entire street on which it stood bombed out of existence — in error, they told her — by a British aircraft in a night raid in 1940.

She'd left the newly set-up Office of Titles and Records — it is too soon, too soon, they told her, to know much else as yet — and returned to her hotel room to sit there alone and consider the savaging of cities. Waking each morning to the sick sound of pigeons, watching them preen their green-and-purple plumage on the line of windows across the street. Here was nothing for her to return to, she was now a stranger amidst the rubble of a foreign city. Every Kessler she sought is gone She has lost the flavors of her past.

She has lost much more. Throughout the war, because she'd held herself from accepting anything that others were too willing to believe . . . for who could know? Who knew, then? . . . She was nourished by the hope that Kesslers, being Kesslers, would somehow have managed to survive. What is the harm in hoping?

The harm is that only now is she saddled with a grief that is immense, fresh and raw, and which she knows should long since have been laid to rest. She must draw around herself the mantle of a family suddenly, impossibly, newly heavy with its dead.

Only see how attentively the child listens to everything! Everything, that is, but her mother's instructions, though even in these she discovers interesting overtones. There are sounds even in the looks of things — she loves immensely to go with Berti to Saint James Park because of the legato of the lawns. And the section of London she lives in, with a great deal of neglected bomb damage, never suggests blight to her because there are tones everywhere. The trains, especially. An acute delight: she hears an identical effervescence in their sounds as, on a certain occasion, she heard in a piece by Edgard Varèse which came over the wireless one day, transfixing her as by the fiery radiance of a seraph. She continued to stand, unmoving, with her face to the instrument long after the music ended, worrying Hedwig considerably.

Her entire existence has become a chain of aural revelation. She loves everything, everything, listens gravely to Gregorian chants, Indian ragas, Mozart concertos.

When she goes to her bed to sleep, the world of night — far from the day-end lull her parents gratefully find it — is a continuation of the world of sound in which she was born submerged. She finds one merely listens to it from a new direction. The trains on the next street but one come through like knives after the usual day sounds have drawn back.

"You are absolutely to promise to *sit still* this time!" Berti's voice is unaccustomedly harsh. He has refused to take her to any more recitals because she kicks viciously at the seat in front when she dislikes what she hears.

"I promise." A world of resignation and falseness in her voice. As she stands in front of him, Gerda's eyes look almost a pure black; she's got a gypsy's cap of curls, and eyebrows nearly dense enough to sit well on a man. Her face is locked in determination.

"You must absolutely give me your word."

"I *have* said, haven't I? I promise."

She's a liar, and he knows what her promises are worth. They glare at each other. Sometimes Berti has the uneasy thought that he fears his daughter. A little. Never in his life has he been attacked physically, not by man or dog, but the depths of his daughter's tears and temper tantrums — and she's capable of either in an instant

— petrify him. She's eleven now, and he senses something inside her that makes him think the day will come when this child of his *will* bruise him, possibly break some bones.

He does her an injustice. Gerda is preternaturally fond of him, appreciative of something undefended and fragile and loving in this man who is her father, but she is never able to express emotions like tenderness when she is away from the piano. How she would like to tell him what it feels like, to make music on the piano! And that she has discovered that every one of her ten fingers has a little brain of its own . . . but she can no more put these things into words than she believes her father can comprehend them.

Now she wants him to take her to hear the American pianist Enid Sickles. Only see, she's torn the programme from the newspaper and shows it to him. With an inward sigh, what he sees is that it is a long one, the first half given over to composers he's never heard of — Byrd, Rameau, Couperin. Not until after the interval is there the name of someone who's known to have existed.

Berti himself has begun a timid approach to music. Though, like Hedwig, he finds it incomprehensible that people can enjoy sitting in a room through two or three straight hours of piano playing, he will admit there are some pieces of music that sound good to his ears. There's something to be said for Beethoven and Schubert. Also for that Polish chap. Chopin. Though he still can't manage to carry a tune in his head for longer than a minute after he's heard it, even that very good thing he likes so much that Gerda plays. He can't at the moment think what it's called or who composed it.

The pianist is fat and looks exactly like the woman — she may *be* the woman — Gerda saw in a tea shop, piggishly putting away six cream-filled gâteaus while swilling down an entire pot of tea. During the Rameau, Gerda studies Enid Sickles carefully. She's certain it's the same woman. If she were to go up on the stage and press her hands to both sides of the pianist's face, yellow custard like the insides of a caterpillar would gush from her mouth and nostrils.

But she plays the Rameau beautifully. And the Couperin, and those that follow. Gerda, forgetting gâteaus and the insides of caterpillars, is transported. Up to now, of the few pianists she's heard in the flesh, only Myra Hess at the National Gallery has had the power to move her in this way. She folds her hands in her lap and gives a deep and rapturous sigh. (Berti throws her a warning look.) Her pipe-stem legs stick straight out in front of her as she sits stiffly, like a doll, beside him. Her eyes never leave the woman at the piano.

Meanwhile, Berti is tired to death. It has not been an agreeable day, he has had to put an attractive little dog to its final sleep because of involvement in a traffic accident, and he has come here entirely without pleasure to sit two hours or more beside this difficult child. He turns slightly in his seat to peer at the people to the sides, behind him, and in the rows ahead of him, every one of them appearing unaccountably to be bursting with happiness at being here.

The piano pieces being played sound childlike to him and he knows, from the programme and the bursts of applause following each one, that there will be three more following this one before the interval. He almost groans aloud. He has always nurtured the hope that his daughter will suddenly feel as tired as he, and not last the programme through. Once, when she was five, she'd fallen asleep in her seat halfway through a piano sonata and he'd carried her home, unwaking, against his chest. He has never forgotten this.

They sit out the interval in silence, then watch the pianist return. Trailing draperies, she lumbers hugely from the wings, positions herself once more on the piano bench, and languidly adjusts her layers of black gauzy skirts. She lays her wrists against the keyboard and waits.

She is elephantine only until the moment she starts to play. Now it is Beethoven, and sounds slightly like something Berti thinks Gerda used to play, but he's not certain. Slowly, slowly, his eyes begin to close, and with utmost care he gives himself over to a blissful descent into sleep. But suddenly the pianist begins flinging strings of things off the keys by handfuls, and against his will Berti is pulled from the abyssal depths. Gerda is digging at him painfully with the point of an elbow and he opens his eyes into her scowl.

"She's not doing that *right!*" Gerda is indignant. What the woman is doing in unspeakable. She'd no right to do the left hand that way, it wants to be brought up much softer.

He should never have trusted her. "Shhh!" Berti says, giving his usual fearful look round. It won't be long, he feels, before his daughter's conspicuous behavior will have made her known to every concert audience in London. Soon, they'll refuse to sell him tickets.

"But she's doing it simply awfully!" the child nearly howls. In front of them he begins to see a familiar restless twitching of shoulders. Gerda shifts to her left rump, then abruptly pushes herself forward and now is standing. In an instant Berti puts his palm across her mouth and with his other hand pulls her back into the seat. He feels positively vicious; what he'd actually like to do is make a ring of his hands and press tighter . . . and tighter . . . and tighter . . .

"You — will — sit — still!" he hisses into her ear. "Or I will pull you, by the hair I will pull you, up the hall and out of this place forever!" He no longer cares whether people hear. Something has miraculously been released in him.

It has usually been his nature to unresistingly allow events to wash over him. Now, suddenly, life seems to have taken this moment to demonstrate how it has constantly wronged him. He has never been let do what he wanted, never even been asked what he wanted. Not once, not once! Even in the bed, the nights when Hedwig gropes for him, his wants are made to grow from her wants. He is hungry when he's told he is hungry. He goes to bed when it's told to him that he is sleepy.

He knows the picture he presents to the world, of a man asking permission to breathe, a world that has forever denied him any means to fortify his soul. But now something has miraculously been released in him. It may be the anger at his daughter. It may be the Beethoven that has done it.

Gerda stares into her father's lunatic face. His eyes are not his eyes, they are baleful and furious, and for once in her life she is frightened of him. She sits back wordlessly in her seat and they endure the remainder of the program in silence.

The last encore finished, Miss Sickles rises
and bows again and again and yet again. The
audience is clapping for her wildly and as
she acknowledges the tumult her head and
arms can barely be seen through the flying
billows of black chiffon. Two attendants
sprint down the aisle carrying red roses
which they stuff into her arms, and which
she then carries off into the wings.

Gerda joined in the first applause only —
this for the Rameau and the Couperin and
the Scarlatti — but sits steadfastly silent
during the clamor for encores. Her hands
clutch the armrests of her seat so fiercely
that Berti can see, from the pressure, the
dark splotches on her fingernails painted
there by Hedwig — bitter-tasting stuff, she's
trying to break her daughter of nail-biting.
Surprisingly, Gerda has allowed this, for she
agrees that the bitten stubs of her fingers
look ugly. One nail, however, she has insisted
be left alone: this is the one she bites when
she finds the temptation too great to resist.

Pushing her arms into her coat, "I'm

going to see her," Gerda announces to Berti.

"No!" her father cries. He is filled with a terrible apprehension. His daughter, who he knows has abominated the last half of the concert, is going to run to Madame Sickles and pull her hair. "She is tired after so much playing on the piano, she will want to go home directly. A cup of tea is all she wants, not you."

"I'll be quick about it."

"I tell you, no!"

"But I *will* go!" Like Hedwig's, her voice can get a particular thrust to it. No need to raise it. Catching the familiar note, Berti knows there's nothing he can do to prevent Gerda from heading like a rocket for backstage.

"Does the little girl wish to meet Madame Sickles?" An old gentleman, his white head plumed like a ripe dandelion, leans across the seat from behind them. "She's receiving in the Trent Room this evening, I believe," and he smiles encouragingly at Gerda. "Just follow those people down the corridor, off to the right, d'you see where I mean? You'll find a stairway there. Just follow the crowd." Gerda turns to stare at him. "Remarkable performance, was it not?"

"Filthy," answers the child, and with a couple of snakelike twists of her flat body she has already maneuvered herself past their rising neighbors and is out in the aisle almost before Berti has raised himself from his seat.

Berti is late in reaching the artists' room, he's had to push himself against the press of people heading up the aisle toward the exits, and then eventually through the dense cluster of well-wishers filling the passage to the room. What pushes him forward is an intense foreboding, so deep that his apologies are inaudible.

He spies Gerda. She and the pianist, surrounded by people, appear to be in deep conference. Seen from close, Enid Sickles, a woman clearly well beyond the flush of youth, has a kind of nobility in her manner of leaning down toward Gerda. This comes from success, Berti imagines, from a history of conquering. It is being accustomed to adulation that gives the American pianist that air she has — he senses, even, a faint amusement in her manner. Thank God, he thinks, thank God! She has a quantity of rich, fine, light red hair, and her throat is the color of milk.

Gerda is waving her hands and talking to her rapidly, her face managing to look at the same time both animated and sullen. How he would like to give her a *frosk,* a hard one, across the face!

Madame Sickles listens, then suddenly puts her hand on the child's head and erupts into fruity laughter. Above the multiple black gossamer layers of her dress, her milky throat is heavy and tremulous. Her shoulders look powerful, and put Berti rather in mind of Hedwig's.

"This child says" — her throat ripples in a convulsion which may be laughter, but Berti now suspects could be irritation — "I did the Beethoven too loud and too fast." What an odd accent the woman has. Strange to say, Berti has not, up to this moment in his life, met up with or heard an American. This must be how his cousin Bruno speaks. To his ears, it somehow has a raw sound, as though the words needed chiseling.

There is some chuckling in the group surrounding them, and also possibly an unamused ripple of sound. The pianist leans down again, seriously. "The first movement, you say? Or the whole sonata?"

Gerda gives a jerky nod and says something more. Berti shivers in the genteel murmur that follows. Some laughter. Enid Sickles echoes the nod soberly, straightens, and says to her companion, a woman standing beside her, "The whole first movement."

"I'll show you," Gerda says. A small grand piano, its top closed and shrouded in a throw of buff-and-grey brocade, has been pushed into a far corner of the small room. She goes at once toward it, removing her coat along the way, dragging it on the floor. Berti, watching in agony, notes how her small pointed buttocks epitomize her totally: imperious, purposeful, intent.

"No, dear, not now. Not here." Madame Sickles, who has tried to capture the child, sends the throng of people — many more have come into the room by now — a desperate look.

Gerda eludes her. "I *want* to show you."

She's at the piano, throws back the cloth covering, opens the lid, and standing — there is no chair — puts her hands to the keys. She knows the sonata well, she's also heard it played twice before and has read the music with her eyes and internal ears countless times. She knows what it should sound like, it should sound like music from a highest Alp. She presses the keys. There is no faintest sound. The piano has had its anatomy removed.

"Blast!" She stamps her foot and glares across the room at Madame Sickles as though this is her doing. Stupid cow. And bursts into tears.

"Incredible." The pianist is shaking with laughter.

Her companion joins her. "Nasty little toad," she says in a slender English voice. "She really should be removed. Surely someone owns her?" And Berti creeps forward, and in a sea of disapprobatory silence, takes his howling daughter by the hand and plunges through the crowd, up the packed corridor, up the overcrowded stairway, which is jammed with people — and finally out of the building and into the intense welcome of the cool night air.

On their return home Gerda stalks to her music cabinet to search for the Beethoven. She can still hear Madame Sickles's spherical laughter swirling horribly — horribly! — in her ears. It's the sound of wickedness, a wickedness having to do with soft white flesh and flying black chiffon and pale red hair and playing romantic music too fast. And those green eyes — a clue to her nature, which is no mystery: the woman will have no one else play the piano in her presence for fear of being shown up, hence her orders that all adjacent pianos be disemboweled.

"She said *that* to her?" Hedwig's voice, from the kitchen.

Hedwig comes to stand in the doorway, arching her brows, glowering at her daughter. "You should not have said that."

It's not like her father to report her conduct to her mother. Though they rarely have much to say to each other, for years Gerda has accepted that she and Berti represent an alliance on the side of the house opposite to Hedwig's. To Gerda, she and her father share a single seat on a seesaw, with Hedwig firmly settled on the other, her mother's side usually the one closer to the ground.

How such thoughts would amaze Hedwig, who sees her daughter as the tyrant of the household, with everyone at the mercy of her whims. She will never understand how it is that good German discipline can dissolve into nothing in this house. Very likely it has to do with the English climate.

"How could you speak so to such a lady? To such a high lady, and so famous? To have said *that* to her!" The name of Enid Sickles, who used also to come to Berlin to give concerts, is familiar even to Hedwig. The Fürstenwalde Kesslers always journeyed in to hear her play.

Then to Berti, who has appeared in the doorway behind her: "And you. You should at once have taken her out of that place. I can see how you were standing there, letting her say such terrible things. Standing like an ox."

Gerda has found the sonata, and opens it. Here's the spot, the beastly woman did this whole patch allegro, and then had the bad taste to repeat it a page later. To say nothing of the whole rest of the movement.

She throws her parents a look filled with bitterness. Does she ever feel affection for them? At the moment, all she knows is that they have no more perception of Beethoven than a canary.

Berti receives her look and imagines it is for him alone. Sighing, he sees again how women are the natural enemies of men but within that recognized framework it is necessary — even possible — to live. "I will not ever again take you to a concert," he tells his daughter, as he's already told her a dozen times.

"I will not go anymore," his daughter replies. "There, only cows play, anyway." Still affronted to her marrow, she goes crashing off to bed.

Hedwig has told Mrs. Markey, possibly —
now that it is safely in the past — with some
laughter, of Gerda's conduct at the Sickles
recital, and the two women have a giggle
over their gin. And Mrs. Markey no doubt
has delivered the story to Mrs. Sponce, who
speaks of it at the next lesson: "You didn't
care for Madame Sickles's playing?"

"Of course I did," Gerda, seated at the
piano, replies sulkily, thinking of the first
half of the concert. Indeed, Enid Sickles
later had also played some Schumann, a
piece new to Gerda, and which Gerda loved
entirely. It was only the Beethoven . . .

"Might you want to hear her again
sometime?"

"I expect I might."

"Well, it's possible you may, I hear she's
going to remain in England. The newspaper
said she's giving master classes at the Royal
College of Music and has taken a lease on a
house in Reigate. What do you think of that?"

"Where? Where in Reigate?" Gerda asks
swiftly.

"Hmm." Mrs. Sponce rises from her seat beside the piano and begins to rummage in the bulging bag she always carries with her, a thing which easily holds a couple of volumes of music as well as clothing enough for a weekend stay. She pulls out a rumpled newspaper.

"Here it is. The house is called Hunicutt Hythe; I've no idea where it is. Why ever do you want to know?"

Gerda shrugs. "I don't know. May I see the paper?" She knows perfectly, and stares at the news item. Reigate. Not far at all from London. She will practice up the Beethoven, then take the train to Reigate and find the house — she'll take a taxi — and demonstrate to that woman how the first movement of the Beethoven demands to be played. For she hadn't got it at all, not at all.

She does that very thing. Takes the bus to Paddington Station one afternoon, and then the train to Reigate, and during the short journey entertains herself rapturously with fantasies of clutching Madame Sickles by that disorderly haze of red hair — pink, actually, and probably dyed — and forcing her head to face the keyboard, to listen. A feat requiring three hands, unfortunately. Then, on the instant, as the

202

train pulls into the Reigate station, Gerda recalls the Couperin. And the Rameau and the four little Scarlattis. How is it possible for such a gross woman — so fat, so monstrous — to play with such delicacy and sweetness? She cannot get the little pieces, like sprays of birdsong, out of her head, where they are going to dwell forever.

The taxi driver, after two inquiries, locates Hunicutt Hythe, and when they draw up to it Gerda will not look at it but alights, pays the fare, and only then faces a tall, thin house of stained yellow brick. It looks withdrawn and unfriendly. The narrow front lawn is surrounded by a tall spiked grille behind which stands a stiff-cut perimeter of box hedge. Everything looks angular and unwelcoming. A straight walk of bricks mortared together by some sort of brown spongy moss leads to a short flight of stone steps. These she climbs to the front door.

She can find no button to push, no bell-pull, nothing but a huge tarnished knocker high in the middle of the door, inches beyond her reach. The door itself is prodigious, of heavy, buff-colored oak that looks to be a foot thick. She gives it an angry knock, knowing before her knuckles touch the wood that it had been fashioned to swallow sound as well as force.

She'll kick it, she decides angrily, her mind set like flint against having come thus far and then being bested by a door, and is on the point of raising her foot when out of the blue she sees her mission as ridiculous. She's given no thought at all to what she'll say when Madame Sickles comes to the door. She stands, staring at it, then turns and sits down cross-legged on the top step.

It's already late afternoon, the sky looks like rain, and she realizes she hasn't enough money to get home. There had been enough for the bus and train fares, but then there was the taxi. She hadn't even considered the return trip. Her day had aimed at but gone no farther than a defiant march over Enid Sickles's threshold, straight to the piano.

Now comes the sound of a piano. So she's with a pupil. This means, at any rate, that within the hour the door will open to let someone out . . . She listens. There's a bit of spirited piddling about with a dozen or so notes, repeated over and over. Immediately Gerda hungers to be at a piano . . . that particular handful of tones . . . the fingerwork . . . something she feels she could do easily . . . and then the pianist swims directly into a piece. In a few seconds Gerda realizes this is very likely no pupil, but Sickles herself. Awfully good playing. She listens, captivated, but doesn't recognize it. Something of Mozart's. Glorious.

"Heavenly," Gerda whispers. She finds the word lovely, too. "Heavenly," she says again, and hugs her knees.

There's a sudden loud burst in the music and she raises her head. The door has opened grudgingly, only enough for the curious housemaid, who'd been peering through the window in perplexity for some time, to push her head out.

"Was there something you wanted?" the head says in total disapproval, angling to get a better look at the girl sitting there — skinny, dowdy, possibly hungry. Some gyppo child.

Gerda leaps to her feet. "I've come to see Miss Sickles." The words come ungraciously, echoing the distrust she reads in the woman's face.

"And what would you want to be seeing Madame Sickles for?" The woman looks her frankly up and down, placing her explicitly. "Madame Sickles is very busy, you can hear —"

"I have to see her!" Gerda cries angrily. "Tell her I'm here, please."

"And who might you be?" Delivered with such insolence that Gerda's world goes red, and with the violence of a small wild animal and an enormous shriek of rage she fires herself at the woman, ready to tear her head off. The fracas pushes the door open and the Mozart comes to a stop.

Enid Sickles comes pounding into the entrance hall. "What the hell's going on out here?" Instantly the two battlers — well inside the door by now — draw apart. Miss Sickles takes one look at Gerda and claps a hand to her cheek. "My God, I don't believe it, it's the little devil from the other night."

Gerda wavers on thin legs and puts a hand to her own cheek, which feels abominable: it throbs, and one ear is hot as fire. "What are you, some kind of nemesis or something?" Madame Sickles demands. "How on earth did you track me down?"

Gerda can find no voice. That filthy woman had got in a good hard pinch on her face, which is now half numb, half sore. She has a nasty ache behind the eyes, besides. The woman herself is whimpering.

"Good Lord, Amy," Madame Sickles says, "you'd better go and wash your face. Did this imp hurt you?"

"Nothing to what I'd've done to her if you hadn't just come out, ma'am. She just come at me. I'm sorry." The housemaid's hair is at all angles, and the bodice of her apron is torn. She fumbles in her pocket and produces a handkerchief, which she puts to her eyes. "I just wasn't expecting it, ma'am, it all come as such a surprise."

"Okay, run off, I'll take over." Madame Sickles turns to Gerda and stands regarding the girl thoughtfully. A bigger woman than Hedwig, though not as tall, and without Hedwig's mountainous bosom, she has the identical manner of crossing her large arms in front of her. Gerda feels a dangerous trembling in her legs . . . she is going to have to sit down, right where she is, in the middle of the stone-flagged hall. And then she spies, against the wall, a narrow straight-backed chair which, chair-shaped though it is, is plainly not meant for sitting on. Still, she limps over to it, breathing unevenly, almost sobbing, and sits down.

"All right. Now suppose you tell me why you attacked Mrs. Farrant."

Gerda leaves off her heaving. "She looked at me."

Enid Sickles nods, as though this sounds reasonable. "All right, I'll buy that. And now suppose you tell me why you came here in the first place."

Gerda opens her mouth and then closes

it. What is in her mind is too tangled to fit words to. The only thing she can hear in her head is the tune of one of the little pieces Miss Sickles had played, and now she sees what has really brought her here.

"I wanted to find out how you did it."

"How I did what?"

"The Scarlatti piece. The one that sounds like a string of little bubbles."

The pianist looks at her intently. "You little pipsqueak. You had some fault to find with the Beethoven, I remember."

Gerda stares down at the floor in agony. She wishes the woman would forget the Beethoven. What has brought her here is a muddle of things. Partly, it is envy, she's jealous to the point of not being able to see straight because this gross, ugly woman is able to make a kind of music at the piano that she herself cannot. She's tried, she's been trying since returning home from the recital, and it is impossible. From lowered lids she throws a glance at Madame Sickles's hands. They're squashy — her fingers look like fat white maggots. How ever could they do what they did? And partly, the other side of how she feels now, with her whole heart what she wants to do is throw herself into this woman's arms and weep, sob, have her hurts seen to lovingly, and her hair stroked . . .

"Are you studying the piano with someone?"

Miserably, the child nods.

"How old are you, by the way?"

"Eleven."

"Eleven. Pure piss and vinegar, too. Fantastic." Sickles surveys her as the housemaid had done, openly, up and down. But unlike Mrs. Farrant's examination, hers is pure, neutral appraisal. "Okay." She gives a jerk of her head to the left. "Come on in and play me something. No Beethoven, thank you. What are you studying?"

"I can do the Revolutionary Étude."

"Can you really! Okay."

Gerda pushes herself from the narrow chair and, stumbling a little, follows Miss Sickles across the high-ceilinged hall, which contains nothing but a square rug in the middle and the chair she's been sitting on, and into a large room with dark-coffered walls, empty of everything but two long black triangular boxes on legs. She stops in awe — never has she been this close to a piano of such size. Two of them! And nothing else.

"Take that one." Sickles seats herself half-sidewise on the bench of the farther instrument, closes the lid over the keys and leans her elbows on it.

Placing her skinny rump on the leather-covered seat, Gerda screws her buttocks to the edge and, once assured she can reach the pedals, anchors herself into place. She gives a wriggle and launches immediately into the étude. She's spent weeks and weeks learning the tricky thing, but the volume that bursts from the piano at her first touch stuns her. She throws herself into the splendid crashings. Her face is throbbing — one cheek blue, one ear a flaming red — but she's thrilled with demonic delight at this new power she has, and in less than a minute, totally absorbed, forgets anyone else is in the room.

Sickles folds her hands in her lap and looks down at them placidly. As she listens to the clamor at the next piano her lips twitch once or twice. Occasionally she darts a glance at the child. How amusingly she'd ground that little butt of hers into the seat! And how red that ear is! How absorbed, how rapt she looks; here's one who'll have no trouble with stage fright. Glancing now and again at the flying dark little claws (a nail biter), she smiles.

When Gerda finishes she finds it impossible to raise her eyes to Miss Sickles and begins, instead, to brush her fingers soundlessly over the keys, as though removing dust from them.

Sickles gives a clap of laughter. "Are you trying to eat up the piano? You certainly can slam into that keyboard, can't you?"

Gerda purses her lips and continues stroking the keys, which now to her look flat and exhausted after the fusillade of artillery she'd pulled from them and the screams of falling bombs, doodlebugs, the blitz, sounds well remembered from the subterranean nights of a few short years ago.

"Do you like Bach? Do you play any?"

"No. I mean, I've never."

"Never played Bach." There was silence, Sickles stroking her chin meditatively. "What else can you play?"

"I know some Schubert waltzes."

"Okay, let's hear them." Miss Sickles settles back as before. The child plays three of the waltzes and is starting on a fourth when Miss Sickles says, "All right, that's enough for now."

More silence. Miss Sickles, eyes closed, drums her plump fingers on the piano lid for a little, the nails tapping in rhythmic succession, like horses galloping in the far distance. Outside the uncurtained windows dusk is closing in.

"You've got those rhythms all wrong, you know. The beat is pom POM pom, not POM pom pom. Like this, listen." She raises the lid of her piano and reaching lightly and indolently into it, plays the first waltz Gerda had given her. The child finds herself in the room of the twelve dancing princesses where crystal chandeliers blaze in joy over waltz gowns in blues, greens and violets like the gauze of insect wings; everything is color and movement. And flowers, from somewhere she can smell flowers. Her nostrils quiver, she nearly weeps to hear what this woman weaves with the threads she'd given her.

"Get the idea?" Sickles's voice comes to her through the mist. "That's how you play a Viennese waltz." She takes her hands from the keys, closes the lid once more and turns her body on the seat until, folding her hands on her lap, she again faces Gerda.

"Would you like to study with me?"

"Yes. Please." That is why she has come.

"I never take children." She cups her chin in her hands and stares at the girl for a long moment, then: "But we'll consider it" and stands up, shaking her fleshy arms and hands vigorously, divesting them of all affiliation with a piano.

"Please . . . might I learn the Scarlatti piece?"

Miss Sickles looks at her in astonishment. "What Scarlatti piece?"

"The one you played. At the concert."

"Oh, that. Possibly, possibly. Now tell me where you live."

A fee has never been discussed.

The pianist speaks often of Gerda to her companion, Miss Pizer, whose chief duty appears to be to stand in the wings with a lighted cigarette at the ready for Miss Sickles to take a deep drag at between bows. She's mentioned Gerda also to Sansen, her agent: this poisonous child she's teaching, the daughter of German Jews, a dark little thing stuffed to the ears with talent. "But she's appalling! She's got the lousiest disposition I've ever come up against, worse than they say de Pachmann ever had. Sometimes she goes absolutely against my grain, I swear I could belt her one across the chops. And then again she knocks me for a loop with her musicianship. And she's still only a child, for God's sake! In just a few years you might want to take her on, George. Though maybe we'd better hold our breath, we've both had experience with these little geniuses who simply sparkle with promise, flower early, and then just as early go to seed."

Hedwig's at the breakfast table, a disordered pile of newspapers at her feet and a pair of scissors and a heap of folded, separate pages beside her. She's just finished clipping something from one of them when she hears Gerda's step in the hall. Hastily, she pushes the clipping beneath her plate, and as Gerda enters, pours and hands her a cup of coffee.

"Here it says," says Hedwig, "here in this paper, where did I put it?" She riffles amongst the heap beside her. "Here I have it." She reads, her full voice breathless: " 'What has come upon the scene this season is a young pianist of extraordinary achievement.' "

Gerda has given her first public concert the evening before. She is sixteen.

"What's that thing you've just put down? That you've buried there?"

"Later, we'll read it later. I have more here first," and again Hedwig paws at the papers. But Gerda has caught the blue flicker in her mother's eye.

"Give it over."

"No." She sees Gerda's face. "Well, all right, I will read it." She pulls the clipping from beneath her dish. " 'In time this fairly able young musician may learn that strength of arm and brilliance of fingerwork will not long compensate for what one would most kindly . . . characterize . . . as' — what is this word? . . . erra-tic? — 'erratic interpretation.' "

Gerda has set down her coffee. "That's because I did the *Moonlight* second movement first."

"You did? Why did you do that?"

"I happen to like it that way."

"And Madame Sickles? She approves?"

Gerda gives a short laugh. "She says she can hear Beethoven grinding his teeth in his grave."

Hedwig stares at her for a moment in silence, then returns to the clipping. " 'Her Schubert is particularly unconvincing.' "

"The Schubert? Who is it wrote that? That hag in the *Times*. Hand it here. I notice that's the one you chose to cut from the paper."

"I'm cutting out from all of them. It's only that one that came first in my hand." Hedwig gives over the clipping, and as Gerda reads it, studies her daughter intently. How extraordinary to know that people are writing about Gerda. It turns her daughter into a stranger. And suddenly she tastes a bitterness in her mouth as when juices sometimes rise up from the stomach. Why, Hedwig reflects, her eyes on the girl, why, while G—d was about it, could he not have given this stranger a clearer complexion and a face perhaps a little less disagreeable in the way the skin fits around the mouth? And without so much dark hair, perhaps, on the arms and legs? Considering that many, many people are from now on going to be looking at her. Under bright lights, besides.

Gerda crumples the review and drops it into her coffee. Hedwig leans a little, and the two of them watch it expand and darken in the cup. As though this is purely a natural thing for Gerda to have done, her mother says to her, "Shall I pour you another cup?"

As clearly as she sees this room, Gerda can see Miss Sickles at what she likes to call her "English breakfast," the table spread with the loathsome things she so adores — kidneys, kippers, bacon, sausages, mushrooms, toast dripping marmalade and butter, forever eating, forever eating; the woman is already the size of two houses. And reading that thing this very minute, probably, and smiling. Because the cretin in the *Times* agrees with her. It's possible she even knows the silly bitch. It's entirely likely that she does.

"What you ought to consider is that if Beethoven had wanted the allegretto to be played first, he would have put it first," Sickles had said when Gerda told her of her intention.

"Well, if he'd thought about it awhile, he might have done."

Sickles shook her head. "You take too many liberties, if you ask me." And looking at her pupil's stony face: "Listen, Gerda, take it from me. Beethoven would never have wanted it done that way."

"Well, there's not much he can do about it, can he? I'm alive and he's not." And Madame Sickles, looking at her intently, had suddenly begun to laugh. Gerda is always startled by this laughter, always unexpected but actually rather frequent, when one came to think about it.

But oh, doesn't the Sickles adore to say, "I always allow my pupils to see a piece of music in their own way." Doesn't she love saying that! "I will never inflict my own views of a piece on a musically serious student." Odious, sententious woman. It's a lie, besides.

Well, reading reviews like this is the price one pays for parading oneself in front of people. Of stupid snobs, rather; there are probably no more than a handful of listeners in all of London who are committed in the way she is, and aren't these the ones she actually plays for? No. She plays for no one. She plays for herself.

Pushing back her chair, she rises and leaves the room. This very minute she needs one thing only — to get out into the air. Away from the flat and away from the beastly piano. At this moment she feels she'd like to rip out its guts.

Out of the blue, her American uncle sends Gerda a buckskin jacket, every edge shredded and fringed as though clawed by a frenzied animal. She raises it from its wrappings, looks at it uncomprehendingly, then holds it across her chest and regards herself in the glass. "I suppose children wear these things over there? One is supposed to look like Minnehaha? Isn't it too . . . well, idiotic, don't you think? I wonder how Uncle Bruno sees me. And whatever made him do it?"

"It is because I sent him your concert programme," Hedwig says. "I suppose this is his way to congratulate you. Bruno was always tremendously silly. Unless it's that wife of his who chose it. Probably it is the wife."

"Oh, here's something." Gerda pulls a slip of paper from one of the pockets and reads it aloud: " 'All our felicitations on your first concert, and may there be many more. The program looks great. Do you play the Schumann *Carnaval*? I'd sure like to hear you do it sometime. Nina reminds me to ask you to send us your picture. I see you as a Kessler princess with golden hair, or do you have your mother's head, pure as the driven snow? Anyway, here's our best and warmest. Your Kansas aunt and your Kansas uncle.'"

"I've no idea what he means. What is a Kansas aunt and a Kansas uncle?"

"Kansas is where he has moved to, it is a place in America." Hedwig contemplates her brother, a tall, skinny boy exhumed from the far past. She imagines him as he must be now, a tall man but otherwise unchanged, with the same flaming hair and eyebrows, a color that somehow exemplifies the most profound foolishness. "With a man like that you never know what he's talking about."

"I suppose I must write and thank them. Whatever is this thing called? And what's his wife's name again . . ." She pulls the note from the pocket once more.

"Nina," says Hedwig, and makes a formidable, and unpleasant, noise in the back of her throat. "He married her out of spite."

"Why d'you say that?"

"She is Russian. It had to be a Russian woman. Only a Russian woman."

Gerda looks at her in surprise. "But why?"

"Why? Why?" A glitter in Hedwig's eye. "To spite the family, that is why. To spite Grosspapa. Why else?"

"You'll simply have to explain —"

"There is nothing to explain. Because our mother was Russian. Bruno has always hated our father's side of the family."

Gerda folds the jacket over her arm. "I fail to understand how his hating . . . oh well, never mind. I'll write and tell them that my hair isn't golden."

"And maybe you will tell them that it isn't red, either."

One critic calls her a fury at the piano. At twenty-one, her technique is dazzling. But Miss Sickles still holds the reins — Gerda is allowed to include Wales, Ireland and Scotland in her touring schedule, but not the Continent as yet.

And there's constant disagreement over her choice of programmes.

"Campanella's okay, and the Schumann, but honestly, Gerda, skip the Rachmaninoff this one time. Allow for some letup. Forget your own pleasure — why do you want to leave the poor audience gasping in the aisles? Show some mercy, child."

"I don't care to play things that are no challenge."

Sickles looks astonished. "No challenge? You're not serious? Mozart's no challenge? Bach's no challenge?"

Gerda spins to face the window, stony.

"And I must tell you it's positively . . . eerie . . . how you keep putting that Balakirev thing in practically every program, or else use it for an encore. How on earth d'you view a recital, anyway? As an act of war?"

Gerda is silent.

"For instance, after the toccata, if you insist on it — though it's a hard wallop following the Paganini — why not two or three Chopin nocturnes? They'd be a lovely relief. And then maybe . . ."

"I won't play mawkish stuff."

Miss Sickles's face reddens, then becomes mottled. Generally she's a woman with a soft voice but Gerda, more than anyone, seems able to put a rasp into it. "I swear I don't know why I ever took you on!"

Gerda turns from the window swiftly. Tears are pouring down her cheeks, she throws herself upon her teacher. "I can't play things I don't like, Miss Sickles, can't you see? I know how it seems to you, but if it has no *meaning* . . ."

Sickles pulls a handkerchief from the neck of her dress and, shaking her head, mops at Gerda's face. "All right, I can't fight your logic. Only, you've got to give some thought to the reviewers, darling; they need as much catering to as the piano buffs who come to hear you. You understand? You've got to show some regard to the critics' limitations. *They*'re the ones who need a bit of rest after some of your selections. Honey, sometimes I *fear* for you!" With both arms she holds the girl out from her, and her look holds both earnestness and doubt. "You've got to be careful not to make your concerts into a circus."

A period of intense silence.

"You *do* make them go wild, I have to admit it. And of course it's the sort of thing that will probably make you pots of money . . ." She pauses. "Well anyway, thank God you don't draw the line at Beethoven and Schubert."

Quite evidently Miss Sickles hasn't read the latest by the reviewer from the Liverpool sheet (a fellow whom Gerda routinely tears up, after reading him), who claimed that Gerda trivialized the adagio in Beethoven's Opus 101 and then had gone on to suggest that he can't be the first to detect a great deal more facility than depth in Gerda Kessler's brilliant playing. Immediately upon her reading it she'd felt the whole of England thrust into malignant relief. The review fed some flame that has always been burning steadily and quietly within her, and now she sees that none of the critics have ever really liked her playing. Those marvelous adjectives they've assigned her (when they have done) are because they know she's sheltered beneath Sickles's mantle. It's Enid Sickles they adore — everyone, everyone adores her, though the old trout, close to the end of her prime, emphasizes those moony things she chooses to play because she really can't trust herself to manage the more difficult stuff onstage anymore. Actually, who any longer listens to her? The famous American-pianist-turned-Briton — who played smashingly, once, no doubt — has now become an institution, whereas the fact is she's no match at all for Myra Hess. She's never really gotten beyond the Baroques. She has no real concept at all of Beethoven or Schubert — or Chopin, in spite of what she says, and whom she plays frightfully.

In the dark of her being, Gerda sometimes admits to the treachery, the grave shame of such thoughts. But not often. Not often.

"Sansen's after me to go on extended tour."

For a second Enid Sickles is speechless. "Sansen said that? He must be off his head. Without a word to me first?"

Gerda shrugs. "Perhaps he intends to. He says he can book me into first-rate halls in The Hague. And Paris. And Milan."

"I'll tear his hair out. The underhanded so-and-so. You *know* you're not ready. You must wait another couple of years. Oh, I'll kill that man!" Sickles's pale, acute eyes look straight into Gerda's, as though the girl will be able to read there some of the things it would be unkind to put into words. "I can't think what's got into him. He certainly should know better."

A competitive silence. Then:

"D'you mind if I speak to him about this?"

"I think I do, rather," Gerda says.

Sickles claps her hands together, then places them in her lap. "I'm not a dictator. I can't rule you. But it would be a totally serious mistake for you to do anything like that now. Gerda, you're still so young, there are so many things . . ." But Sickles can't go on. The plain fact is, she can't say the things that need to be said. Not to this one, not to Gerda.

And what is Gerda thinking at this moment as she stares at Enid Sickles? That the old thing really is getting on, the skin of her face is white as bone, and Miss Pizer ought to tell her not to use such white powder so that, putting on her concert face before going onstage, she needn't always have to pinch both her cheeks hard to put a little color in them.

"At least, Gerda, you'll give a little more thought to it before deciding, won't you?"

"You really don't think I'm ready for it." Gerda speaks in a very low voice.

"Not for Europe, not yet. Not yet. Oh my dear, quite apart from adding more stage experience to what you already have, you've first got to develop a thicker skin. You mayn't be able to take . . . well, you already know what anyone's up against when they have the audacity to place themselves at a piano in front of an audience." As though she's made public admission of a private, shameful failing, Miss Sickles gives a huge sigh, throws her hands widely to her sides, then lets her arms fall heavily against her. "You open yourself to the world, you hand it a gift . . . and then the critics are upon you. I'm not sure you . . ." She stops to regard the brooding girl beside her. "Honey, are you angry with me?"

"Of course I'm not."

"You know, I rather think I'll take Sansen up on his idea," Gerda says briskly to her mother the next morning. She's thought the night through, really thought deeply; and she'll do this with or without Sickles's blessing. Like beautifully lettered cards — shining, embossed black on purest white — there are the names. Brussels. Paris. Berlin. Rome.

Suddenly Hedwig detests London. It is rain, rain — always rain — or else the days cold and yellow, the fogs raw and with that color of brown in them that she sees more and more often swirling around the lampposts. "Breathing. I have always trouble breathing," she complains to her daughter, she complains to Berti. It is from breathing in London that she has got this heaviness in her chest — even pain, sometimes.

Maybe America *will* be a better place to live, as Bruno often writes. He lost his Russian wife, Nina, three years before, which somehow removes an impediment to the journey. In any case, the air is better there because there is more of it, and it is newer, not so much breathed in and out. "I am writing to Bruno," she announces to Berti. "Here there is no future."

In fact, she wrote to Bruno weeks ago, and has his answer already. He is living in a place called Kansas, where, she somehow has the notion, he builds things like prisons.

Berti's first thought is of leaving the dogs, whom he loves. It will break his heart to give them up. Only today they have brought in a little dachshund, with eczema that looks like a map of Europe all over its warm pink belly. And Dr. Quillinan gave the little plush fellow straight into Berti's hands. Berti has by now learned an enormous amount of animal medicine, which Dr. Quillinan acknowledges with his trust. He absolutely cannot endure the thought of leaving the veterinary.

"Future? How, future? What future is there in America more than here?"

"For one thing, I have a brother there. My only living blood relative," Hedwig says, who has forgotten — Berti too, probably — that her husband is her first cousin. Of course, a brother is closer, look in any of the Kessler books. "When you begin to get older, things like that matter more."

Eventually he knows there's nothing for it: they will move to America. When will they leave? As soon as they will get their affairs in order, she says, and instructs Berti and Gerda to kindly see to their end of it. Gerda can give her concerts there. Hedwig has already applied for passports. And on the Friday, at eight o'clock in the evening American time, she is to ring Bruno up.

Except: "I'm not having any," Gerda says. "Sansen's already arranged part of my tour. It's quite settled. I've no idea how far east it will take me, quite possibly to Moscow. It may be weeks. Months."

Hedwig accepts this with enormous serenity. Not a muscle of her broad pink face relaxes in relief, which is what she feels. She accepts that she and her daughter haven't gotten on in years. Anything, even a comment on the weather, can set off an argument. And when there is deep disagreement on something, sparks fly — lately, Hedwig's battles with Gerda have become loud, fierce and orgastic. The only element of these ferocities that she'll miss is the delirious physical pleasure they give her. Nevertheless, relief is uppermost. Gerda will not come with them? Very well, she will not come. It makes no matter, the wheels have been set in motion. She's halfway to the state of Kansas before she's even begun to pack a trunk. Gerda will join them when she finishes her tour.

Gerda keeps her thoughts to herself. America indeed.

Hedwig has jumbled the dates. Or someone has. She and Berti have got to take a boat — she will not set foot in an aeroplane — which leaves Thursday week, a month earlier than planned. Very likely it's Bruno's fault, he has never in his life done anything right. The matter concerns immigration quotas and juggled dates of arrival and something her brother has told or has not told the authorities who make up the boat lists in New York City, where he will meet them when they disembark. There's nothing for it, they have to go. The two of them must arrive before the date of August 15.

They leave in a fury of expostulations and arrangements half-made, apologies. Berti, weeping openly on his last day, comes to say good-bye to the dogs, the cats, a small puma and a ferret which is being boarded. Pansy Quillinan is there, and throws her arms around his neck, kissing him loudly and smokily on the mouth.

Gerda is left standing alone in the flat

and finds the emptiness suddenly coming down on everything like a layer of thick felt. To relieve the crush of silence she goes to the piano and begins to play. But the day is beastly hot and she stops, gets up, draws the curtains and removes her clothes. She deposits her narrow flanks onto the folded towel she's placed over the bench and, naked and dripping, plays over and over and over Bartók's Allegro Barbaro for an hour and more. The longer she plays, the more the piece crashes out, sounding a celebration of freedom.

Enid Sickles is horrified. She insists Gerda come out to Reigate and stay with her until she goes on tour — if go on tour she must, and apparently she must. How can a girl of twenty-odd be left to live alone? What can that mother of hers be thinking of? Sickles is positively bursting with indignation. She'd met Hedwig once — a huge, florid, passionless woman, who clearly smelled as though she'd just knocked back a hooker of gin. She knows that heavy German type. She hates them. Yet how can any woman, even this one, show so little interest or pride in the progress of such a musically gifted daughter? Damned unusual. Not that she hasn't had it up to here with mothers of the other kind, who can't shove their kids ahead fast enough, who practically chain themselves to your doorstep, haunting stage doors and artists rooms, snaking backstage like witches, scheming night and day for the advancement of their children's careers. Better, perhaps, to be an under-loved child and have a mother like Gerda's?

"Do give up the flat," she urges strenuously. "Come out and live with me. There's a practice piano in the attic, and of course these two down here. You know perfectly well if you're left to yourself you'll eat nothing but ginger-nut biscuits from morning to night." Between meals, these are Miss Sickles's chief weakness.

Sickles also suspects that, left to herself, the musically voracious girl will be at the piano twenty hours a day.

She takes Gerda's refusal philosophically. The girl is headstrong and curt and often insolent, and would certainly be no pleasure to live with, though Sickles is inclined to forgive her almost anything: she's never had a student like this one — pigheaded, narcissistic, egomaniacal, and who possibly approaches genius.

Fool that she knows she is, Enid Sickles —
seeing Gerda off at Heathrow — risks a last
caution: "The Schumann, darling, I know
you keep saying you don't want to overdo
the schmaltz, but Schumann doesn't *have*
any schmaltz." She pauses and looks anxiously at Gerda. "Not Schumann. Sweetheart, don't play him as though you're doing
Bach. Be a little . . . elastic? — you know
what I mean — in the second movement?"
She speaks almost mournfully.

"I know what you mean," Gerda says.

"Well." Kissing the girl enthusiastically,
ashamed, eager to mask her total disapproval of the whole trip. "I know you'll
wow 'em. You're going to be terrific, it'll
go like a house afire. Good-bye, dear, I'll
see you in October."

She looks pale and somewhat thin in the
face, and, arms around her shoulders,
Gerda feels stricken for a moment, and
wonders whether any of this can be her
doing. Of course not.

Aloft, she settles into her seat, feeling deflated, and scowls out at the sky. A pale glow of light is coming from somewhere — the sun? Yet no matter where she looks — directly above, below or straight out — there's nothing but heavy white. Not a blasted thing to be seen through the window but her own face echoing back at her. Most particularly, her belly's taut with nervousness. This thing she's sitting in might well crash, mightn't it? Splash, rather, into a million wet splinters, since they're over the Channel. But only suppose Sickles is right? Maybe she *has* rushed things? These cities, hotels and halls ahead of her, in strange places, when she doesn't even know the languages? All she has are dates and lists and directions in her purse. Abruptly it's quite clear that Sickles is right. Gone is the ecstatic electricity she's been feeling for days, weeks. She tightens her lips, tightens her belly and stares with huge anxiety into her face at the window: superimposed upon it, against the clouds, Enid Sickles's bleached eyes — dubious, chiding.

It will turn out that they love her in four languages.

Amsterdam first, where — a risky procedure she'd been solemnly warned against — she spends the full morning and afternoon preceding the concert practicing on the fatigued grand piano in her hotel suite. But the concert goes off without a hitch, and the Schumann is pronounced, later, athletically joyous. She underlines the words of the translation and sends it, with the original review, to Reigate.

Bruno has flown in from Kansas City to meet the ship. He hasn't seen his sister in nearly fifty years but he knows absolutely — absolutely — he'll have no trouble spotting her the second she puts her foot to the dock.

He recognizes her sooner. Here she comes down the gangplank, wearing their grandfather's face. If here isn't Grosspapa! Minus the whiskers, three inches taller, and with a colossal set of tits. Superwoman. She comes nearer, with those eyes Bruno will never forget. And the walk. Even the set to the lips. For hasn't the old man lived with him in nightmares since he was eight?

That bite-sized little fellow following her will be his cousin Dagobert.

Immediately there is a quarrel.

"Someone must be told. The boat is filled with thieves," Hedwig says after assuring herself this man is her brother Bruno. His hair is gray and brown — no longer the red she remembers, and already plenty gray. The face is very American but she can see her brother Bruno in it. And his voice booms. A cowboy. But he knows them at once, and in no time she hears how he sounds like his letters. They don't kiss, but shake hands like strangers.

"Completely filled with thieves," she says, giving him back his hand. Her nostrils flicker; the jacket he is wearing has a sweetish aroma of pipe tobacco and treacle, a smoking mixture she has smelled someplace before and dislikes.

"One I found yesterday, in our cabin. Actually." Is she speaking of roaches? "Trying to make off with our trunk." Her English still has a strong Berlin accent, and from indignation her face has become red as a tomato.

Bruno is skeptical. "Baggage handler, probably. Somebody's got to get the stuff off the ship."

"No." Standing foursquare on the dock, arms folded, she's an island of obstinacy. People stream out from behind them and away to the sides in V-formation. "He was making with the lock, I saw him. And" — triumphantly — "now the lock is broken! I will go to lodge a complaint. The only proper thing to do. For the sake of others."

Berti thinks that in London he noticed the lock of the trunk looked broken but now he has nothing to say.

Bruno refuses to enter into his sister's fantasies. "I tell you he must have been a baggage hustler. They've got to get those things ready to go the day before, it's a big ship. Let's find a place where you can wait and I'll try to get your stuff picked up."

"Tell them it is still in the cabin," she says. "I have strapped it to the bed. With the padlock from my purse. Come, please, I don't trust to leave it for long. You and Berti will carry it down."

So they quarrel. Dumb greenhorns. He'll go back, but only to unstrap it. It will be handled in the right way, nobody's going to let him wrestle a trunk down the gangway and across the dock. Give him the key. It's the ship's responsibility . . .

She blazes at him. "But it is the one with the books! In it are all the books!"

It takes a mighty restraint on Bruno's part to hold back from screaming into the Grossvater face of his sister. He can only glare at her. Whereupon she now knows Bruno very well again, that stubborn boy face she remembers, and she's suddenly despairing and heartsick and flooded with family longing. The grandparents are packed in the trunk which her brother cruelly hands over to the ship's porter with instructions to have it delivered to their hotel. And then, angrily, he pushes them ahead of him into a taxi. They have no idea that he's within an ace of packing the two of them into a plane and sending them on to Kansas City, without him, that very night. Actually, the hell with them both.

EVENTS IN NEW YORK. The notice board confronts Hedwig on her way to the dining room the next morning, and she gives it a passing look, then stops to read it again. Victor Hammerschlag. There cannot be two people, two musicians, with that name. He is conducting an orchestra, in The Town Hall.

Victor had been a frequent visitor in Charlottenburg. Now it seems to Hedwig that he came once a month, at least. Fleetingly, she recalls that at one time she was in love with him. Even then, very young, he was already recognized in Berlin as a highly talented young composer. He played an instrument, some instrument. The piano. But also another. The violin? No. The name almost comes to her, but she cannot remember the sort of thing it is. Something that one blows, perhaps. A kind of flute, perhaps. No, not that either. Now she sees him, sitting, almost caressing a large stringed instrument that stands up between his legs. Aha! It is called a violoncello, and now there he is in her mind, sitting and playing it in Grosspapa's drawing room.

Hammerschlag, whom she hasn't thought of in years. And suppose she had, who would have supposed he'd gotten safely out of Germany? "Look, you will not believe this!" she cries to Bruno. "Victor Hammerschlag! You remember him. The composer. Here in New York, can you imagine such a thing! He was such a good friend of Grosspapa."

"Never heard of him. Let's go eat."

"Oh, you were already gone." Hedwig recollects. "I wonder, would he remember me. But of course he will remember me!" Bruno is startled at the sudden ultra-blue of her eyes. "I remember how he played for us once, for a whole afternoon, some opera on the piano, all of it, singing the parts. *The Beggar's Opera.*" She wrinkles her nose. "I never liked it. And not Grosspapa either. Vulgar music. But Victor said we must listen." Smiling, Hedwig closes her eyes.

"Let's go eat."

They will all go to Hammerschlag's concert, Hedwig announces briskly at the table.

That will be impossible, says Bruno, glaring at the two of them, Berti staring down into his plate. The plane to Kansas

247

City leaves in the afternoon; there won't even be time for lunch, they feed you on the plane, if you can call that food. To clinch it, he rises from the table, goes to the lobby, then returns to show how it is even more out of the question. The concert date is two weeks away.

But she will not leave New York without seeing Victor. An old friend, an old, old friend. Such people you do not fly away from. Bruno cannot budge her. Three reservations on a plane mean nothing to her.

"All right, get it out of your system, let's see if you can find him this morning. I'll look him up in the phone book for you."

Victor Hammerschlag is not in the phone book. And the telephone company does not have him in their records.

"His impresario!" Hedwig almost shouts. "He will know!" He will be posted on the program outside and Bruno will put through a phone call and perhaps, yes, she will get to see him this morning! Only tell him it is Hedwig Kessler calling.

Again Bruno is consumed with fury, then thinks, to calm himself, it will at least take her off his hands for the morning. He discovers in himself a nearly uncontrollable itch to choke this woman he hasn't seen for so many years. She's fleshing out, and in spite of the large face under that coronet of white hair, she's everything he remembers but had forgotten for years. In spades. His sister Hedwig was born a pain in the ass and she's going to be an even bigger one when they get out to Kansas. Why in God's name had he agreed that they come over?

The manager is Chase-Gorman Associates and they refuse to give him Hammerschlag's address or phone number. His sister can write him a letter and they'll be glad to redirect it.

Hedwig takes the phone from him. "I am here for only four hours!" she shouts in agony. "He is an old friend, from back in Germany!"

"Sorry. Rules. That's the best we can do."

"But I tell you —"

"They're always an old friend. Write him a letter." The scoundrel at the other end hangs up. Hedwig, her face distorted with rage, possibly grief, turns to her brother. Remembering that look in her eye, he steps back.

"Forget it." He forces a laugh. "Come and I'll show the two of you the sights. We'll take a rubberneck bus. New York is famous, you must have heard of it in London."

"I do not leave this city without I see Victor Hammerschlag." And she folds her arms resolutely over her bosom, exactly as she had on the dock yesterday.

"Well, I'm flying back to Kansas City on the three o'clock plane. You can come with me or not." His face is dark, purple and bumpy with wrath, and he'll be damned if they start off life in America with his shitty sister calling the tune.

He flies back later that day, alone.

So suppose they don't go to Kansas City.

Why had she ever given a thought to living anywhere near this beastly brother of hers? He, as Harry would have put it, gets up her nose. Imagine her forgetting the insensitive monster he is!

He must know how few are the things that are dear to her anymore, he knows her history, that she has lost and lost. And here it happens that Victor Hammerschlag is in New York. Never mind what this must mean to her, it is less than nothing to Bruno.

She doesn't need him. She has still many things from the trunks, she has always kept back objects of great value, though some bear small connection to the family. It will not kill her to sell them. There is the Bohemian glass decanter which Grossmama bought from an estate sale, and which had stood for years on the oak table on the landing in the house in Charlottenburg. It is precious, perhaps, but only to the family from which it came. Beautiful though it is, she will easily consider selling it. It is from the year 1750, and she knows its value very well. She has also saved a few of the Meissen figures. Only let someone put her in touch with the right person here and she'll guarantee that before this day week she and Berti will be comfortably settled. Who needs Bruno?

It takes all of two days for Hedwig to find a flat in New York. She and Berti end up with four rooms in the Bronx, a pleasant enough little place, three of whose windows look down upon a wide paved boulevard with grass and trees on either side. These are what put the seal to her choice; she has never been really happy, she tells herself, without something green to rest her eyes upon.

When the building superintendent showed her the flat, he threw upon the door to the bathroom triumphantly: it was only just redone, and all the fixtures are new. Why, Hedwig wondered, would anyone want lavatory fixtures of maroon-colored porcelain? The commode, particularly — how is one ever to know if there is blood in the urine? Also one has to sit too high for proper evacuation.

The four smallish rooms with their low ceilings and the badly engineered lavatory, together with the strange unmusical way she hears English spoken on all sides of her — she can barely understand many of the words in the shops — all of this she accepts grimly as the consequences of the past. She feels she has always known she would one day be cast adrift in a totally foreign land to fend for herself, repudiated by what is left of her family in the present, yet still buoyed up by the family of the past. Her stay in England was only a tempering for this.

The trunks brought from Germany, still with her, have the endless resources of Baucis's pitcher. She'll take good care to see that Berti finds work. In the meantime they eat and there is a roof over their heads.

She has left no forwarding address at the hotel.

Munich, the last concert but one. They clamor for encores, but she's tired and decides, tonight, she'll give them one only, a Mozart rondo. As she prepares to return to the piano she imagines she catches a glimpse backstage of someone, someone familiar, far behind her, who seems to duck behind a column as though not wishing to be seen. Sansen! Surely it's Sansen!

She plays the Rondo, then stands to take her bow while pages run up to thrust yellow roses into her arms. She holds these, bowing again and again to the tumult, and finally walks offstage. The yellow roses must look revolting against the apricot-colored gown she's wearing. But what brings Sansen here?

He lets himself be seen now, and she moves toward him carrying the flowers awkwardly, hampered somewhat by the length of her gown. Sansen has become a dry old man, tall, crease-faced and always worried-looking. As he comes to her, his glasses glinting in all directions, he lays his hands gently on her arms. "Enid . . ." he says.

Oh! Enid's come over with him, is at this moment seated in the audience, and now will have heard, by benefit of a concert hall, that the Schubert sonata they'd also been at loggerheads over *should* be played exactly as Gerda played it. What good luck! What —

". . . died of a stroke this morning."

"Oh my God."

"So I thought I'd better nip across and tell you before you read it in the papers. Especially with the concert in Paris coming up." He folds his long thin arms and looks at her in deepest sorrow. "You're just a young girl; after all, you ought not be left like this, alone . . ." Gesticulating wildly, a young man runs from behind the curtain entreating her in German to come out and take another bow; can she not hear the noise out there?

She leaves Sansen standing, mournful and uncertain, and is forced to take two more curtain calls. The Germans positively howl for further encores and finally she seats herself at the piano and drapes her skirts to both sides of her, well above the ankles — through her still uncomprehended grief she nevertheless can grizzle that the beastly gown's too long, the hem gets in the way of the pedals. Without pause she raises her hands and commences the second movement of the *Kreisleriana,* the keys a single blur, but she knows the thing with her eyes closed and does indeed play it with closed eyes, as Sickles had always begged her to learn to do it, the way Sickles herself plays it. Played it. *Nicht zu rasch.* Not too fast. Into the long moment of breath-held silence at the end she opens her eyes to see Enid Sickles's knotted blue-veined hands resting on the keys.

Sansen delicately bends his long arthritic legs and folds himself after her into the taxicab, which speeds off through lamplit rain-wet streets.

"Shall I go on with the Paris?" she asks.

He looks at her somberly. How remarkably the child has comported herself throughout the tour, traveling with no companion, no one to lean on should the necessity arise. Unheard of. He'd naturally assumed she would be accompanied by her parents, at least the mother. But no. Of course, it proves he was right, to begin with, in assuming she was ready, and certainly her reception at every one of the concerts bears him out. Still, what does the girl feel? Her straightforward demeanor after he'd given her the news had rather shocked him. Totally unsuitable, he thinks, and then recalls the Schumann, and her wet face when she'd come backstage after the encore.

The rain has commenced again, a slapping rain that drums down on the taxi roof so hard that it might be, suddenly, a hailstorm. Here, inside, the rattles make it difficult to speak and be heard. He raises his voice.

"I'd say it depends. On whether you think you can. Swing it, I mean. Under the circumstances." They are both silent. "I think they'd understand if you canceled this last one. You were both so close . . ."

"When's the funeral?"

"There's to be no funeral." He removes his glasses and looks at them as though in surprise at finding them on his nose. "She has always expressly said, and she's put it in writing to her solicitor, that there's to be a private cremation and no fuss." He folds the glasses, tucks them in his breast pocket and now looks completely blind. "There's no need to hurry over for that sort of thing."

"But that's unbelievable! She's so well-known . . . there are so many people . . ."

"There'll be a memorial service, I'm sure. The College will hold one. Not immediately, because of her expressed wish of no fuss. Now how do you feel about Paris?"

"I don't know."

They proceed in silence through the thudding violence of the rainstorm. Then

Gerda says — he has to strain to hear her — "Do you suppose . . . I could have her ashes?"

He is astounded. "Why, Gerda?"

"Well . . . what will they do with them, do you know?"

"No, I don't know."

She won't tell him why she wants them. She has a vision of a golden urn — simple, slender — like something she's seen in one of her mother's trunks. She'll enfold the precious container to her breast, "May your ashes forgive me," she will whisper. She'll take them to Vienna and strew them over Schubert's grave.

They have reached the hotel and Sansen peers blinking through the cab window. Her hand on the door, she says, "Don't get out, I'm going to run straight up . . . About Paris . . . I rather think I will, you know."

In the dark she cannot read his expression. He clears his throat. "Enid would agree with you, I think. She'd say it was the professional thing to do. If you feel up to it."

"You think I ought not."

He makes no reply. She turns to him suddenly, and pulling his hand brutally to her lips, she kisses it, kisses it many times, she has no idea in the world why. The last link to Sickles, possibly, and in silence the tears flow again. He pats her hand a bit awkwardly. "Come, let's go into the bar. Have a little drink with me. Eat a little something, perhaps."

"No thank you." She opens the door. "I have to be by myself. Please."

"I understand." He leans out after her. "I didn't tell you. You were magnificent tonight. She would have been proud. Magnificent." Through the driving sleet she waves a hand at him and is gone.

Berti, carrying his lunch in a paper bag, leaves every morning for the subway, and later takes the tube to New Jersey. He's working in a textile mill, Hedwig tells the few neighbors she's become cautiously friendly with. His job involves, mainly, sweeping floors of threads and fluffs and textile ends. This she does not tell them.

The composer Hammerschlag has twice come to dinner. Hedwig did not immediately recognize him — large-bodied, craggy-faced, he has a mane of gray hair reaching to his shoulders. On his first visit he wept at the table. Hedwig, innocently asking about his family, learned that he had lost his beautiful young wife at Dachau, where they had performed medical experiments on her. Like Hedwig, he has practically no family left other than a brother who managed to reach England in 1940 but by accident was put on a ship to Australia, where he now lives.

On his second visit, Hedwig says, "You are a famous man. A conductor. A composer. I am not surprised, I still remember when you were very young . . ." She stops, alarmed. Will he cry, like last time? She has taken the loss of her own family stoically. There are more ways to handle sorrow than with tears.

But Hammerschlag has had his cry. Now he wants to know about Gerda; he has several of her records. She is a fine pianist, her Bach is superb. How is she doing in Lon— And he sees that Hedwig has gone white.

"Do not ask a word." She is unable to talk.

"Hedwig, what happened? Is she ill?"

Suddenly her large face is inflamed. "Let me tell you. Only you. She has done a terrible, terrible thing!"

Berti quietly gets up and leaves the table.

Hammerschlag cannot believe what Hedwig is saying. Her daughter has been arrested. Or is on the point of being so, as of the last telephone call from England. She has done a terrible . . . but what has she done? *This* is what she has done. She has ruined a young man. A pianist. Broken his hand. Always, this girl has had a terrible temper, it could be seen on the day she was born. She is nothing but a — Well, now she will have to answer for it.

"But exactly what has she *done?*" cries Hammerschlag.

What Gerda has done is, she picked up from the piano the big metal lamp that a cousin had given them — had given to her and Berti on their marriage; Hedwig brought it front Germany in her trunk. A fine bronze lamp. This, this lamp Gerda lifted up and then brought down hard on the hands of a pupil. The young man will absolutely no more be able to become a pianist. Four of his fingers, she broke.

"You know her temper. No, you do not know her temper. She takes after Rosa Kessler. Of the Munich Kesslers." Like a child, she bends her wrist and wipes away a tear of bitterness. "At least it has so far been kept out of the papers."

"But how did she come to do such a thing?"

"How did she come to do it? Ask her! From her temper, that is how!"

"A young man, you say? Perhaps he . . . if with his hands he was . . . you know, perhaps she could only . . ."

"His hands! She hit him in the hands, they were on the keys! With the lamp she hit him on his hands, on the keys!"

Hammerschlag's recollection of Hedwig, from the Charlottenburg days, is of a somber, elegant, pale-haired young woman with sympathetic and intelligent eyes, a world away from the woman who faces him now. Yet why should this surprise him? They are a world away from those times. Has he not accepted the fact that every-where one goes, fate is waiting with razors? So. She, too, has had her share. He can only regard her mournfully.

Hedwig, meeting what she interprets as an accusatory look, thinks: like Berti. He has the same look as Berti. Men.

"So who knows now what will be? My famous daughter. Who may find herself, tomorrow, in prison."

After the Paris recital — like the others, a success, but somewhat muted, in Gerda's mind. Understandable. She returns to England and learns that Enid Sickles has left her a small income. Not enough to live on, but she'll teach. Her name attracts all the students she cares to handle. She hates it, but does it. She's also begun making recordings — the Beethoven sonatas, chiefly, which have a very good following.

She's resumed concertizing locally, and though Sansen mentions America, she has no interest in it.

Teaching turns out to be a revelation. She finds every student in some way physically repulsive. Why, Gerda wonders, does any degree of musical talent seem to go hand in hand with some bodily peculiarity? Perhaps she's just never looked closely at people before?

She decides that a pianist looks ridiculous when viewed from behind. Her women students are lumps, most of them, with derrieres that billow out on the bench, bulbous as pumpkins. Or they're as gaunt-rumped as Afghan hounds. And their elbows: pointed knobs that appear to travel inanely up and down the keyboard.

As for the male students, most have very strange ears. Some are limp as folded bats' wings. Or else they're hairy, or they're crisp-looking, so that she often has to throttle an urge to lean forward and bite into them.

She wonders if there's something wrong with her.

One day Bartley Munson comes to her, a tall young man, rather good-looking, with dark rampant hair, and whose narrow flanks are encased in trousers so tight that she has great trouble in removing her eyes from the largish bulge in front. Her cheeks flaming, she leads the way into her studio.

He has a big head, big hands. "I studied with Madame Enid six years ago," he tells her, "but my father died and I had to leave off; I had my mother and three sisters and a brother — very young — to see to. Now Mum's remarried. Chap with plenty." He gives her a quick, brilliant smile. Would she consider him for a pupil?

He's around thirty, probably, the tallest man she's ever seen. But it's his hands that make her marvel. They're huge and ungainly-looking, butcherish, something she associates with musical idiocy, but the fingers are long and strongly knuckled and immediately bring to her mind the presto con fuoco of the Chopin F-major Ballade.

"Let me hear you play something."

He surprises her with a Mozart rondo, doing it warmly, the tones rounded as globes. As though it were Schubert, in fact. At the finish she gives him a charitable smile and motions for something more. He rolls into the Shostakovich Piano Preludes and she lets him play them to the end.

She was right about the hands — he already has a prodigious technique, and she feels something close to a stab of envy, and perversely enjoys this. "Would you do the Mozart again, please, and don't romance it quite so much." For a second, his look is startled, then it switches to amusement and from there to what appears to her to be intelligent humility. Considering that he must probably have been playing it the first way for years, he doesn't do at all badly in lopping off some of the honey. "Ever so much better," she says.

"Now about the Shostakovich," she begins, but he shakes his head: "I'm not going to change a hair of that. Are you game to let it stand?"

"You haven't heard what I have to say!" cries Gerda.

"I can read it in your voice. There's a thing or two you don't care for."

"There certainly is. The whole conception —"

"I want to let it stand. I'm not frightfully keen on changing it. If you don't mind. I've been worrying the things for months and I've got them exactly the way I like them. Is that a terrible thing to say to you?" He gives her the most delightful of grins. Intelligent humility, her eye.

"I thought you asked to study with me."

"Oh I did. I do. It's only this special thing — tell me, honestly now, d'you think there's only one correct interpretation of a piece?"

Hah, a slap at the Mozart, too. But he excites her. "All right. Let me fetch my engagement book and we'll get you scheduled, shall we?"

Afterward she watches him go off. What hands.

He's indolent, something she'd never have imagined. Many a thing she might be willing to overlook in him but not that. It bewilders her, and enormously cramps the teaching sessions. To add to that, she can never manage to meet his eyes without the most unspeakable thoughts rushing to her head, making her dark face flush to raspberry. For this reason she never looks into his face when she talks to him.

Nearly throttled by her fantasies, she sits bolt upright beside him and regards nothing but his hands. He's doing the *Carnaval*, and suddenly it has become impossible for her, when he plays any of the heroic parts, not to imagine those stupendous hands of his cupped to her hips.

She thinks she cannot continue having him for a pupil, yet finds it impossible to send him off. In fact she lives for the days when he comes for lessons. She detests teaching as much as ever and there are times when it's all she can do to stick it out with the more blundering ones. It's not her idea of a way to earn a living. But this laziness of his — she still can't bring herself to accept that he refuses to practice, and almost airily attempts to slide through with the least preparation possible. Because his technique is so prodigious he does astonishingly well. Yet each time he leaves she tells herself she's a thundering idiot to put up with this kind of thing from a student.

"Would you do the page over, please. The melodic line wants to be a bit cleaner," she tells him for the second time, when he's done the *Reconnaissance*. How absurd that that, or even the *Davidsbündler* finale, should give him trouble. With hands and muscles like his — again that massive throb in her groin — it should be easy sailing. Yet for two lessons in a row he's done little more than stumble through them. The sheerest sloth; it's obvious he doesn't look at the piece from one lesson to the next, and each time he departs she's resolved to tell him, the following week, that it's all up.

He intends to become a concert pianist! He hasn't an earthly . . .

The day comes that is absolutely *it*. She tells him: continuing with him is pointless, he may as well chuck it, this will be his last lesson. She says this, facing him squarely, anger mounting as she speaks, overcoming her discomfort. How dare he appear each week, week after week, totally unprepared . . . and how ready she has always been to work with him, to work hard, to her very limits. As she speaks her anger turns to fury. He wants to become a concert pianist? He hasn't a hope. He's looking at her with a revolting smile, regarding her as though from some unscalable height and she an . . . an insect down below. Unbearable, unbearable . . .

The policeman — perhaps another kind of officer, he was not wearing a uniform — had come to the house, asked several questions, listened to her, then sat with his hands in his lap, his thumbs working round and round each other. After a moment he stopped the twiddling long enough to sign to her, by raising one thumb, that she was to say more.

But she had already given him the details. She could only stare at him.

"I really think you'd do better to have a bit more to say, miss. That is, a bit more to say than nothing. The young man's going to press charges, I've no doubt. I mean to say, you appear to have done him a bit of damage."

She met his eyes, held the stare, then lowered hers. "It's just that I'm so awfully . . . ashamed." Her voice very low.

"Ashamed," the policeman said. He sat back. "Now, was that before or after you did what the chap alleges?" He regarded her misery, then started with the thumbs again.

273

Was there any way she could have told him, in a way that he could understand, how her throat had filled with gorge — she could still taste the bitter fluid — how he had sat down to the Prokofiev and given her the identical, error-ridden, slap-dash version he'd played the week before, the violent chords as patently unstudied, the rendition as technically wanting as it had been the lesson before — yes, and the lesson before that! And then, when he'd come to a stop, allowing his hands to rest on the keys, the indescribable way he'd raised his eyes to her and smiled. *Smiled* — tauntingly — what was she going to do about it? The bloody, bloody, bloody rotter.

The lamp was the closest thing to hand.

Tears spilled from her eyes and ran down her cheeks. She made no effort to interfere with their progress.

"Well, suppose I put it this way," the officer said. He spoke kindly. "The two of you were alone. You mentioned just now you were ashamed. He said something to you, did he?"

At the moment she was lost in the feel of the cold tears on her face, like rain trails down a window.

"Said something improper to you, did he?"

"Whatever do you take me for?" she'd shouted at Bartley Munson. "Do you know who I am? How insulting! How positively —" And then the lamp.

When the blood was wiped away she saw that she'd cracked two of the ivories.

"That's what I suppose must've happened, mmm? Made you an indecent offer, had he?"

What a row that ox had raised down at the station after coming from hospital, his hand done up in bandages as far as the elbow.

"You're not a very big lass, are you? And he's a bit of a hulk, if I might put it that way. Physically. And also by comparison, if you see what I mean." Was he telling her that he could understand her recourse to the lamp?

"Said something indecent to you, did he?" the officer persisted. Musicians weren't like artists, not in his experience, they weren't. If it was painting she taught, now, she'd be used to all sorts of things, seeing people in the buff, all that. What a tiny dark bit of a thing she was, though he couldn't see there was much to look at in her — bit on the ugly side, in fact. Chap must have been pretty hard up, he'd say.

Ahead of her and on all sides, in space

and in time, she saw the results of what she had done. Shock. Scandal. Disgrace. She was alone in a dory on a precipitous sea. With rocks.

"Yes," she had whispered.

And when she later countered his story with her own, she never looked at him. But his indrawn gasp would stay with her through her life. The case was never brought to law.

"Yes," she whispered, and had come safe to shore.

Her career in England is finished. As a recitalist, perhaps everywhere. One of the tabloids has got hold of the story, never mind that they managed to mangle it.

"Love and music are the two wings of the soul," she is reported to have said to her student, at once inflaming him to lascivious frenzy. Presumably he had chased her several times around the piano, until in desperation she had had recourse to the lamp. "Is that what she's trying on with me?" His hand swollen and white in its bandages, he is reported to have exploded with laughter. "What in the world could make her think I'd ever give a fish's tit about her in that way? Her, of all people!"

Reading this, she gave a gasp. Could he have said such a beastly thing? Of course not. Yet true or false, the entire episode, however dreamed up in some newswriter's head, remains there in permanent black and white. Who, reading it, would think to doubt it?

She can never again appear on a concert stage.

Munson decided not to pursue the case, in the face of her own slightly more temperate charges, a matter she has no wish to dwell on.

"Do you think you could manage some room in your flat for me?" she writes Hedwig. "It will be only temporary, of course, until I find a place of my own."

Hedwig has started a catering service but it doesn't go so well. She'd seen herself as famed for her *Sandtorte*. And *Bundkuchen*. Instead, only occasionally does she get an order, very sudden, for enough *Paprika Schnitzel mit Kartoffelklössen* to feed twelve — someone is caught with guests coming. But this doesn't happen often enough. The things people put in their stomachs in this country — what her cousin Harry, G—d rest his soul, used to call the cat's breakfast — cannot be believed. Food from the Chinese. Greeks, even. Mexico!

And now Gerda arrives, coming through the door with a mountain of suitcases. Hedwig trembles. *"Mein Gott, tell me exactly what happened!"*

Gerda's eyes are stormy. "We will speak no more about it. Ever."

"But —"

"Ever. Is this to be my room?" Gerda walks into the room where Hedwig has led the way with some of the luggage. She sees her mother out and closes the door.

Nothing is said again, ever, of the piano

affair. It seems not to have got into the papers here. How fortunate that Gerda never concertized on this side of the ocean, Hedwig thanks G—d. Her daughter is unknown in New York — from all the time of being so famous in Europe, and on phonograph records, too, she can still walk in the street and nobody looks twice in her face.

Hedwig sees Berti off each morning. With his pale smile and lunch in the paper bag, he walks down the street to the subway and, from someplace farther down, takes the tube to New Jersey. Sometimes, after the door has closed behind him, Hedwig goes into their bedroom to look at the trunks. As in Harry's place, she keeps them stacked against the back wall.

A few of the pieces she has removed and put about the flat — the marble-and-bronze ormolu clock from Berti's mother's house in Berlin, now on the bookcase shelf, and Grossmutti's Bavarian hand-painted fruit dishes, on the dinette stand; but none of these treasures, and they show it, can live properly in a place like this. The flat, though it fairly well suits her, lacks a certain feeling.

Far better though this neighborhood is than the one in London, she cannot seem to rest easy in it. All day long the building is surrounded by the sound of pigeon-warble that brings back the memory of her hotel room in that last Berlin visit. And downstairs on the ground floor lives a man who stations himself on the street corner every morning, and from her window Hedwig has seen that a car stops, and after a little talk it goes away, and back he comes to the house. She has watched very closely and cannot see that anything has changed hands, but often she sees him lean his elbows on the car window, talking. "That man is a narcotic," she has told Berti darkly.

From experience she knows she is able to make do in all sorts of circumstances but still and all, is this the kind of existence, Hedwig asks herself, which she can expect to the end of her days? She has a husband but has forgotten why she married him. She has a daughter who is as bad-tempered as ever and who has always been a stranger, if not an enemy. And then there is the semi-genteel ugliness around her and the terrible way Americans have of speaking English. Though she's not a woman given to dejection, sometimes Hedwig thinks there is so much pain to living, she doubts the pleasures are worth it. Even her little private solaces, like the small nips of *Schnaps* she takes now and then, no longer liberate her spirit.

He has a conscience, after all. Bruno tracks his sister down in her Bronx bower and sends her a gigantic box of Droste chocolates and a bottle of good Scotch whiskey from Macy's, whiskey being a universal currency — he remembers the pathognomonic pink of Hedwig's face in New York. All this he follows with a letter.

"A letter from Bruno today," Hedwig announces at dinner over the steaming *Nockerln*. She pats her apron pocket where the letter rests and raises her eyes to express, possibly, resignation.

They're sitting in a dining room whose original and probably handsome wooden panels have for decades been covered over, and over yet again, with sheets of paint, a fact that chills her every time her eyes rest on them. At this moment what her eyes are resting on is the narrow ledge below the ceiling where the paneling ends, and where she can detect an uninterrupted line of gray dust. Always, she keeps forgetting to attack it with a covered dust mop. Should she get a woman in to clean or should she not? She, who came from a house with up-stairs and downstairs maids. They ask an arm and a leg, cleaning women.

Gerda, listless, follows her mother's eyes upward and then looks down and across toward the apron pocket. She cannot stand unfinished things. "Well," impatiently, "what has he to say?" Beyond that he paired off with a Russian woman who has died, she knows almost nothing of her uncle Bruno.

"He says . . . what Bruno says is . . . that we should come out to where he lives in Kansas. He says there is lots of space. And wheat."

"How heavenly."

"I don't know how it is with you," Hedwig says coldly, "but I find nothing in this city to hold me here. It is a thought." And she looks speculatively at this satur-nine, untouchable woman who is her daughter.

Is what she has done so terrible?

What has Hedwig done? Only invited Victor Hammerschlag to dinner. A friend of the family. Is there a reason Gerda shouldn't meet him? They are both musicians, he is already world-famous. Positively all she has in mind is to make the poor man some *Gans mit Äpfeln,* some *Linzertorte,* perhaps — dishes she's positive Victor hasn't tasted since he left Europe. She would like to do something for him, his face is so sorrowed. Instead she is accused of trying to matchmake, or whatever words the wretched girl used. Such a beautiful goose she has bought from that thief of a butcher on the avenue. Besides, Gerda is already twenty-nine.

They think highly of Hammerschlag's music in America, Hedwig has seen many of the concert reviews. Absolute raves. Though modern, his music is supposed to be good. Anyone would think the girl would be pleased. So what if Victor is sixty? Her Tante Gert, Berti's mother's sister, married a man from Mannheim, a cantor with a wonderful voice, who was thirty-five years older than she, and it was a blissful marriage. Besides, certain things are imperishable — the Kesslers have known the Hammerschlags for three generations. And they have shared a cavernous loss — his people have joined her own, and doesn't G—d look down from heaven upon them all — many, probably, in the same grave?

"I've seen him on the telly," Gerda says. "Loathsome. All that fat dripping over his neck."

"He is a good friend and a famous man," says Hedwig angrily. "You should not speak like that of him. He says he has just finished a new piano piece; I think he likes that you will play it for him when he comes. It will be an honor."

She's astonished at the scornful smile the girl presents her with, that same look as when Hedwig had suggested she wear the burgundy-colored velvet, the only dress she owns that doesn't make her look so yellow.

To her mind, it is totally unnatural for a girl always to speak so nastily to her mother. Whenever they talk now, on whatever subject, it ends in fighting. The girl is like a dog: anything her mother says is immediately grabbed in the jaws and worried for five minutes, like an old rag. She sighs bitterly, and there is a taste in her mouth as though she had just licked brass. She has even rented a piano for Gerda — a very good large grand, it is expensive — and had it tuned, and there's been no thank-you for it and Gerda hardly touches it. Is there anyone in the world the girl likes? No. Except maybe herself. No. Anyone who hates others hates themself, Hedwig tells herself sagely.

No matter. Gerda can appear at table or not. Victor will come to dinner. If only she can get the right apples, like the hard green sour ones she still remembers from Berlin.

Like her brother Bruno, Victor Hammerschlag refuses ever to go back to Germany. In fact, he will not put a foot anywhere on European soil. An educated man, he has nevertheless concluded — exactly like her brother — that because monsters and apes once ran over a land, the language of Goethe and Heine can suddenly become a bad language.

Hammerschlag arrives, a package and a flat music case under one arm. As he'd done on his first visit, he gives Hedwig a European bow, a kiss on the cheek, and a box of fine English chocolates. He repeats the bow and the kiss to Gerda who, wearing the burgundy velvet dress, comes to meet him. Before her stands a short man with the receding hairline of a cellist and, as he bows, a tender-looking bald spot toward the rear of his head. His shining purple face proclaims a blood pressure that is not what it should be. He smells of pipe tobacco, his suit looks unpressed, everything about him announces a man who lives alone, aging and vulnerable. He looks warmhearted and kindly, he is a famous composer and conductor. Gerda, recalling the one piece of his that she knows of, "Stratagems for Strings, Brasses and Percussion," finds it hard to imagine such music coming out of such an overwhelmingly ordinary-looking man. He lays his music case down on a table.

"You cannot know what an honor it is that

I meet you and for me to come tonight." Hammerschlag's accent is heavier than her father's. He regards her with an enormously interested smile, then takes both her hands into his. "I very much, *very much*, like your Bach. You are still recording?"

"No. Not yet. Not here." There's no way she can explain to him that music is the last thing in the world she wants to talk about, but "You will make me so happy if you will play this," and picking up his music case, he thrusts it into her hands.

Hedwig runs Berti off to help arrange chairs in the dining room and Hammerschlag almost entreatingly leads the way to the piano.

She must tell him she can't. She's barely touched the piano in weeks. There's something wrong with her right thumb, she really ought to seek medical treatment. Dare she chance it? A quick glance at the music he's thrust at her stirs her curiosity, and though she feels the familiar warning in her right wrist she seats herself and spreads the music on the rack. The thing is to give it no thought. Plunge in.

His notation is scratchy and narrow. She snaps on the brightest bulb of the piano lamp and starts to play. Promptly the pain begins, spreading from the wrist to the thumb. For a while what she's playing allows her to ignore it, particularly in her surprise that music like this can have come out of this man. Rhythmic, rattling stuff — very good, really, though his use of every register forces her to make frenzied leaps in and out of the keyboard. Her hands are like lions sent in awkward directions by a mad trainer. " 'Scuse me," she mutters as that filthy thumb of hers slides from a key into an unintended dissonance.

It's terribly good. Who would have thought the old man to have so much blood in him? She wonders suddenly how she looks to him, sitting at the piano under this filthy light. Of course she has always known she's no beauty, yet what of that? Should one expect the exteriors of musicians to be touched by angels? Look at Beethoven, with his traplike mouth, or Brahms with that enormous paunched belly, those ridiculous whiskers. And Enid . . . so fat, so . . . The pain is relentless now, though she continues playing; it's spread up her arm, and immediately, like a canoe entering calm waters after great turbulence, she enters a melodic passage — a beautiful melody — though a swift glance shows more breakers up ahead.

The pain and heat in her arm are intolerable. What might he be thinking, standing beside her — that he's never seen a homelier woman playing the piano? Here she is under this remorseless light. She knows how the lines at the sides of her eyes look laid on with a pencil. And the heavy down on her upper lip, which she keeps trying to lighten with peroxide, is, she suspects, beaded with sweat, thanks to this athletic stuff he's given her to play.

She finishes the thing, wringing wet and in agony. But it's good! And she turns her face up to him to smile, to smile genuinely, on the brink of telling him how really awfully good this piece of music is. She thinks her right arm is paralyzed.

She meets his eyes on her face, and though he quickly opens his hands in a gesture of admiration, she's caught the expression she's interrupted. She will never forgive him that pitying look. She will remain unforgiving until death. She crashes her hands furiously back into the keyboard, banging like a maniac — anything, anything, some furious Chopin, to very hell with the pain, until Hedwig comes to call them to dinner.

"Your playing . . . I don't know what to say . . ." Hammerschlag walks beside her to the dining room. "To think you have never seen it before, and you play, like . . . like . . . It is hard to believe. You are a great artist, Gerda. I hope you know that." Pointedly, he makes no mention of the music itself. Radiant, Hedwig watches as he holds back the chair for Gerda to seat herself.

Her right hand is useless. She will have to eat with the left.

He's waiting for her opinion of the piece, is he? Well, he can wait until — how do they put it here? — till hell freezes over.

"I have today another letter from Bruno," Hedwig announces a month later, again at the dinner table. She removes the folded paper from her apron pocket and with care lays it beside her plate. Berti looks at her guardedly — something is in the air, she doesn't generally announce Bruno's letters, though he's spotted them now and then when he brings the mail up from the lobby.

"He wants that we take an aeroplane and come to visit him."

Berti looks down at his plate, recalling how the two of them had parted. This is a very bad idea. It is a better idea that half a continent continue to separate this brother and sister.

"I think he is lonely that his wife died," Hedwig says. As carefully as she had set it down, she lifts the letter, folds it, and returns it to her pocket.

She doesn't like New York any more than she had liked London. Here she is in her middle life and with still no real place to call home. This city is mad and pitiless.

She has gotten to know more of her neighbors, or has heard stories about them. In the very flat next door lives a woman who refuses to handle subway tokens because she says they are irradiated; a group is doing it, she's told Hedwig, to kill off the human race. A German woman, too, Jewish. She will not put her name on the roster in the lobby. It is Pfulb, Hedwig thinks. Or Pflum. That is next door. And somewhere on a floor above lives a pinch-mouthed Irishman whom she has seen in the elevator carrying an instrument that fits into a small box, some kind of a horn on which he is always practicing. All day he practices, the building is filled with his sound, a sound like a baby wailing. And out in the streets, things are worse. People walk toward you, talking violently to themselves or to someone no one can see. What frightens Hedwig is that they seem to be increasing in numbers. The women are the worst. There is one in particular whom Hedwig sees often, the words she says must surely blister her tongue. When she passes, chills go down Hedwig's back, as though she were walking on sugar.

She decides she happens to be one who doesn't care for large cities. She still has Charlottenburg in her blood, and the villa and its grounds keep returning with painful fidelity. Sometimes when she is out in the street, for no reason ferny garden smells like the ones at home come at her, and she has to stand still until her heart stops missing beats.

She has described to no one her visit to Charlottenburg, where she found everything gone — the villa, everything, bombed to the same kind of rubble as Harry's house with Harry in it. Not a tree was left.

Animals. People are animals. Animals on all sides. When all she really wants is the green of lawns and the smell of phlox on a summer night.

A dozen times she's sat down to answer Bruno's letter but never does because she's so unused to putting her thoughts in writing, especially the thoughts she's thinking now. Today, again, Hedwig sits with paper and pen before her, leaning on her elbows at the kitchen table with her chin propped on her fist, and gazing at the wall opposite, revolving round and round in her head all the things she wants to say to him and cannot find the words for. She wants him to know how sorry she is to hear about Nina, but how can someone outside, even a sister, say anything to help make the hurt easier? And she sees now how maybe it is her own fault that she did not get to meet his wife. All these years, and she did not do it. And knowing that his Nina came of Russian family brings their own mama to mind, and at so late in their lives she wants to tell him again that he is wrong in what he thinks of Opa and Oma and how they felt at her and Bruno's father also marrying a Russian woman. They did not hate her, as Bruno seems to believe, she will never know where he found such an idea. Of course, being older than she when their parents died, he must have felt it more, the older child always does. So it is understandable to Hedwig that he married also a Russian woman, and now she blames herself that they did not meet.

Is it a pretty village he lives in? She doesn't have the first idea, now, of why she came to New York, and she doesn't mind telling him that this so famous city which many say is supposed to be the capital of the world — one has heard it even in Europe — is terrible. Simply terrible. She is not happy here. How she misses village gardens! She wants to get a little bit of green in before she dies. What she wants to ask him is, does he think there would be a place in Drummond for them? Do lilacs grow out there? She and Berti will both work, they are used to it and they are not proud. Berti will take any kind of work. Has she already mentioned that he is hired by a textile mill in New Jersey? It is across the river and he goes there every day. Actually, he is a janitor there. Perhaps Bruno can find a small house for them in Drummond? Because suddenly she wants to make sauerkraut. Does he remember Oma's barrels with the sauerkraut and the cranberries and the ice crystals in? How she longs to live in a house again, even a small house.

Gerda will not wish to leave. She doesn't mind the lunatics and the *Schmutz* here. Hedwig herself can't do much with her, there is always a look on that girl's face as if she has just licked brass. She has started playing the piano again but it seems that she always plays in anger. Hedwig herself believes Gerda will be happier living away from them; it was perhaps a mistake that she left London, so they must not mind giving her the chance again. What does Bruno think about their moving house to Drummond?

Why is Hammerschlag phoning her? Possibly he imagines himself in loco parentis, now that she's seen the two of them off, watched the plane roar across the field, take off on a tangent and lose itself in the murk? And just as was the case when they'd left London, Gerda feels herself alive in the pure oxygen of freedom. She realizes now that anywhere in the world suits her as long as she can be alone. Heaven is that place where everyone is a stranger to everyone. She walks blocks out of her way to buy her food in different shops so that the clerks won't wear faces she's seen before.

She wishes Hammerschlag lived in Samarkand.

"You are going to be all right?"

"Of course I'm going to be all right."

"Your mother tells me you are taking pupils?"

"Yes."

"You must forgive me. You have enough money to live?"

"Yes. Quite." Please, let him ring off.

"Such a pianist as you are, you should have no troubles. Do you want I should send you a few pupils? I have many contacts, Gerda."

"No, no thanks. I have as many as I can handle." She has barely enough to cover her rent and food, but she hates every hour of teaching more than she hates poverty.

"Ah, I am glad to hear that. I will tell you that I must fly down to Dallas. That is in Texas. The symphony there is playing a thing I wrote for them."

"Oh, how very nice!" And she means it, he can hear how her voice warms.

"You will take care of yourself all right? We will meet when I come back, to see how you are getting along. I will call you. I promised your mother."

So that's it. "Of course. There are thousands here in New York who live alone and manage quite well, you know. Hundreds of thousands, I dare say."

"You are right. I have only one thing to say — do not close yourself off. You must get out, meet people."

"I shall. I promise."

"I want you should get my meaning." His voice, heavy with paternalism, is slightly muffled — he's brought the phone too close to his mouth. "New York — you must realize what a wonderful place it is. No one needs to be lonely."

At this moment for some reason she remembers her mother telling her that when he was twenty-five, Hammerschlag's young wife was gassed at Dachau.

". . . a collection of cities, really. You must put yourself *into* them. You know what I mean?"

"I know. I do know." There are tears in her throat. Can he hear them?

"Here is everything in the world. Chinatown. Little Italy. Harlem. The Cloisters. Such a variety. Carried here like . . . like spores on the world's winds."

"Yes, Victor, I know all that. I promise I will visit all those places."

"I will call you when I come back. Maybe we will go together next month, hear Serkin play."

"Yes. We will. Now I have a pupil coming, I must ring off. I wish you good luck in Texas. Very good luck." She hangs up the phone.

He, too, lives alone. He cooks for himself, he told them at the dinner table once, he actually enjoys cooking. He has always liked roast chicken, the way his wife used to make it. Her hand still on the telephone, Gerda suddenly sees him in his small kitchen wrestling with a chicken. How must it feel to a man to remember his wife's cooking? She was young. Beautiful, probably.

But she *has* been getting out. As in London, the city is full of free concerts — she hears chamber groups, symphonies, choruses, soloists. Going to them is like living on thick, rich soup. She's discovered also there is a devoted drove of concert followers, she sees the same ones almost every time she goes.

And so, of course, do they see her. She recoils at the notion of being considered part of that herd, most of whom appear to be at a loose end. One hag, always wearing a hat made of what looks to be shellacked grass, attends the noon-hour recitals with her lunch in a filthy cracked patent-leather handbag and sits nibbling while the players carry on. There are also beastly-looking old men dressed in tag ends who obviously come only to find a place out of the cold and rain or sun. They drowse in their seats, for the most part. Certainly they find the sounds of violins, violas and cellos preferable to the din of traffic.

A few weeks ago she'd gone to hear a string trio at one of the museums, and a flea-bitten old man came in with the same woman she'd seen munching an apple and a banana through the Goldberg Variations the week before. Poor freaks, they'd taken seats in front of her and the old fellow had promptly dropped off, his head nearly grazing his lap. When the trio came on-stage with their instruments, the applause brought him to. Groping to consciousness but still in some bizarre old man's dream, he spoke, the words quite distinct to Gerda's ear. "Dogs have been known to eat cat food," he mumbled to his tatty com-panion before he snapped awake.

Occasionally she can afford the big halls, and thinks of giving up the free concerts entirely — she's noticed that one or two people in these raffish audiences have taken to nodding to her when she comes in.

Berti remembers the books in his father's house — not by their titles but by their bindings, especially those with their endpapers marbled like oil on a pond under sunlight. His brother Reiner (born a cripple — one of the first to go in the German mercy killings in 1940) was the true bookworm, but it was Berti who handled the books lovingly, opened them, stuck his nose into the center crack, and inhaled deeply. More than anything, it was their smell that he loved . . . it might have been the glue pinning the pages to the back binding, or chemicals in the paper, but smelling books was one of the loves of his youth. He can still today recall the celestial aroma certain of them had — one, especially, had the purest, strongest, most transporting odor — Friedrich Gerstacker's *Germelshausen*, its red-brown binding the color of the chocolate his mother drank every morning. Today, Berti vaguely remembers the tale of a phantom village which once every century materialized in the midst of an enchanted forest, a story which for some reason he's always associated with the history of the Kesslers. But mainly he prized the book for its beautiful smell. He can still see himself as a child sitting contentedly, his nose pressed to the center of the opened book, ecstatically inhaling.

All this lies behind his taking a job as night clerk in the Transient House on Wintergreen Street in Drummond. This happened shortly after his and Hedwig's move to Kansas. Answering an ad Hedwig had cut from the newspaper, Berti opened a door and walked into his childhood. He approached the desk to speak about the job to the proprietor, a man named John Wessel, and then, with a feeling close to faintness, had to grab at the counter quickly. There was the inexpungible smell of *Germelshausen*, straight from boyhood.

"You have a job advertised in the newspaper?" Berti inquires, but he doesn't see Mr. Wessel. There is a haze of mahogany and glass and leather bindings between them, and Berti knows that should this man refuse to hire him, he will fall to his knees and beg, implore him to let him work here. For whatever purpose, fate has brought him halfway round the world to become night clerk at the Transient House.

There's no need to beg for the position. He is the only one to apply. Mr. Wessel, looking down into Berti's gentle eyes, is satisfied he can do the job, matter of fact, he can start that night. Berti thanks him, inhales deeply and turns with joy toward the front door.

He's been here for three months now. The work is pleasant and unexacting, particularly after two in the morning. And the odor greeting him each midnight when he reports for work is still a rapture for him. He thinks perhaps it is produced by the greenish-yellow liquid the night cleaning woman puts into her floor-scrubbing water.

He knows everyone who lives in the place — a few students from the local college and several working women are, in the main, fixtures. Also, an occasional man comes for a night now and then — or a girl may check at the desk during the evening, and when this happens Berti hands her a key. It is none of his business what they do. Everyone here is cheerful, they seem like good people, and the nights are quiet. Every town and city in the world, Berti knows, has places like this one. The women are pleasant. He calls them dollies. He calls them popsies. He spends the calm early-morning hours reading — magazines, newspapers, books — and almost regrets when it is time to leave and go back to Bruno's house.

Why the hell he's fired by this particular need Bruno Brodsky can't say, but every few years he's afflicted by a sufficient muddying of memory to imagine he loves his sister Hedwig. He experiences a wash of pity for her (why pity?), or it may be guilt (why guilt?). But whatever it is, periodically he has to offer himself to her in one form or another. In the early part of the war it was with food parcels, packages so stuffed with chocolates and Spam and coffee and tea and maple syrup that it was a wonder any of them ever reached her and Berti. He'd started again as soon as the war was done with, while England was struggling back to its feet.

As the years passed, he kept writing letters; he's certain he wrote two letters to each one of Hedwig's. And what was every letter from her but a sopping blanket to his well-meaning, his good intentions? Every one of them brought home to him her essential Germanness, her other-world upbringing, her inflexibility. He suspects now she's always been a little bit askew, even as a child. Now that he comes to think of it, it's curious that he hasn't one single friendly memory of Hedwig from when they were children. Not even before the deaths of their parents — which Bruno remembers very well — after which the old folks had immediately and successfully whisked his sister off into a fairyland of manufactured events that they also knew — looking into Bruno's eyes — they'd never get away with, with him.

So why his well-intentioned interferences? Why his constant urgings that they come to the United States? The instant he saw Hedwig, with the braids wound round her head, he knew what was to be the outcome of the meeting in New York.

So why has he always been doing this? Is it possible there's something, after all, in the famous Kessler tie? Could the first eight years he'd spent in that barbaric house filled with heavy Heidelberg furniture in the Berlin suburb have so wound up the clock of his life that he's got to spend the remainder helplessly letting the spring uncoil?

It must be so, for he's cajoled this forbidding, spacious sister of his and their cousin, the little fellow she married, into moving to Drummond. And now, with his wife — who'd been the very cream of his life — gone, he seems to have settled himself firmly into a future of misery. All his own doing.

He'd picked up Hedwig and her husband at the airport and then drove the eighty miles or so to his house. Hedwig, immediately upon getting out of the car, lifted her big head and drew a mighty breath.

"Ah! The smell!" she cried, her nostrils twitching like a rabbit's. "How fresh is the air! How clear. It smells like wine. No, not wine. *Apfelsaft!*" And turning to her brother: "How healthy to breathe! We have been living in a miasma, that is the only word to name what it is like in New York City. Choking! Everyone there is choking! The same in London!"

He'd grabbed some suitcases and turned to lead them into his house, but his sister, in all her firm amplitude, continued to stand on the walk. "The good green earth," she murmured, and after an interval followed him up the steps.

She keeps hoping Hammerschlag will finally get the message, and leave her alone from now on. In any case he's too busy a man to keep pushing solicitudes, for her mother's sake, on the sullen bitch she knows he must think her, always in temper, and with no looks at all, and a quirk in both her thumbs, so that she cannot play the piano anymore. Perhaps never again — how does that make her feel? She doesn't know.

"I have found something today!" he announces, shaking a finger at her in the same kind of ponderous merriment her mother is sometimes given to. It must be a German trait. He's bullied her again into coming to dinner with him to another of those rotten restaurants he so fancies — Baltic, Lithuanian, Hungarian . . . wouldn't she like some wholesome English cooking for once!

"How is it you have never told me you recorded the Beethoven Variations!" He has the record with him, his arm pressing it tight against his rib cage.

"Oh, that," she says. It's the Opus 34, and she's right to be offhand about it. She'd done the recording in London two years back, and listening to it after it was released, never wanted to hear it again. They'd given her an unforgivable piano at the studio, with an uneven tone and a temperamental damper pedal, but unfortunately she didn't have what they call, in this country, enough clout to demand a better.

He has whisked her off briskly to a restaurant, and they duly eat. Hammerschlag drinks aquavit with his *njoki* and talks the whole time about his concert series, horrendous experiences with his agent, with conductors and their dull orchestras, and two commissions for orchestral works. Then he escorts her back to the Bronx. She watches him go off into the night, carrying the recording with him. Well, he's got a nasty example of her playing to listen to. Does she care? She doesn't care. How absurd and stark a person's life is, she thinks — rather like a set of hooks for the hanging on of dreams and fantasies. Even her fantasies wouldn't stand up well to examination — imagine her mother's having ever given half a thought to Gerda's considering in a physical way an untidy-looking old man like that, with a noodle-filled belly. Actually, when she came right down to think of it, she doesn't want anyone's tendrils winding around her. She wants to be free and clean.

Today Gerda hands over three onions to the white-jacketed boy who weighs things at the produce counter. "Hi there," he says, "how ya doin'?" His face, polka-dotted with acne, is creased in a smile, and she sees in his eye a glint of recognition. He remembers that he's seen her before. Only because she hadn't got the energy lately to travel farther for her groceries, she's come three times in a row to the neighborhood supermarket. For turnips, on the Wednesday last; for a couple of oranges a day later. And now today. His daring to remember her is more than she can bear. "How much do these weigh?" she asks pointedly.

"You're English, aren't you?" He keeps holding the onions, grinning at her like an ape, and she has to turn and run from the store, down the street, around the corner and into the vestibule of her apartment building. She cowers in the elevator, barely managing the strength to press the button for her floor. They will not leave her alone. Hammerschlag, thank God, has left the country to become guest conductor of a symphony in Liverpool, but now there's this. They will not leave her alone. Even a filthy stranger. They will not leave her alone.

She's ill, she knows she's ill. The pain in her thumbs starts up if she so much as looks at a piano, and many's the day she swears she sees blood on the keys. Yes, she's ill. There's nothing for it — she'll get rid of the piano, give up teaching. She hates concerts, hates listening to music on records or the wireless. Radio, that is.

Last week she'd wakened one morning and turned on the radio at her bedside and lain there, half awake, listening to a *Brandenburg*, weaving shreds of sleep in and around the orchestration, totally without joy. She realized then that music had become nothing but a mathematical exercise — without beauty, emotion or meaning. Her well has dried up. All she asks is that the world leave her alone. And now she must go far beyond the boulevard for her food purchases, to find stores she's never entered before.

Hedwig certainly has no intention of stopping here in her brother's house for the rest of her life. Since he's retired, he's home all day, and no matter that he closes himself up in that place he's built for himself in the cellar where she can hear him knocking away at things, and sawing, hour after hour. What does he make down there? Shelves. More shelves for more books. He is always bringing in books.

But the feel of his being constantly in the house nags at her like a tormenting child. Occasionally he will come up to the kitchen for a cold can of beer or a glass of milk. And then there's luncheon to be made for him, which she does not enjoy; yet she does it in spite of Bruno's insistence that he's used to building his own sandwiches. She's here, isn't she? Nothing will keep her from messing around in the kitchen — Bruno's words. Nothing. It is a duty she recognizes.

Berti is here too, of course, but is usually upstairs, sleeping. He comes into the house at half after eight each morning and goes immediately up to bed and does not rise until late afternoon. By then she has a good dinner ready. Men are unwelcome in a house until there is evening food on the table.

It's not a house she cares for. It's a wooden, old-fashioned American thing with many small rooms, seven or eight of them, and all — the bedrooms, too — filled with books lying anywhere, and stinking ashtrays with half-smoked tobacco and white ashes; from any room she can hear her brother banging his pipe into the one nearest him. The smell of a burning pipe is revolting, and even more so the odor of cold tobacco ashes, which fills every room of the house so that even her clothes smell of it. But there it is. Hedwig sighs bitterly. This is not her house.

Anonymity. Now Gerda feels she can walk the streets like a stranger. She *is* a stranger — this might be the day of her first arrival in the city from some unnameable place. Only her handful of piano students know her and she wishes she could greet them veiled.

Then why does she feel such loneliness? Truthfully, an enormous loneliness that transcends misery. The no-man's-land she's gained entrance to shows itself to be empty also of the peculiar and neutral peace she's sought.

She begins attending movies in the evenings. Once, a man in the seat adjacent to hers places his hand on her own resting on the chair arm and her body freezes rigid. Her hand flies to her lap and the neighbor changes his seat.

What is there to do? Gerda recalls Enid's having once confided to her that she'd visited a psychoanalyst for some sort of help, early in her career. She'd never mentioned the problem. One didn't go into details about that sort of thing, of course. Yet Gerda can't imagine Enid's ever needing what you might call help of any deep nature. It might have been nothing more than stage fright.

One day, during a particularly agonizing moment in one of her interminable walks, she spots in a window the placard of someone proclaiming himself a spiritualist and on impulse, in an unbearable shaft of pain, finds herself running up a short set of steps and delivering herself into the hands of a whiskered, dourly intense-looking man who invites her to be seated.

At the beginning he tells her things that seem surprisingly apt. He talks to her for half an hour. Then — has anyone ever told her, he asks, that she has strong ectoplasmic possibilities? He senses a power in her that is simply extraordinary. Has she ever given thought to becoming a medium? The odd thing is, when he looks at her what he sees is a man with a head of wild white hair, clutching one of those sticks conductors wave about. A baton. The true ideal world is sexless, she knows that, doesn't she? He wishes he could be the one to call her forth after she dies.

Gerda looks toward him, at his sharp, thin face with its deal of ornamental face hair, its shiny forehead with bristly black caterpillars for eyebrows and the black whiskers outlining his face, curving down to a fine-clipped Vandyke. For the moment she can't tear her eyes from his facial land-scaping. She hopes to detect a smile, but he is serious. For twenty dollars, he says, he can help her map her life. She has re-markable potentialities, even the chair she's sitting on is pulsing. But she must recognize that she needs help. What luck that she's come to him.

"Is this session over then?" she asks.

"I'm afraid it is."

"I think I've heard enough," Gerda says.

"I can really help you. Really, really help you. It happens I am also a parapsychologist."

"Thanks, no."

"You don't meet someone with my abili-ties every day in the week."

"I quite see that." She gets to her feet. "Thank you. And I'm sorry, I'm afraid I can't afford any more."

"A pity. A terrible pity. You have so much. You know what I see when I look at you? I see a misfit."

"What a beastly thing to say!"

"I'm telling you that you need help. Come back again. Let me give you another appointment. You'll come back. Tuesday afternoon at five."

"I shall not."

"I wish you were open to seeing what a terrible mistake you're making."

"Thank you anyway." She's reached the door.

"Go, then. It's only a whole lifetime you're throwing away. Go back to your raggedy gray life."

She's vibrating with rage. "That sounds a very good idea. And I think most of what you've said is absolute . . . twaddle." She's got the door open, her heart ripping through her chest from the thrust of her anger.

"Let me tell you something for free, Miss Britisher." He is as angry as she, the skin of his face, what can be seen of it, a blazing, mottled red. "You know what I see when I look at you? A woman tormented by her virginity. It stands out all over you. You're dying to get laid. You want to be loved, but you're not lovable. Okay, there's enough truth there that fifty dollars wouldn't cover."

Hedwig, continuing to do what she has to do for her brother and his house, also continues to keep her eye out for something else. Each evening after she's washed up and set the dishes away, while Berti readies himself for work and Bruno sits stinking up his reading room with pipe smoke, she opens out the local newspaper across the kitchen table and carefully reads the classified ads. That's how she found the job for Berti. And she hasn't been in Drummond three mouths before something in the paper leaps to her eye: a men's fraternity house wants a housemother to live in, supervise the kitchen and direct the running of the establishment. She writes the address down carefully and next morning sets out to find the street. She will look for thirty minutes, she tells herself, before asking someone.

She has to admit that she finds the streets of Drummond rather pretty, most of the houses small but each with its bit of lawn and a yard in the back. She passes beyond a section of small stores and comes upon a tiny park. Here there are benches at random, and tired from her walking, she selects one and sits down, purse on her lap. Naturally she might not take the first position she applies for, she has plenty of time to pick and choose, but what a pleasure it will be to be out from under!

Boys are snickering, looking at her, passing. She returns their stares distastefully. What is there about her to be funny? They should be in school. American children have no manners. Little beasts. When she's sat enough she rises and sees for the first time, along the backrest, awkwardly printed in white block letters: THIS BENCH FOR HOORS. She leaves the place, but is forced finally to ask the way to the street she's looking for. Of course. It is in the section where the college is. Not so far, actually, from Bruno's house — she has merely walked in the wrong direction.

She finds the street, then the number, and stands on the walk to get a look at its architecture.

It is a largish white wooden building with two spacious porches, front and side. With approval she notes the wide windows and French doors opening out onto the porches. By now she has seen enough American houses to recognize the oldness and beauty of many of them, and the penchant Americans have of delivering over fine family homes to funeral parlors and other sorts of businesses. She particularly likes the look of the immense front door — it brings certain houses in Charlottenburg to her mind. Small panes of glass of different colors border the central pane, and at the very top are three Greek letters.

It will be nice to live in a house with Greek letters above the front door.

Slowly she goes up the walk and mounts a set of stone steps which badly need attention — she'll set someone to scrub them straightaway — then looks for the bell. There is a hole in the wood beside the door, where there must once have been bell. Another thing that must be attended to. She raps on the door in that manner of hers: Ba-ra-rom! Ba-ra-rom!

And departs, smiling, twenty minutes later. They are desperate here, they have suddenly lost their housemother, and she has agreed to move in over the weekend.

Bruno: "So you're deserting me."

True enough. Hedwig, her coronet of braids gleaming white and more tightly disciplined than usual, stands waiting in the lower hall by the front door, three packed suitcases beside her. Berti may decide to stay with Bruno, no decision yet. The two of them seem to get on. It is all one to her. She sees none of the distress in her brother's eyes she'd read in Cousin Harry's when they'd left the flat in Hackney. She thinks that her brother looks like a devil, with their mother's red hair going to gray now and his eyes the color of coffee.

He's not exactly heartbroken that Hedwig has found herself a job elsewhere. Since the day of her coming she's given his house the feel of being stuffed. Each night he's seen her, stiff with grievances, climb the stairs heavily to her bedroom, no doubt to sit on her bed and count over all the injustices ever done her, a miser counting her gold.

"Don't tell me lies," Hedwig says, giving him her sky-blue look, "you will be relieved when I go." She waits an ominous moment. "We both will be. I wonder where is that taxi? I phoned them up an hour ago. You will tell Berti when he wakes. I will see if he can move in with me."

"You phoned fifteen minutes ago. I could have driven you, you only had to ask me. And why leave so early? It's Saturday. Those louts will still be in their beds."

She consults her wristwatch. "It is half after nine. They will not still be in their beds."

"You mean they'd better not be, eh? Planning to make some changes at the Phi Gam House, are you? I should warn you —"

She looks at him sharply. "You think I will try to change everybody. When the boys sleep is nothing to me. My business this morning is with the housemaid." The front bell rings. "Ah, here must be the taxi." And she opens the door.

Gerda is standing there, a hand valise beside her.

"Mother."

Hedwig is speechless.

"I hope it's all right. I've left the city." Then Gerda bursts into tears. Hedwig, whose hands have flown to her cheeks, swoops forward and encloses her weeping daughter in her arms, pressing her head to her breast, for that is what a mother's breast is for.

Prepared for a grumpy uncle, or even, from the way her mother has always spoken of him, a rather beastly man, Gerda finds she rather likes the old thing. His hair is a kind of halfway ginger, graying now here and there, and curly as her own; and his face, arresting, dark, is lined and cross-lined like a grid, and with what certainly appears to be a warm, even charming, smile. Is he lonely? What bad luck — his wife dead, his sister gone off house-mothering in a fraternity house the other side of the campus, and her father, who surely can't be much company, either asleep upstairs or at work on his night job in some nasty little place her mother assures her is a bawdy house.

"I realize I've come out here without an invitation . . ." she starts to say to Bruno the day after her arrival. They're sitting over coffee at the table in his kitchen. Hedwig had moved out yesterday.

"Don't worry yourself about it." He smiles. Such a wide, creased grin. His eyebrows — oddly, still a fiery red — arch in a comical fashion. It's easy to see he's actually a large-hearted man. "Look at all the room I've got here." He waves an arm widely, inviting her into a limitless expanse. "You're very welcome."

"Thank you." Perhaps he really means it? "I've got this need to sort myself out, rather . . ."

"Forget it. You're one hundred percent welcome." He scrapes his chair back a little, perhaps to get a truer picture of her. "You know, you don't look like a Kessler."

"How d'you mean me to take that?"

He looks around him stagily, then leans toward her. "It's a compliment, honey. I don't know how you avoided it, seeing that

326

you got a double dose." In a hoarse whisper, as though against the possibility his sister might be standing in the hall near the doorway, "I don't know how Hedwig managed it. There are people who can't always be sure of their father, but you don't look related to either of them." With an impish wink: "Congratulations."

She laughs. "Well, there's no doubt I'm hers. We're the same blood type. All the subtypes are compatible too, I'm told."

"Now, how would you know that?"

"I can't really say why it was done." He sees how she clasps her hands hard and looks down on her knuckles. A very tense young lady, this one. And not too well, he'd say — the child has circles around her eyes likes a raccoon's. Obviously she feels his eyes on her, for she inhales and exhales deeply and pulls herself up, sitting very erect. "It has something to do with when I was born, they ran these tests in hospital. Perhaps I was ill."

He looks again at the near-black wiry hair, the dark complexion, and smiles widely. "Well, I guess you and I are the renegades of the family. Kesslerism runs thinly in us."

She smiles back. "Mother's hair has always been close to white, she says, even when she was a child. Where did yours come from? Were there other redheads in the family?"

"Only my mother. Hedwig's and my mother. Your grandmother. Our father delivered a punch in the face to family antiquity and brought a redheaded Russian Jewess home to our grandparents. As could have been predicted, it was instant hate."

Something stirs within her, a thing her mother had once said?

Instant hate. Now she recalls Hedwig's vociferous disdain for redheads, and her insistence that Bruno had defiantly married a Russian-born woman who looked like their mother. "Is there some reason our family doesn't care for people with red hair?"

He looks at her slowly, appraisingly. "You've only just got here, sweetheart, I don't know why I should be haranguing you with —"

But "Oh, please," she cries out, "what is this family thing that's always so hush-hush? Please. What is it about people with red hair?"

Still regarding her thoughtfully, "It goes beyond that, I'm afraid. Our mother — Hedwig's and mine — was a Russian. The color of her hair has very little to do with it. It was a pretty Russian girl my father brought home, not particularly well educated, spoke no German, read no philosophy or poetry, played no instrument. Oh, yes, her hair was red, that's not uncommon among Russian Jews. I trust by now you know how the German Jews felt about the Ost-Juden, the Jews from Poland and Russia?"

"Well, I guess I do, actually. Somewhat."

"And probably still do, I wouldn't be surprised. Oh, yes, there's one more thing. She was pregnant with me when he brought her to Charlottenburg."

"Ah."

"Well . . ." He studies his fingernails, then looks up at her. "So I was born. And three years later, Hedwig was born. And a few years after that, our grandfather killed his daughter-in-law." He opens both palms out at her, smiles.

"How did he — how could you possibly know that? Did he shoot her?"

"He poisoned her."

"You saw him do this?"

"No, honey, I didn't see him. The day my mother died I heard my father accuse him. Now look —" Bruno puts both his elbows on the kitchen table and leans toward her. "There's no need to go further into this. The old man's dead, Hedwig needn't know, it's done with —"

"It is not done with! Please, Uncle Bruno, tell me the whole story. I'm not a child. Once and for all, may I not know everything? Am I not a member of the family?" Her voice is tight, she's managed to make herself sit even taller, has an air of total, grim self-possession. This is a different Gerda and at once he accepts it.

"All right. I'm afraid there's no slightest doubt about it. She had a hard time with Hedwig's birth and afterward was in failing health. The old man — you know, don't you, he used to be a doctor in the German army sometime in the 1890s? — insisted on preparing tonics for her. To strengthen her. Slowly he fed thallium to her in small doses, over the next few years. Never enough to cause suspicion, though she seemed to get worse rather than better. She suspected something, for she wrote letters home to her family, who were by then established here in America. Years later I read those letters."

She leans on the table, eyes closed, and rests her forehead on her hand. "My God," barely whispering.

"My father discovered the whole thing, but from what I overheard I can't say how.

330

I was in the upstairs hall outside my grandfather's room and I heard what my father said to the old man — that he had destroyed the one thing in life that he loved. My mother disappeared — there must have been a funeral, but I don't remember it. And so did my father. I suspect now that he may have killed himself, but of course I'll never know. It just seemed to me that Hedwig's and my parents vanished in a single day. The story in the family was that they were killed in an automobile accident."

She stares at him steadily. "I'm not sure what to believe. You were so little — is it possible you didn't really understand what you thought you heard? How would you know what thallium meant?"

He smiles at her very gently. "Yes, it's possible I didn't understand what I heard. Now, my dear little Gerda, we'll put it out of our minds. I only tell you all this at your insistence. Let's talk about important things. Do you know how to drive a car?"

The subject of love is something Berti's given some thought to. It's connected with many aspects of life, he knows, though not always of the man-and-woman kind. Nor child, nor friendship. He owns a pocket watch, for example, once the property of his great-uncle Frederick, Hedwig's great-grandfather. It has been among the Kesslers for many years. Ornate and richly burnished, it has a small latch on the back which, when pressed, gives out a small chime announcing the nearest hour on the face of the watch. The sound of the chime is silver, the watch is gold. Berti knows how precious it has always been considered by the family, and that it was last owned by Max Kessler from Magdeburg, before coming to Berti upon his marriage to Hedwig. After Max's death. Between Berti and this watch, which he carries in the inside pocket of his jacket, love exists, a love having nothing to do with Kesslers. It is something between the heart and metal, and the sound of a tiny chime, and the thing goes under his pillow at night.

He thinks, also, that he once loved Pansy. Until recently he used often to hear her smoky, caressing voice in his dreams, though she appeared always as a young and graceful horse. Happily — for he is still afraid of horses — these dreams have now stopped.

And now there is . . . well . . .

Behind the counter where he sits is a small carpeted cloakroom and here, on the electric plate, several times during the night Berti makes coffee for himself in a cracked enamel pot. On this particular night — in fact, it's three in the morning — he has just brought forth a steaming cup which he has set on the counter, but even before he's seated himself a woman hurries through the door. She looks shaken. He recognizes her — one of the dollies — strongly built and not very young. She's always given him a smile as, key in hand, she's headed for the stairs. All he knows is that her name is Madge. He has always considered the brilliant smile she flashes at him as something she puts on professionally, like the short, flaming dresses she sometimes wears. But at the same time the smile always seems to him rather shy. "Oh Berti, honey, come quick; oh Berti, there's a dog hurt, lying outside on the sidewalk!"

At once he's off the tall stool, lifts the hinged countertop, and the two of them run through the front doors and out into the night. It's a bad one, the wind is thin and sharp, and fine hail mixed with a slamming rain pings like needles over his skin and eyes so that he can see almost nothing, but she takes his arm and pulls him, leading him to the side of the building where something large and dark is lying. It looks to be a heap of burlap beside the hotel wall. Then by the fitful light from the lamppost, he sees it is a large animal lying there, making a steady panting noise and looking at nothing. "We've got to do something!" Madge cries.

"We'll carry it inside," Berti says. His first thought, too, is that the poor beast has been hit by a car. Now he notices how bloated it appears, and that a part of its body is moving spasmodically. He stoops down, lays a hand and then an ear to the belly, and waits. "I think she is having babies," he says. He tries to lift her. The dog is very wet, very heavy, and stinks.

"I'll carry her in," Madge says. "You hold the doors open, honey." Berti blinks at her. She gathers the dog to her, lifting, staggering, clutching her to her chest. But she's a muscular woman and as he watches, manages to get herself upright, adjusting the animal's weight so that it's in balance against her body. The rain battering at her, she semi-trots toward the hotel entrance. Berti runs forward then, holds open the outer and inner sets of doors, and in the small back office she deposits the dog on the rug. There, over a period of half an hour, with the woman hovering in anguish behind him, Berti helps deliver the dog of four pups, no two alike.

She likes the job well enough. The frat house, the boys call it, a place as old and decrepit-looking as Bruno's own, with furniture much battered, but which she has ordered polished and is now in better order. Somehow, here she has developed a sense of proprietorship. For some reason it is more her house than Bruno's can ever be. After much searching, she's found and installed a brass door knocker which the housemaid is ordered to polish once a week.

As in everything Hedwig undertakes, she's magnificent as housemother. The meals improve tremendously, the boys bring their dates here instead of carting them off to the local restaurants. She is imperious in her governing and she bullies them, and they like it. She has plenty of plans with regard to the running of the house and will gradually put them into action.

Nor has she failed to make necessary adjustments herself. She has quite gotten used to the lively smells of boys' bedrooms. And with no one consulting her, the boys have decided the house needs a mascot to go with the three Greek letters above the door and have brought in a clownish large brown dog which, after some small initial resistance, she has accepted. They've made a party to celebrate, and placed bowl after bowl of beer on the floor which the creature obligingly continued to lap up and then proceeded to stagger about and sit on people's shoes. Now there are hairs everywhere, even in the soup. Soon the beast will be a forest of leaping fleas. Well, she will adapt herself to the animal. Incidentally, she has seen him make pee down the hot air registers. Let them only wait until the cold weather starts.

Madge doesn't use the room upstairs very often — twice a week, maybe. She works in a bakery, days, she tells Berti, but doesn't make nearly enough to keep her soul pasted to her body. What she does upstairs doesn't bother her in the least. He thinks she looks at him a little anxiously as she tells him this, but he appears to be only half listening, and pats her hand. They are again in the little back room which now has a thick, not unpleasant smell of dog, and Madge has come in early to have a look at the pups and to chat with him.

"What are we going to do with them?" she says. "We'll have to find homes for them, won't we? I couldn't bear it if we . . . if we . . . you know what I mean. Oh Berti, you wouldn't . . . would you?"

"It is too early," Berti says gently. "They must stay with the mother. Later we will see."

He's never really looked at her before. Now he sees how her hair is soft and cloudy, a rusty brown mixed with a little gray, cut short and very nice. A very nice face she has, too, with quiet, friendly eyes. A kind face. He feels entirely easy with her. Men must like her, Berti thinks, and it is not only because of the sex business which, by his standards, is a business like any other. Only it must surely be hard and sometimes unpleasant work? Nothing that a woman would *choose,* exactly, if there were other opportunities . . . ?

Madge stops by each time she comes to the Transient House, descending the stairs after her night's work, usually carrying a box of freshly made crullers she's brought with her from the bakery. Berti has already made coffee and the two sit in the little room, eating and drinking, often in silence. Every now and then she likes to stoop and lift a pup and nuzzle it against her cheek, their built-in amiability often reducing her to tears.

She says to Berti one night, "You know, it just come over me the other day — how I spent a good half of my life being walked over? I wanted to go to secretarial school but the folks claimed I was needed at home. My sisters went but I never did. And then they pushed me into marrying somebody I didn't want to marry, he was a widower and I only learned later that he already ran two wives into the ground. I left him years ago. Now I do what I want to do, when I want to do it. It's terrible, just terrible, when you suddenly realize all the years you spent being walked over." Berti, the coffee cup close to his lips, pauses, then carefully lowers it and sets it on the little table. Shaking his head up and down vigorously, "The same. The same. It has been the same with me."

Sometimes, at three, four o'clock, the two of them noiselessly ascend the wide, time-pitted stairs to the second floor.

Comes a certain Saturday, they call it here Parents' Day, when families will arrive from all directions to stroll about the campus and view the rooms where their sons and daughters sleep, study and carry on. The frat house gleams from its special sweepings and scrubbings, with Hedwig having triumphantly exorcized the smells of the boys' bedrooms, flinging open doors and stepping back to savor the gasps of mothers. She also presides over a special midday dinner for the visiting families of her boys, serving up *Sauerbraten mit Kartoffelklössen,* also *mit* pineapple kraut, and accepts their awed accolades with a slight, queenly bow of her head.

And now, in the evening, her boys are holding a house dance. Hedwig is amazed at how the living and dining rooms have blossomed into a ballroom by means of wide doors that roll away into the walls. Constantly moving lights in all colors attack her balance, while three young men play brass instruments new to her eyes and ears, and also one who plays on drums, the total of all this enough to split open her head. It's a relief to her that she spends the time in the kitchen, on her way to which she has extracted, from below a black-velvet-draped table at the end of the ball-room, a bottle of vodka among others which should not be there, and which she carries off and places beside the stove.

One visiting parent alone comes to the dance, a man named Cyrus Witterhorn. His normal speaking voice is very loud and he greets Hedwig with a mock formal bow as he shakes her hand. He thanks her for caring for his son, he's glad to see the boy in such a nice-looking house, and he has certainly enjoyed that dinner, magnificent dinner! She thanks him, she is glad he enjoyed it, and within herself wishes he'd leave. This is not the kind of man she likes. He is too large, and has thinning, lifeless hair that looks greasy; it had probably once been blond and thick and, very likely, rippled. In addition he is florid-cheeked and, Hedwig thinks, dirty in the eye.

The front hall and ballroom are filling up with arrivals, and the noise, almost visible, swirls around them. She excuses herself to go back to the kitchen. Witterhorn follows. "No point in my being out there with all those kids. Sure is a nice-looking place you've got here, I like these old houses. You're German, am I right?"

"Yes." She pulls an apron over her head and stands watching him as she knots the ties in back.

"One of the herring folk, ha-ha." In no hurry to leave, he gives her a grin and watches her place tidbits on a tray. With a chuckle he lets her see that he snitches one.

After an interval Hedwig says "Maybe you would like to sit down?" and pulls a chair from a nearby table.

"Thanks. Hey, what's that I see there?" He looks toward the stove. "Booze? I don't mind if I do."

She pours vodka into a small glass for him and he leans against the back of the chair with a broad smile. He admires her white hair and that way she has it arranged in a crown of plaits. He likes women with colossal bosoms. "Don't make me drink alone, you're going to join me, I hope." Hedwig hesitates, then brings a second glass from the cupboard, and as he fills it, seats herself in another chair beside the table.

He raises his glass and nearly drains it in one swallow. "I gotta compliment you again on the looks of this house. I was here last year for Parents' Day and the place looked as ratty as the one I'm staying in." Appropriating the bottle, he pours himself another drink. "And my boy tells me the meals here are terrific."

"I thank you." The man seems actually not quite so unappealing as she had thought. "Also I like your boy. Stephen. He is one of the good ones, I will tell you." She sends a quick look toward the door — the noise, the talk and the laughter seem positively to crash through in huge chunks she can almost touch — and she rises to close it as he replenishes her drink. "But it is nice, to keep house here."

"Noisy, though. Tonight."

"It is nothing. It is usually not like this, of course."

"Of course not." He helps himself to the food on the tray and they sit and drink in a companionable silence. The woman amuses him. Germans amuse him. Frenchmen amuse him. Romanians amuse him, even Englishmen amuse him. A part of him considers all foreigners freaks, proof of nature's whimsies. The noise from beyond the kitchen door is enormous, but even when it tones down, the floor and walls continue to vibrate. She fills his glass and her own once again. "Donkey shane," he says, laughing. She laughs with him, then regards the tray of canapés absorbedly. Preparing them was entirely her idea and she hadn't really known if such things would be expected for an evening such as this. So the two of them will eat them. She holds the tray out to him, picks up a lobster patty and pops it into her mouth. "What is the work that you do?" she asks.

"Oh, I'm head of a firm out in Omaha, we're financial advisers to institutions. I'm a member of the Board of Trustees here at the college. One reason why I like to keep my eye on the place. 'Sa good place."

"It is! It is! From the first day I have liked it." This is actually a most agreeable man. She puts a hand to the table to steady herself.

"Hey, am I hearing right? By God, they've stopped playing that glop and — do you hear what they're doing? It's a waltz! C'mon, Mrs. Kessler, let's go out and shake a leg before they find out somebody switched the music. Come dance with me, my lady!" Laughing, Hedwig allows him to pull her from the room.

It is recognizably an old-fashioned waltz, only played by those strange instruments she'd seen them unpacking in the front hall, and to her ears more than a continent removed from the familiar Strauss rhythms she vaguely recalls. Her boys and their girls are laughing at the music but they are dancing to it and so is she, though she's not done such a thing since she was quite young. Witterhorn guides her gently and knowledgeably over the floor and she allows herself to be led. Somehow her feet seem inclined to step one on the other. Her head swims, and she talks to him continually, chattering like a girl, telling him what she's planning for next day's dinner, her amazement at the size this room has suddenly become; did he know they did it with doors, entirely with doors? And she thinks now, please, she would like to return to the kitchen.

This they do, and with exaggerated gallantry he seats her on her chair. Pouring himself another drink he asks, "Didja happen to meet the housemother they had last year? Nah, of course not, she's in the jug. They nabbed her, she was stealing things hand over fist. Nice-looking gal, fooled me. A redhead."

"Please, you should not speak of redheads!"

"Y'don't like redheads."

"Mein mama was a wedhead. Red. A redhead." Again she puts a hand to the table. He can see the woman's getting sloshed. He stands. "Well, I think I'll run along now and —" but "Oh!" Hedwig cries, "oh!" Yet again she clutches at the table, but falls from her chair. She lies on the floor with her eyes closed.

"Jesus Christ!" Witterhorn stares down at her, then looks around desperately — maybe this could be something more than the drink? — and heads hastily into the swirling bedlam beyond the kitchen door.

He returns to the kitchen with his son to find Hedwig lying in the same position and indeed looking very peaceable. "Holy shit," the son says. They stand looking down at the woman on the floor. "I suppose we should call an ambulance?"

Breathily, Witterhorn gets to his knees beside her and puts an ear to her chest. "Seems to be breathing okay. Plenty loud. I think she's just out. Had a bit too much, if you know what I mean."

The boy regards the nearly empty bottle. "Yeah, we know she likes the stuff. Now and then. No problem usually, though, not really."

"Well, what do we do now?"

"I know she's got a brother lives across campus. Let me give him a call, name's Brodsky" and the boy heads for the telephone.

It's Gerda who responds to the summons. Stephen Witterhorn, waiting for her outside the front door, places an arm under her elbow and guides her through the turmoil inside. They reach the kitchen, where she stops abruptly in the doorway. Her mother is still on the floor.

"We thought we'd better just leave her that way until someone came," Cyrus Witterhorn explains. To his own ears this sounds pretty lame.

"Mother!" Gerda cries, flying to Hedwig's side.

"You know," Witterhorn continues, "it might be nothing at all — I'm afraid she's been at the bottle a little too much, I hate to say . . ."

Cradling her mother's head in one arm, Gerda lifts it slightly. Hedwig gives a huge and tortuous sigh, flutters an eye open and stares up into her daughter's face, then turns her head as though the sight is more than she can bear. "I do not feel so very well . . ." Her voice is thick.

Gerda sits back on her heels. "I think we'll take you up to your room."

"Sure, sure, we should do that!" Witterhorn almost shouts. "You leave her to Steve and me, we'll get her upstairs. Where's her room, Stevie?"

"I'll show you, we can go up these back stairs. Need help?"

"Nah."

With another sigh Hedwig has subsided, both eyes closed. She's folded her arms across her abdomen, lying in the ageless serenity of a medieval knight on a cata-falque. Witterhorn attempts the lifting but this is a big woman, and it takes the two men finally to carry her, one at each end, across the kitchen, up the stairs and into her bedroom, with Gerda following.

They place her on the bed and stand looking down on her. Her braided hair is in thick disarray, her pink face is placid. She is sleeping like a stone.

"I'll stay with her," Gerda says, "and I want to thank you both very much."

The men leave the bedroom with no re-luctance, but outside in the hall Witterhorn turns to Gerda. "Y'know, I think I'm to blame for this. I shouldn't've let her drink so much. I didn't realize she couldn't take it. Honestly, I didn't give it a thought."

"It's quite all right." Gerda, having followed them, leans tiredly against the doorjamb. "In any case, I'm afraid she's not exactly new to 'the stuff,' as you call it. You're not to blame yourself."

"You're one fine missy, I want to shake your hand." He does this, his relief enormous, his smile wide. "But you know, I still feel sort of responsible. I'll call tomorrow, see how she is. You going to be here?"

"Yes, of course, I'll stay the night."

She pulls from beside the window a peculiar American-styled chair with legs that seem purposely to be spread-eagled, and placing it close to the bed, seats herself. Suppose this is more than drunkenness? Suppose her mother really is ill from something or other — a heart attack, a stroke, anything that could fit the still figure on the bed? How would one know? Yet how unutterably revolting to call up an ambulance, have her taken to the emergency room of Drummond Hospital, and then be told that her mother is in a drunken stupor. She scrapes the chair nearer to the bed.

Hedwig appears perfectly at peace. Now her face is pale and looks fine-carved, with a kind of classic simplicity. Her breathing is quiet and not in the least sonorous, as one might expect from someone in a drunken stupor. But what does one know of drunken stupors?

Her uncle's information of a week past has been washing about in her head like sloshing waves, back and forth, forth and back, and — viewing the figure on the bed — she tries to imagine Hedwig's reaction if she were to tell her the story of her mother and father, and of that most beloved grandfather, and . . . she need go no further. Gerda smiles. Her mother's reaction? Like bringing a flaming torch to a pile of dry leaves.

Ah, her mother is stirring. Hedwig brings a hand to her face, as though brushing off a fly. "Mother?" says Gerda. Leaning toward her.

Hedwig gives a huge heave of her bosom, opens her eyes and stares at the ceiling. "Mother?" Gerda says again.

"Is it done, is it over, the downstairs?"

"The what — oh, you mean the ball? The dance? Yes, I'm sure, I heard sounds of people leaving. And a lot of tramping noise coming upstairs. I think the boys have returned to their rooms."

"I should go and see." But she makes no move.

"No, of course not. I'm sure everything can wait till morning. Why don't you —" But Hedwig has returned to sleep.

For the first time Gerda gives her attention to the room, this place where her mother actually lives. She's surprised at its austerity. It contains no more furniture than one might think absolutely necessary. The bed. A wooden bedside table and on it only a small clock, a brush and comb, and a round celluloid bowl holding a number of white metal hairpins. Against the farther wall a narrow, cretonne-covered cot with many small pillows. It is perhaps very American, but none of this fits with the comfort-demanding amplitude she associates with her mother. Here she cannot see a single one of the Old World treasures her mother has always surrounded herself with.

It's on the cot that she'll spend the rest of the night.

The house, at eight o'clock on this Sunday morning, seems totally silent. Gerda opens her eyes, makes no movement, but lies quietly scanning the patterns on the tatty-looking ceiling. Pale gray continents, clouds and rivers, products of ancient rain leaks. She knows immediately where she is and why, but is too lassitudinous even to look toward her mother's bed. She realizes she'd forgotten all about her uncle Bruno, who may or may not know she's not in the house. But the two of them, with mutual thankfulness, are used to going their own ways, and the thought doesn't distress her.

Now, unmistakably, there's the delicious resinous smell of coffee. Has her mother gone downstairs? Raising herself on an elbow, she looks toward the bed. There is Hedwig's large motionless form, covered by a blanket. But as though her own slight movement has acted as a prod, her mother stirs, sits up abruptly, then immediately puts a hand to her head.

For a long moment Gerda regards her.

"How are you feeling, Mother?"

Hedwig gives an immense start, her hand still to her head: "Why are you here?"

"They came for me last night. One of the boys. I slept here on the cot."

Hedwig throws off her blanket, then looks down on herself. "I have slept in my clothes."

"Yes, we thought it best not to bother you too much. You were . . . anyway, how do you feel this morning?" Sitting up, she swings her legs over the side of the bed.

"Gerda! You must explain this. Why does it happen I am in my clothes? And you are here. Why?" looking gloweringly across at her daughter. "You have had a fight with Bruno, yes? Yes. Now you listen to me, Gerda. You have followed us from London to New York. And then from New York to here, to Drummond. And now from Bruno you come to this house where I am. You want maybe to move in here? No. It cannot be done. Here are only boys. Young men." Her usual color has returned, she faces her daughter grimly and folds her arms across her bosom. Speaking with the familiar pink righteousness that is hers alone, "You must go back to Bruno and learn to live in one place and not always to come running to me."

Gerda is swept with such a wave of irritation that she nearly bounces on the cot. Has last evening entirely disappeared from the woman's head? Is this the sort of thing to be expected the morning after one falls to the floor from drink? The accusatory look in her mother's eyes raises something in her breast she hasn't felt in years. It's almost as though they're in London once more and with that savage pleasure she can almost taste, she says, "I have not had a fight with Uncle Bruno. I might expect you to think such a thing. If you want to hear it, the fact is you drank too much last night. And I don't mean tea. They found you on the floor in the kitchen. Drunk." She waits a moment. With relish: "Dead drunk." And there's the deep satisfaction from long ago, reading the rage beginning to kindle in her mother's face. "They called me and I came over. They picked you up from the kitchen floor and carried you here to your bedroom. How . . . shameful. How humiliating."

Amazingly, instantly, Hedwig seems to have swallowed her anger. She raises her hands to her head as though to pat her disarrayed hair but returns them to her lap. "Yes, now I remember last night. I . . . yes, it is true, I am not used to so much drinking. Yes. When you will be my age you will perhaps understand — let me tell you — no, I cannot tell you, you are a girl who will not understand. I . . . have had a very hard life. Very hard. I will not say it all to you because you will not understand, you have never been a one to understand anything. I will say only that for me in my life there have been no pleasures. Not with any place, not with anybody. Nobody. Did I ever have pleasure even from you? Never. Always people are set against me. I do not know why. Bruno? No, not my brother either, even when he was a boy. No one. Ever." As though she has been remarking on some everyday matter of small consequence, she raises her hands and begins to remove pins from her hair.

Gerda, cheated of her battle: "You cannot say that Father was ever mean to you. Quite the other way round, if you ask me."

Silence.

"I think I'd best get back to the house. You don't need me? I must be there before Father wakes, otherwise . . . well, I certainly have no intention of telling him this . . . this sordid story."

Hedwig is uncertain of what the word

means, but notes the curl of her daughter's lip.

As for Gerda: she has not slept well, her neck aches, the fact that her mother will not rise to anger baffles her beyond bearing. "In case you don't remember, you were in a drunken stupor last night, from drinking too much with that filthy man, that father of someone or other here in the house. They had to pick you up off the kitchen floor . . . imagine! . . . and carry you up here to bed. Not the sort of thing I could very well explain to Father, is it?"

"Hah!" Hedwig almost tears herself from the bed. "You could not explain to Father! Hah! Shall I tell you something, you *Zänkerin*, you devil: HE IS NOT EVEN YOUR FATHER!"

Gerda stares at her mother steadily. "I suppose you mean that to shock me, don't you?"

"*Mein Gott.*" Hedwig raises her hands to the back of her head, draws the immense straggle of hair plaits forward over each shoulder and clutches them, her hands shaking. "So you know."

"I came to that conclusion long ago," raising her head grimly. "Long, long ago." Rising from the cot she walks to the window and stares down onto a broad stretch of lawn which, she can note even now, badly needs mowing.

Hedwig gives a tight laugh. "Hah. Have you then wondered sometimes maybe about your real father?"

"Actually, I've given it little thought, if you must know. I only wonder whether Father . . . does Father know?" Turning from the window, she faces her mother. And starts to cry. Shaking, she puts her hands to her face. "Poor Father. Poor Father."

Hedwig: "Not poor me, is that it?"

"What do you mean? What can you possibly mean by that?"

"What I mean is that you will hear how this has happened. What I want is that you will sit down in this chair and listen to me. Do you hear me? You will sit down in this chair."

Gerda leaves the window and seats herself in the chair. Hedwig, the two braids of hair still in her fists, pulls them forward as though trying to part them from her head. She continues to grasp them, her hands trembling. "This goes to the time when Berti and I left Germany. The time when I went to see Otto von Heisermann. He was a longtime friend of our family, it goes back many years. Very close to Grosspapa.

This man, this good and long friend of the family, I go to him because he is a high-up man in the Nazi Party and I ask will he help to find Opa and Oma and then maybe he will help us all to leave Germany. I throw myself upon his friendship with Grossvater. I cry. I beg him. He tells me he can know nothing about Grosspapa and Grossmama, it is out of his hands, but for me and Berti maybe yes. He tells me yes. I must do one thing. He will then see that Berti and I leave Germany. He will see that we get on a truck and then on a boat and he will arrange it. Things like that he can do." She stops, looks at her daughter. Gerda is stone.

"I must allow that a man, a man he will have ready, to have intercourse with me. Otto wishes to watch. That is all. Wishes to watch."

Gerda bites her lip, looks down into her lap.

"And so I must come again to Otto's house and there is the man, a gypsy man. He is not wanting to but he must. It takes time. He is not wanting to but he must. All our clothes we must take off. For a whole long evening we are there. Three times he must enter into me. And Otto watches and . . . And then I return home and in a few days comes a big long automobile with a chauffeur and I leave Charlottenburg with Bert and the steamer trunks." Throughout the delivery her voice in a straight line, neither rises nor falls. Has she said all this to herself in her silent throat hundreds of times, thousands of times? The two of them are quite still. Finally Gerda rises from the chair and stands. In which direction to go? To her mother who is staring at the window, her head raised, the braids of hair still clutched in her hands?

Gerda walks from the room quietly.

She's not prepared for walking into Cyrus Witterhorn's arms. With a hand raised to the knocker, he's standing at the porch door as she opens it and plunges into him.

"Missy! It's you!" He puts his hands to her shoulders to hold her up. He straightens her. "Here now, don't you fall down." Something funny about the girl. Her eyes. "What's the matter, honey, you look like a zombie. Is it your mother? She okay?"

Gerda stares at him, blinks, shakes her head. "She's fine."

"You're on the way out. How about a cup of coffee? C'mon, let me take you to breakfast."

"Oh no; no thanks. I just" — she puts a hand to her forehead — "I just need to get home. Really. I've had a . . . bad night."

"Sure, I understand. Jesus, I'm real sorry. All my fault."

She glances at him in surprise. In her mind she's seen him as rather a clot but he's now a picture of contrition — indeed so disturbed, she feels a stab of guilt. "No, really, you mustn't think that. Really you mustn't. It's nothing to do with you, actually."

"You sure she's all right?"

"Of course she is, she's this moment getting dressed. Now, please, I think I must get home," and she turns toward the steps.

"Okay. You look kinda . . . you able to drive?"

"No, I'm going to walk." And because he continues to stare at her worriedly: "The air will do me good."

"Let me drive you." Gently, he takes her by the elbow. "My car's over here, on the side. C'mon, just tell me where to go."

Her head is full of webs, it isn't in her to resist. She follows him to his car.

They draw up in front of Bruno's house and he gets out hurriedly and reaches the side door before she's properly got it opened. They begin to ascend the walk when Gerda suddenly stops. There's the sound of a piano — a rollicking tune, a bit familiar. Some American folk tune, played none too fastidiously. She opens the door and Bruno greets her, smiling. "Come in, sweetheart, I thought I'd have the old piano tuned, maybe you'll start . . . oh, how d'you do?"

She performs the introductions, then is

made to shake hands with the tuner who turns from the stool, smiling, a wizened old man in a black dusty jacket. Except for the frozen little smile, his face seems hidden behind glinting glasses. He rises and begins to pack his battered case; he's just leaving, maybe she'd like to sit down and see how the instrument sounds?

Absolutely not. But she sees Bruno's importuning eyes, and still in the fog which she's brought with her from the fraternity house, sits down on the old round piano stool and puts her hands to the keys. She's barely played in weeks. Never mind. She plays a short Schubert thing, her head miles away from her fingers.

When she finishes she stares gloomily at the keys. The old fellow actually hasn't made a bad job of it, and she thanks him. "You can play," he says solemnly, then stoops and picks up his case.

Witterhorn is beside himself: "Holy cow, little lady, you sound like a real professional. Who would've thought —" But Bruno interrupts. "Gerda, you've got to get back to it, I thought maybe getting the thing tuned would do the trick."

She puts her face in her hands. "Uncle Bruno, thank you. Just don't . . . but thank you, thank you."

Witterhorn senses that something's up. "Look, I'm gonna go. Gerda. Nice name. I'm gonna come back, say seven o'clock, I'm taking you out to dinner, you hear? To a nice place I know. See you at seven. Nice to meet you," he says to Bruno, and follows the tuner out the door.

"Who's the guy?" says Bruno when the front door has closed and Gerda, removed from the piano stool, has taken a seat on the couch. Her head feels twice its normal size — maybe it's her need for sleep. Suppose she tells her uncle what Hedwig has related to her. Right now, that way he's regarding her, he looks expectant, or it might be slightly concerned. Perhaps it's merely curiosity. She could begin "I've had a jolly rotten experience this morning . . ." No. Possibly at some later time, after she's digested it? No. Probably never. Suddenly she feels a rush of pity for everyone in the world and every thing, and especially for Berti; she wants to lower her face into her hands and let loose a torrent of tears.

Her uncle is still waiting. The guy. "He's the father of one of the boys at the fraternity house. I went over to see Mother and he offered to drive me home."

One of Bruno's eyebrows shoots up quizzically. "You're going out to dinner with him." This appears to be more than a statement, and Gerda imagines, if she took the time and gave herself over to it, she could read a multitude of things in it.

"Oh I don't know," she says tiredly. "Probably not." She pulls her dress farther down over her knees, smoothes it over her lap and folds her hands. "I've no idea why he said that, probably he felt sorry for — well, I don't really know. I doubt I'll go, actually."

Bruno says nothing more but pats his shirt pocket, looks around for his pipe, sees it, picks it up and shooting her what seems to her a very sweet smile, walks out into the hall.

"It's called an Alexander," Witterhorn says. "You like it?"

Gerda very slowly twirls the glass and gazes down into its dark smoothness, about a quarter of which she has drunk. "It's rather . . . rather good, actually. I've never had one before."

"I wouldn't be one bit surprised if you told me you never had a drink before." He gives her a large and perhaps slightly apprehensive smile.

"Well, I have had a bit of wine now and then. Not often." She tries to return his smile. "I suppose you're thinking about my mother . . ." She says this lightly, all she really means to do is reassure him. On the drive here from her uncle's he had insisted on explaining last evening, his admiration for Hedwig and all she'd accomplished at the Phi Gam house, and the really miraculous dinner she'd served up, and more, and more . . . all of this presented to her within the framework of contrition, so that what she'd just said was purely to help him put the whole episode of last evening from his mind. Instead she notes a flush begin to mount his cheeks and in some consternation puts out her hand and for a barest moment touches his where it rests on the table. "*Please* don't blame yourself. Mother's quite all right. She's always been a bit of a . . . tippler, I believe is the word. I tell you this quite honestly. The whole thing has absolutely nothing to do with you."

They regard each other in silence and she's certain the look of gloom in his eye seems to have departed. He lets out a tremendous sigh. "Okay, Gerda, I believe you. We'll forget about it." He sits back. "Now I want to tell you how much I appreciate your coming with me tonight. I was afraid you wouldn't show when I got to your uncle's house."

However little of this Alexander thing she's drunk, it seems to have lightened her head. She welcomes it, actually, it does seem to keep the thoughts hovering over her from alighting, so mightn't it prove she'd done the right thing in deciding to come out to dinner with this man? Though she has no slightest wish ever to see him again, she can recognize the oil of friendship that alcohol provides, and in a swiftly gone moment almost comprehends her mother's need to drink against the world. Yet the cocktail seems to have brought a bit of an ache to her stomach — it's probably rather strong in spite of its warm brown velvet feel. Why does it bring Brahms to her mind? Perhaps she'd best not have any more.

"And something else, little missy. The piano. You sure can hit those keys. You could have knocked me over, I really mean it."

"Well. Thank you." It *must* be the drink — his eyes, that way he has of staring at her, seem peculiarly intense: pale brown and slightly speckled, like the agates the children she'd grown up with in London had used to play with.

"You gallop like a little goat. You know —" But at this moment the waitress arrives and sets their dishes before them and the subject of her piano playing is dropped. As they eat, he tells her what life is like in Omaha nowadays and he tells her the story of his marriage and how his life has changed since his wife's death, and how a lot of bilge has sure passed under the bridge since then, and he's plagued with worries about his son, an only child, who might be smoking pot at those rap sessions they have nowadays and life is sure one helluva gamble, isn't it?

"It's early yet," Cyrus Witterhorn says, "let's see what's doing roundabouts." They've left the restaurant and are in the car, and Gerda receives a strong whiff of whiskey as he leans across her to crank her window down — true, the night is warm, and the interior of the car, its windows closed for two hours, warmer still. He sits back, looks through the windshield and frowns. Where to take a little lady like this, the evening's still young?

"Oh, I don't know that we actually need go anywhere," says Gerda. "I've enjoyed dinner, really I have. Perhaps I ought just go home . . ."

"Just let me think." And he thinks. Might take in a movie, he guesses. "There's not that much doing on Sunday night in a town like this, you'd think with the college and all . . . How about a movie? There's a drive-in not far from here, I don't know what's playing but I haven't been to anything in months. Let's go see." And he starts the car.

She's not sure what a drive-in is but makes

no reply, aware that the pain in her stomach, though tolerable, is still there. Perhaps she shouldn't have finished that Alexander after all? But she hadn't wanted to give offense, and besides, it *had* tasted rather good. Also still with her is the inertia that allowed her to accept this dinner invitation in the first place, from a man she doesn't know and under other circumstances would never have known. And so she sits beside him, bathed in a gentle melancholy she doesn't have the energy to examine.

"Oh yes, I remember this place," Witterhorn says as they pass a roadhouse bar with WELCOME RAY AND CLAIRE in red neon over one window. "I wonder who the hell Ray and Claire are. Might stop there on the way home for a quick one. Take in the movie first." On they go.

How odd. In this wide field, where very likely daisies and Queen Anne's lace stir languorously during the day, are a number of cars all facing a movie screen whose size she finds difficult to believe. The movie has already started, their car is far to the back of the well-populated field, and she stares at gigantic human forms and faces, everything meaningless until Witterhorn opens his window and pulls inside a sort of box which he hangs on the window near him. Immediately there are loud voices, the huge faces on the immense screen, a man and a woman, are quarreling and Gerda stares, even leans forward slightly to take in the scene she's witnessing. Then she leans back in her seat and in the swirl of angry scrabble that fills the car ardently wishes herself home and in bed.

Witterhorn, himself with only half an eye directed to the screen, tries to figure out what there is about the woman beside him that has pushed him to spend this Sunday evening in such a manner. True, he has to remain in Drummond for a board meeting tomorrow morning, but the "little lady," as his head persists in calling her, offers little in companionship and seems to direct nothing toward him, beyond an answer to something he says. He might even call her spinsterish. No.

He's taken rather a fancy to her. The fact is, she reminds him of his dead wife. Amelia, during their courting days, had been just as standoffish, though beneath that rather prim manner of hers he'd always detected a coy desire that he trample down the fences she'd erected, and that he wouldn't be disappointed when that day came.

But this one has more to her. Amelia had

had an ordinary sort of bringing up: her parents ran a chicken farm, and she herself had been a member of the 4-H program and also ran a small children's Bible study class Sunday mornings. He'd found her a comfortable and reliable-enough wife, though he doubted he'd want to repeat that marital experience exactly.

No, this one definitely has more to her. There's nothing about Gerda to suggest chicken farms or the singing of "Jesus loves me, this I know," though now that music enters into it he's on to what there is about Gerda Kessler that sets her apart from all the spinsters or Amelias he's ever known. This one plays the piano like an angel.

And there's also about this one an air of . . . tragedy, he'd almost say. There's something about her that feeds some flame within him, he can't say what, exactly, but he detects a sort of inner well that he desperately needs to plumb. Music is only part of it. He gives her a sideward glance. Has she ever made love with anyone? he wonders. She's facing the screen and he thinks her eyes are closed, but it's dark in the car. Carefully, he raises his right arm and places it across the back of her seat. She doesn't stir.

"Gerda," he says softly. He thinks her head moves a little, against his arm. He leans over and kisses her delicately on the lips.

"What!" cries Gerda, opening her eyes, and Witterhorn is upon her. With a practice that suggests activities not totally limited since the death of his wife he reaches down through the neck of her dress, and as she rears to the side away from him this Amelia-like gesture inflames him.

"No!" Gerda cries, exactly as had Amelia. She raises both her arms. This appears to have a galvanic effect on Witterhorn. Abruptly he enfolds her. "Let me! Let me!" he pleads "Oh Gerda, you little Gerda!" Again he plants a kiss on her lips deep, hard, as he pushes an arm up beneath her dress.

She's in absolute shock. What to do? What kind of man . . . With one hand he's pulling strongly on her underpants and with the other doing something with his own pants. The voices from the movie seem to rise in a crescendo as: "Oh, baby, I need you. Let me! Let me! Oh let me!" Witterhorn cries. She's positively frantic, then suddenly turns, lunges toward him and thrusts both her hands around his neck. Tightly, tightly: all the little brains in her strong fingers intent on one thing. Tighter.

Witterhorn can't even gasp. The circle of force culminating in the pain at the front of his substantial neck is unbelievable. With a need far more intense than the one he'd felt below, he tries pulling her fingers from his neck but they seem to have sunk deep into his flesh and their strength is enormous. His head begins to swim and a small, hoarse cry is all he can manage.

Gerda removes her hands and folds them quietly in her lap. After an interval Witterhorn, his throat blazing with pain, starts the car. He doesn't speak, he can barely swallow, the bitch has probably busted his larynx. They reach her uncle's house and he makes no move but keeps the engine running as she opens the door, gets out, closes it and without looking back goes up the walk. She hears the car drive off.

At two in the morning Gerda wakes to discover herself in a sheath of vomit, her abdomen in flames. Likewise, her face is burning. Lying in the damp trough of her bed, she has no thought beyond a quiet wish to remove herself from life.

After that she must have fallen asleep, for she's next aware that the room is yellow, filled with daylight, and she can hear her uncle descending the stairs to the kitchen. Through the pulsing sound of the waterfall in her ears she hears voices, recognizes one of them as Berti's and dully acknowledges that he has just come in from his night work. Her pain has very slightly abated but she decides she will lie there until . . . she doesn't know until what. Until Berti climbs the stairs to his room.

And so she continues to lie in her bed. Indeed, Berti does climb the stairs and she hears him go first into the bathroom and later into his own room. His door closes, and only then does she realize what it is she must do.

Very slowly, easing herself partway from the bed, she puts her feet to the floor and manages to sit. What she will do is, she will go into the hall and at the top of the stairs softly call to Bruno. By the time she reaches her bedroom door there's the sound of Bruno's car. He's off to somewhere.

Well, she's able to walk, after all, isn't she? Though she feels herself a walking slab of pain she slips on a robe and clinging to the banister, hauls herself a step at a time down to the lower hall. There she puts her hand to the telephone when a broad wave of nausea sweeps over her. By a force of will she's never known she had, she dams the nausea and dials for a taxi.

The cabdriver doesn't have to be asked. At the emergency room he darts out, opens her door, and in utter passivity she allows him to lead her inside. Luckily, for she's brought no purse, he gives no thought to the fare but leaves, once he sees the admitting nurse put an arm around Gerda and lead her off down the hall.

"I'm taking you right in to the doctor, honey, we'll do the paperwork on you later." She opens a door. "Here's Dr. Raskin. Doctor, I've got a real case here. Just walked in." She brings a chair forward and scoops Gerda into it.

They've interrupted the doctor, who's at the window pouring birdseed into a feeder. "Sit down, please, be right with you. Just want to get this —" He peers over his shoulder, straightens, puts a box down, and closes the glass. He walks to Gerda and puts a hand to her face. "Ouch," Dr. Raskin says.

"I think I'm . . . rather ill," says Gerda.

"Ummm-hm. Where does it hurt?"

"My head. No, my abdomen. And I've vomited. It's because of something I drank last night —"

"Drank what?" the doctor interrupts.

She looks at him in dull surprise. "I think it's called an Alexander."

"An Alexander. What's an Alexan— oh, the cocktail, you mean? Anything in it?"

She gives him a face of bewilderment, then with a broken sigh, rests her forehead on her hand. "Yes. Of course. Some sort of liquid . . . brown." The thought of the drink raises up a revolt inside her and she puts a quick hand to her mouth.

"Where did you drink it?"

"At a restaurant. Here in town."

"Oh. No, I don't think an Alexander's going to make you as sick as you look. Let's have a look at you, we'll talk some more later." He goes to his desk and presses a small button.

"I think I'm going to vomit . . ." she says through her fingers. Instantly he pulls a handful of tissues from a large box on his desk and pushes them into her hand. At the same moment the door opens and a nurse comes in on silent shoes. "Liz, this lady's going to need some help. Get her in the examining room and help get her things off. I'll be right in."

The doctor wants to schedule her for surgery immediately. Probably in two hours, as soon as Dr. Del Nero arrives. "You can take every appendix he's ever removed and they'll make a straight line stretching from here to Kansas City. You're in good hands," Dr. Raskin tells the shivering Gerda, now again sitting before him at the desk in his office. "He's a genius. Miss Williams is going to take you to your room and you'll wait there in bed till we come for you. We'll do a few little tests first and don't you worry, you're going to be fine in no time." He pushes the button on his desk once more. "Plenty more Alexanders in your future. Me, I prefer a good Martini any day. Ice cold. Anything more you want to know about?"

Nothing. She thinks nothing, she consists of nothing but pain, many pains, yet one. She allows the nurse to seat her in a traveling chair and roll her from the room and into an elevator. And she registers nothing of the many things that are done to her, and when they've finished and brought her to this room and this bed and covered her lightly with a blanket and the door to the room is closed, she lies staring up at the whiteness of the ceiling. The pain that is her body is not confined to the present; it envelops her yet encloses all the pain she's ever known and also consumes her future.

Slowly she folds the blanket back and with great care manages to sit herself up. They've hung her clothes in the closet. All she needs is her dress, anything but this white thing they've draped her in.

She manages to stand and then pull off the gown and totter to the closet, where she takes her dress from the hanger and slips it over the pain that is her body.

She shuffles out into the empty hall. The door of the elevator, directly across from her room, slides back immediately when she touches the button. Inside, she selects the lowest indicator and a moment later emerges into the basement. The place is full of pails and ladders and floor-cleaning machines. And doors, the walls are studded with doors. These she forces herself to open at random and is faced with broom cupboards and shelves containing soaps, brushes, bottles. She walks jerkily on down the hall, hunched over, clinging to the wall.

She arrives at a line of huge laundry machines and opposite, a large door, removed from the others. Opening this she faces a room which she enters, closing the door behind her. She selects the farthest back of the piles of rumpled linens on the floor and lays herself down upon it. It is softer than the bed she has just left.

Bruno is overwhelmed at the immensity of his grief. Nights, he does all he can to keep from falling asleep. Every dream is death-tinged. Even each daytime thought is surrounded by the murk of death. Why only now is he aware of the depth of his fondness for the girl? Silently, not a muscle of his face moving, he rails at fate, the world, the everything. Gerda's suicide outrages his every sense. He walks now with a slight stoop, carrying his mountain of blame. Here his niece had come to him from God knows what, saying she needed to sort herself out, something like that. And he'd left her alone to do just that. So blind. She was looking for help and he'd given her room, board and solitude. After the first day, had the two of them ever once sat down to talk?

He can find nothing to do with himself and the days slip by as though oiled. The house is as quiet as before Hedwig's coming.

There's Berti upstairs. The two cousins, roughly the same age, were together frequently during their youth. His chief recollection of the young Berti is that of a fragile child: two big eyes on a thin neck. Look at the little fellow today — he sleeps and eats here but lives elsewhere. Somehow he seems not to mind working in that screw-hole. No, no, that one's not unhappy: spends the day in bed, departs evenings to do his living someplace else. His not so much a life as the echo of a life.

Then to Hedwig, who, soon after her arrival, with that family obsession of hers, had grabbed him by the collar and — never mind that he considers himself 150 percent a Brodsky — forced him to climb the family tree, now so violently pruned. She will never understand how he can be indifferent to the family. Why did that hulking Viking woman marry her mouse of a cousin? For no reason but that he was a Kessler. Poor woman. Poor impossible woman. Can this feeling of his be compassion? "You had a whole lifetime of her, I can imagine what it must have been like, but what do you think we should do, honey, should we forgive her?" Bruno says to the nonexistent Gerda, and pulls a handkerchief up from behind the pipe in his pocket to mop his wet face.

He has lain himself down on the living

room couch, not really to sleep — but somehow a knocking rouses him from a kind of demi-sleep, and he rises to walk slowly to the front door.

Always, it's the unexpected that comes to his house. He throws open the door and beholds there an old man in an untidy dark suit, his head enveloped in a halo of springy white hair. Can this be Albert Einstein standing on his stoop? "Excuse me," the man says, the two words immediately placing him as German, and he gives a very slight bow. "It is here I will perhaps find Gerda Kessler?"

Bruno stares at him, then says "Come in" and stands aside. The man moves unhesitatingly into Bruno's dark front hall, where he crosses his arms firmly and faces him. "You are then the uncle, yes?" Onkel, he pronounces it, the German way. "You are surely Bruno, I am right?"

Bruno turns a masklike face to him.

"I think I remember you. You do not remember me. You were a small boy. I am Victor Hammerschlag." And the man extends a hand which Bruno ignores. "Gerda. She lives here, here with you?"

"No more," Bruno says.

"Ah! So sorry! You will tell me where to find her. I have driven here from Kansas

City, where I am conducting this week. And Hedwig, she is here maybe?" Hammerschlag turns, and squinting his eyes, peers up the dark varnished stairway as though he expects to find his old friend standing above in the gloom.

Bruno is untouched by the man's disappointment. No one may enter his own grief. Still, he indicates the living room and says, as before, "Come in."

Hammerschlag walks in, gives a flick of interest at the long black piano, and the two men seat themselves on the couch. "I want to see her look when I tell her." The gentle old face, very pink now, crinkles into a charming smile. "I am making arrangements at Tanglewood for next year — she will be invited to play a Mozart concerto which I will conduct with the orchestra there. It will perhaps be the Boston Symphony." Hammerschlag stops, places a hand on each knee and leans slightly toward Bruno, continuing to smile into his face. "She has been too long hiding herself out here, yes? I think someone must bring her to attention, you agree with me?"

Bruno folds his hands and says nothing.

"You have maybe listened to her recordings? I make people listen to them. You know how fine she plays?"

Bruno continues to sit in frozen silence. For a lightning instant he has the thought that so long as the man beside him is unaware of Gerda's death, her death perhaps is not totally final. The thought, more grotesque because he has felt his heart give a tiniest leap, fills him with anger at the old man.

Hammerschlag moves uneasily. "Bruno? You will tell me please where I will find her?"

Bruno raises his head. In a rage he flings: "She is dead!" His voice creaky and high, not in any way his own. He turns aside from the old composer and puts both hands to his face.

Hammerschlag has departed, taking his heartbreak with him but leaving in the air words that Bruno will hear each time he walks into the room. "In mine heart! In mine heart!" hoarse with agony, now a part of the place like the long black coffin of the piano and the old couch with its age-shredded pillows. He rises slowly, walks to the windows and lowers every shade.

No need any more to view Berti with that mild pity many had once been moved to. For some years now he's been a happy man, no longer leading a life of incubation. For he has found what many seek and never find: release in work, and in love. True, he's become very slightly stooped and now wears thick-framed glasses, but he has developed a mild, cheerful air and is, in a word, happy.

He's long since made his peace with Gerda's death. To tell the truth, even while still in London he'd begun to feel her life only marginally, for she'd always been off concertizing or practicing interminably at the piano, and even after joining them in New York, had for the most part confined herself to her room. Long gone and even forgotten are those lucent, volcanic days when she'd clung to his hand as they walked or took the underground to and from concert halls, the two of them bound in a strong though unacknowledged league.

Madge, too, has changed; she has the

same sunny voice, but when she's with Berti it has taken on a note of deep and genuine fondness, and each time he approaches her — still somewhat shyly and with that look of his which is always warm with wonder — she folds him into her ample person with an appreciation that never falters.

Then there comes a turbulent night closely resembling the one when Madge had swept into the lobby to pull Berti from his evening coffee to rescue a dog full of pups — it's on just such a night of winter fury, with snow and wind and hail, that they are upstairs and his arms are around his Madge and he is tenderly and sweetly in the act of love when his heart, which has heretofore given no evidence of unquiet, chooses that moment to come to a gentle and final stop.

After much initial kneading and weeping and calling out to him, sobbing, she pulls his clothes on and phones for help.

Always the world is interrupting her life, but Hedwig adjusts, she adjusts, she will not be like the woman in the English poem she remembers from the days of Miss Love, forever weeping on a washed-up shore. No. Actually, in the years since Gerda's death (adjusted to!) she has arrived at a fair degree of content. Let it be put plainly: she is queen of the roost. The Phi Gam House has a comfort and even elegance that no shenanigans seem able to ruffle. As for the meals — ah, the meals. She is famous. The frat house never lacks for eager pledges, a state of affairs arousing much envy and resentment on the part of the other houses on campus.

But the death of Berti somehow does more than throw a spanner into the machinery of her orderly life. Because it is unexpected? Because of its nature, which is among the things she will not think of?

A few days after his death Hedwig discovers, on top of a pile of Berti's underpants in the bureau drawer of his bedroom in Bruno's house, a small Hebrew prayer book.

Berti is suddenly transformed.

And now come flooding back the pieties of the old folks, in spite of whose rigid adherence to strict Judaism Hedwig seems never, herself, to have been deeply moved by. When she'd reached London the old customs fell away naturally, as a coat is shed in a climate no longer requiring it. She'd fallen into a secular life without giving it a thought. By now she's forgotten the prayers, she's forgotten the ceremonies, she's even forgotten the ritual foods.

But she sees it was otherwise with Berti who, though manifesting little, must have inwardly practiced many of the observances she can only faintly recall. It is obviously necessary that he be buried in accordance with Jewish law. Yes, obvious! And now she has a handle on a thing that needs doing so that she can successfully seal this passage in her life.

It is not easy. The burial society of the orthodox *shul* in Kansas City that she gets in touch with refuses to bury him. Neither she nor Berti is a member of the congregation, and the *shul's* burial plots are limited in number. No, she will have to go elsewhere.

But he has been cremated! Hedwig cries. His ashes will surely not take up much space?

Horror. Does the woman not know cremation is forbidden? That G—d will not accept ashes? That the body must remain exactly as it was at death, with nothing done to it beyond washing and dressing? Nails may not be cut, sharp instruments of no kind be used on the body, nor any part of the body be subjected to fire? All this she does not know, and she calls herself a Jew?

Her mistake was to approach such a strictly orthodox synagogue. She next contacts a reformed congregation, also in Kansas City, meanwhile marveling at how many synagogues can be in such a relatively small city in the middle of the United States. This time she decides she will appeal directly to the rabbi, and is quite prepared to describe to him, with proper dignity, the family she comes from, and how there were innumerable rabbis in the Kessler constellation — and their fate she does not have to tell him . . . he will certainly understand. And he listens and he does indeed understand but throws out his hands in helplessness. Though they are not members of his congregation he might, even so, consider her request, but the burial ground is of relatively small size, and their first obligation is to their own membership. She and her husband are —

were — not serious Jews, are — were — they? And he smiles gently and sadly and afterward shakes his head when she describes finding the Hebrew prayer book on the little pile of Berti's underpants.

"Now look," Bruno tells her, "why keep going in to Kansas City? We've got a nice little Quaker congregation right here in Drummond, good understanding people, you want me to speak to them? Berti will rest very comfortably in the cemetery there, believe me." Which is how it comes about that the box of Berti's ashes rests quietly in the children's corner of the Quaker cemetery in Drummond, its tiny marker graced by a bit of trailing ivy.

It's not too long after this that the frat house dog, too, reaches the end of his days, no doubt expedited by a superabundant intake of beer. Hedwig had become quite fond of the animal, and it must come as no surprise that she arrives at the house one day with, under her arm, a dachshund the color of a caramel, and upon this creature, which she carries nightly up to her room since it cannot manage stairs, she bestows all the fierce vigilance, solicitude and affection she is capable of, all of which she has in high supply.

About the Author

FRIEDA ARKIN'S work has been twice selected for *Best American Short Stories* and her first novel, *The Dorp*, was published in 1969 to wide critical acclaim.

She attended the Juilliard School of Music and received her Master's in anthropology from Columbia University. She has written five cookbooks, a gardening book, a number of poems, and articles for *Woman's Day*, *The Christian Science Monitor*, *The Massachusetts Review*, *The Georgia Review*, *The Kenyon Review*, *The Yale Review*, and *Yankee* magazine.

Frieda Arkin's short stories have appeared in journals including *The Massachusetts Review*, *The Kenyon Review*, and *The Yale Review*. After a long hiatus from fiction, when she turned to raising a family and writing a series of cookbooks, Frieda joined the late Andre Dubus's writing group, prospering under his mentorship while completing *Hedwig and Berti*. She lives in Ipswich, Massachusetts.

The employees of Thorndike Press hope you have enjoyed this Large Print book. All our Thorndike and Wheeler Large Print titles are designed for easy reading, and all our books are made to last. Other Thorndike Press Large Print books are available at your library, through selected bookstores, or directly from us.

For information about titles, please call:

(800) 223-1244

or visit our Web site at:

www.gale.com/thorndike
www.gale.com/wheeler

To share your comments, please write:

Publisher
Thorndike Press
295 Kennedy Memorial Drive
Waterville, ME   04901